Death on Herons' Mere

MARY FITT

With an introduction by Curtis Evans

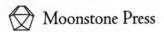 Moonstone Press

This edition published in 2022 by Moonstone Press
www.moonstonepress.co.uk

Introduction © 2022 Curtis Evans

Originally published in 1941 by Michael Joseph Ltd

Death on Herons' Mere © the Estate of Kathleen Freeman, writing as Mary Fitt

The right of Kathleen Freeman to be identified as author of this work has been
asserted in accordance with the Copyright, Designs and Patents Act 1988

ISBN 978-1-899000-46-3
eISBN 978-1-899000-47-0

A CIP catalogue record for this book is available from the British Library

Cover illustration by Jason Anscomb
Text designed and typeset by Tetragon, London
Printed and bound by CPI Group (UK) Ltd, Croydon, CR0 4YY

Contents

Introduction

Over four decades ago, in *Watteau's Shepherds: The Detective Novel in Britain, 1914–1940* (1979), the late scholar LeRoy Lad Panek likened the 'classical' British detective fiction of the Golden Age (roughly 1920 to 1940) to eighteenth-century French rococo painter Antoine Watteau's *The Shepherds*, which winsomely portrays a pastoral scene of French aristocrats cavorting as mock shepherds. In Panek's view, Golden Age detective fiction in its most classic form employs the rural settings of the country house and village as an artificial stage for murder, never intending to achieve verisimilitude but rather striving only to entertain, notwithstanding hard-boiled novelist Raymond Chandler's later dogmatic declaration in his 1944 essay 'The Simple Art of Murder' that 'fiction in any form has always intended to be realistic'. To Panek, the eccentric aristocrats and quaint villagers of classic British mystery are merely players putting on a performance for our enjoyment as readers, engaged in a mere game of murder, where nothing need be taken seriously.

The crime-writing career of classical scholar Kathleen Freeman, who published, mostly under the pen name Mary Fitt, twenty-nine detective and crime novels between 1936 and 1960, both confirms and challenges Panek's thesis. A goodly number of the author's mysteries in fact aim at portraying murder very seriously indeed, including her Superintendent Mallett tales *Death and Mary Dazill* (1941), *Requiem for Robert* (1942), *Clues to Christabel* (1944) and *Love from Elizabeth* (1954), and her stand-alone story *Pity for Pamela* (1950). Others, however, conform more to the relatively blithe country-house stereotype of classic British detective fiction. Indeed, Mary Fitt's final Mallett story, *Mizmaze* (1958), written when Freeman was terminally ill with congestive heart failure, reads like a parody of Golden Age mystery.

When Mary Fitt's Superintendent Mallett novel *Death on Herons'
Mere* appeared in Britain in the second half of 1941 (and in the United
States, under the title *Death Finds a Target*, in 1942), it directly followed
into print *Death and Mary Dazill* – happily soon to be republished
by Moonstone, along with *Requiem for Robert* – which reviewers
had widely hailed as a tremendously original and innovative work
within the crime and mystery genre. *Death on Herons' Mere*, on the
other hand, was rightly deemed a more conventional sort of mystery.
Readers coming to *Death on Herons' Mere* after a perusal of *Death and
Mary Dazill*, observed the reviewer of the novel in the *Birmingham
Post*,

> will find no comparable unconventionality of plan, no reconstruction
> of a long-dead past, but a straightforward tale of murder and detec-
> tion – with a time-table and alibis, with an improved military rifle
> in the background and even (that well-worn expedient) a worried
> man's walk during the night. Yet 'distinction' is still the word for
> Miss Fitt's handling of intrinsically ordinary materials. Her style
> is still polished; her personages are again alive and interesting
> without becoming too big for their boots.

Death on Herons' Mere is a model traditional detective story, in short,
written along strict lines by an able practitioner of the form. Sounding
rather like the late modern traditionalist crime writer P. D. James, Mary
Fitt herself once asserted, in comments on the composition of radio
mystery: 'The highest craftsmanship in any art can only be brought
out by observing rules, the more difficult the better.' Again sounding
like James, she declared that audiences desire an affirmation of moral
order in mysteries. At the conclusion of a properly designed detective
novel, 'wickedness has been detected, innocence has been protected,
justice is to be done… There is no moralizing; but there is a moral.
Law and Order must prevail.'

Death on Herons' Mere takes place entirely on the estate of Herons' Hall, a huge country mansion owned by Simon Gabb, a 'new money' millionaire who hails originally, like the author herself, from Birmingham. At his great industrial works at the county town of Broxeter, twenty miles away from Herons' Hall, Gabb manufactures iron and steel, his blast furnaces ever reddening the darkling sky, along with a sideline in hunting rifles. (The name Broxeter was probably inspired by Wroxeter, a village in the West Midlands county of Shropshire, which was built on the site of the ancient Roman city of Viroconium Cornoviorum.)

Gabb acquired the Herons' Hall estate after the death, three years before the events of the novel, of its landed-gentry owner, Colonel Sir Charles Laforte, a great white hunter who expired tragically (or not) after being gored in Africa by a charging rhino, leaving behind an earnest tome, *The Lure of the Spoor*, to inspire others to follow in his slaughtering footsteps. At the time of his demise, the good colonel was a widower, but he left behind two young adult children – a daughter, Arden, and a son, Billy – as well as a widowed middle-aged sister, Helen Charleroy, and her young adult son, Royce, with much disappointed expectations, there being no money left with which to support the estate. (Helen in particular was ambitious to become de facto mistress of Herons' Hall.)

Thus, out went the colonel's clan, to dwell in a mere lodge on the grounds of the estate, and in came the Gabbs in all their refracted glory: Simon himself; his anxious wife Polly; their brilliant, mercurial son Giles; their hard-working but patently less gifted son Basil; and their discontented only daughter, Jessica. Basil is married to Pauline, who, although she has borne her husband a six-month-old son, is already decidedly discontented in her marriage. Also involved in the tale, which seems to have as many characters as a Victorian novel, are Simon's brother, James, James's dour wife, Janet, and their children Henry and Lucy, the latter of whom expects to marry Giles; smooth barrister Hubert Olivier and his young wife Madeleine; and, as befits a country-house mystery, a gardener, a chauffeur and assorted maids.

When the novel opens a party is in progress, with the occupants of the house having returned to its palatial confines for the first time since the Gabb regime was inaugurated. There is a storm; an elm tree crashes down across the drive, and the guests are compelled to remain overnight. The next morning Giles's dead body is discovered in the boat-house on Herons' Mere. Though seemingly an instance of suicide by shot-gun, earnest series character Dr Fitzbrown – 'a tall raw-boned young man' with 'thick dark eyebrows', 'shiny clothes and a shabby little car' – quickly pronounces that Giles's death is a case of foul play. Soon police surgeon Jones and Superintendent Mallett are on the scene, stirring up a pot of illicit emotions and nasty secrets.

Aside from the fact that Giles, ostensibly attached to his cousin Lucy, had become decidedly attracted to Arden Laforte, there is also the matter of the secretive work he was doing on a special military rifle, with the aim of obtaining a lucrative government contract. (There are rumours of war with Germany, after all.) Could there have been industrial espionage afoot? Just what has been taking place around the little island in Herons' Mere, where a target has been set up for rifle practice? More than pike fishing, you may be sure! It is a most tangled web – or fishing line – but matters both murderous and matrimonial are neatly resolved after a thrilling climax.

Elements from *Death on Herons' Mere* may seem familiar to modern readers. When reading the book I myself was reminded of bits from British mysteries from over a four-decade period, including Patricia Wentworth's *The Clock Strikes Twelve* (1944), Agatha Christie's *Dead Man's Folly* (1956) and Robert Barnard's *Corpse in a Gilded Cage* (1984). Yet for many nostalgic vintage-mystery readers in the beleaguered third decade of the twenty-first century, over one hundred years after the Golden Age of detective fiction began, familiarity makes the heart grow fonder. And certainly one can never have enough of the good writing and strong characterization which Mary Fitt brings to this novel, the first in an extremely welcome series of reissues.

ABOUT THE AUTHOR

One of the prominent authors of the classical detective fiction of the Golden Age and afterwards was herself a classicist: Kathleen Freeman, a British lecturer in Greek at the University College of South Wales and Monmouthshire, Cardiff (now Cardiff University) between 1919 and 1946. Primarily under the pseudonym Mary Fitt, Freeman published twenty-nine crime novels between 1936 and 1960, the last of them posthumously. Eighteen of these novels are chronicles of the criminal investigations of her series sleuth, Superintendent Mallett of Scotland Yard, while the remaining eleven of them, nine of them published under the pseudonym Mary Fitt and one apiece published under the respective names of Stuart Mary Wick and Kathleen Freeman, are stand-alone mysteries, some of which are notable precursors of the modern psychological crime novel. There is also a single collection of Superintendent Mallett 'cat mystery' short stories, *The Man Who Shot Birds*.

From the publication of her lauded debut detective novel, *Three Sisters Flew Home*, Mary Fitt – like Gladys Mitchell, an author with whom in England she for many years shared the distinguished publisher Michael Joseph – was deemed a crime writer for 'connoisseurs'. Within a few years, Fitt's first English publisher, Ivor Nicholson & Watson, proudly dubbed her devoted following a 'literary cult'. In what was an unusual action for the time, Nicholson & Watson placed on the dust jacket of their edition of Fitt's *Death at Dancing Stones* (1939) accolades from such distinguished, mystery-writing Fitt fans as Margery Allingham ('A fine detective story and a most ingenious puzzle'), Freeman Wills Crofts ('I should like to offer her my congratulations') and J. J. Connington ('This is the best book by Miss Mary Fitt I have yet read').

If not a crowned 'queen of crime' like Allingham, Agatha Christie, Dorothy L. Sayers and Ngaio Marsh, Kathleen Freeman in her Mary Fitt guise was, shall we say, a priestess of peccadillos. In 1950 Freeman was elected to the prestigious Detection Club, a year after her crime-writing cover was blown in the gossip column 'The Londoner's Diary' in the *Evening Standard*. Over the ensuing decade several of the older Mary Fitt mysteries were reprinted in paperback by Penguin and other publishers, while new ones continued to appear, to a chorus of praise from such keen critics of the crime-fiction genre as Edmund Crispin, Anthony Berkeley Cox (who wrote as, among others, Francis Iles) and Maurice Richardson. 'It is easy to run out of superlatives in writing of Mary Fitt,' declared the magazine *Queen*, 'who is without doubt among the first of our literary criminographers.'

Admittedly, Freeman enjoyed less success as a crime writer in the United States, where only ten of her twenty-nine mystery novels were published during her lifetime. However, one of Fitt's warmest boosters was the *New York Times*'s Anthony Boucher, for two decades the perceptive dean of American crime-fiction reviewers. In 1962, three years after Fitt's death, Boucher selected the author's 1950 novel *Pity for Pamela* for inclusion in the 'Collier Mystery Classics' series. In his introduction to the novel, Boucher lauded Fitt as an early and important exponent of psychological suspense in crime fiction.

Despite all the acclaim which the Mary Fitt mysteries formerly enjoyed, after Freeman's untimely death from congestive heart failure in 1959 at the age of sixty-one, the books, with very few exceptions – *Mizmaze* (Penguin, 1961), *Pity for Pamela* (Collier, 1962), *Death and the Pleasant Voices* (Dover, 1984) – fell almost entirely out of print. Therefore, this latest series of sparkling reissues from Moonstone is a welcome event indeed for lovers of vintage British mystery, of which Kathleen Freeman surely is one of the most beguiling practitioners.

*

A native Midlander, Kathleen Freeman was born at the parish of Yardley near Birmingham on 22 June 1897. The only child of Charles Henry Freeman and his wife Catherine Mawdesley, Kathleen grew up and would spend most of her adult life in Cardiff, where she moved with her parents not long after the turn of the century. Her father worked as a brewer's traveller, an occupation he had assumed possibly on account of an imperative need to support his mother and two unmarried sisters after the death of his own father, a schoolmaster and clergyman without a living who had passed away at the age of fifty-seven. This was in 1885, a dozen years before Kathleen was born, but presumably the elder Charles Freeman bequeathed a love of learning to his family, including his yet-unborn granddaughter. Catherine Mawdesley's father was James Mawdesley, of the English seaside resort town of Southport, not far from Liverpool. James had inherited his father's 'spacious and handsome silk mercer's and general draper's establishment', impressively gaslit and 'in no degree inferior, as to amplitude, variety and elegance of stock, to any similar establishment in the metropolis or inland towns' (in the words of an 1852 guide to Southport), yet he died at the age of thirty-five, leaving behind a widow and three young daughters.

As a teenager, Kathleen Freeman was educated at Cardiff High School, which, recalling the 1930s, the late memoirist Ron Warburton remembered as 'a large attractive building with a large schoolyard in front, which had a boundary wall between it and the pavement'. The girls attended classes on the ground floor, while the boys marched up to the first (respectively, the first and second floors in American terminology). 'The first-floor windows were frosted so that the boys could not look down at the girls in the school playground,' Warburton wryly recalled. During the years of the Great War, Freeman, who was apparently an autodidact in ancient Greek (a subject unavailable at Cardiff High School, although the boys learned Latin), attended the co-educational, 'red-brick' University College of South Wales and Monmouthshire, founded three decades earlier in 1883, whence she graduated with a BA in Classics in 1918. The next year saw both her mother's untimely passing at the age of fifty-two and her own appointment as a lecturer in Greek at her alma mater. In 1922, she received her MA; a Doctor of Letters belatedly followed eighteen years later, in recognition of her scholarly articles and 1926 book *The Work and Life of Solon*, about the ancient Athenian statesman. Between 1919 and 1926 Freeman was a junior colleague at University College of her former teacher Gilbert Norwood, who happened to share her great love of detective fiction, as did another prominent classical scholar, Gilbert Murray, who not long before his death in 1957 informed Freeman that he had long been a great admirer of Mary Fitt.

Freeman's rise in the field of higher education during the first half of the twentieth century is particularly impressive given the facts, which were then deemed disabling, of her sex and modest family background as the daughter of a brewer's traveller, which precluded the possibility of a prestigious Oxbridge education. 'A man will do much for a woman who is his friend, but to be suspected of being a brewer's traveller… was not pleasant,' observes the mortified narrator of William Black's novel *A Princess of Thule* (1883), anxious to correct this socially damning misimpression. Evidently unashamed of her circumstances, however, Freeman evinced a lifetime ambition to reach ordinary, everyday people with her work, eschewing perpetual confinement in academe's ivory tower.

Before turning to crime writing in 1936 under the alias of Mary Fitt, Freeman published five mainstream novels and a book of short stories, beginning with *Martin Hanner: A Comedy* (1926), a well-received academic novel about a (male) classics professor who teaches at a red-brick university in northern England. After the outbreak of the Second World War, while she was still employed at the university, Freeman, drawing on her classical education, published the patriotically themed *It Has All Happened Before: What the Greeks Thought of Their Nazis* (1941).* She

---

* Under the heading of 'Dictators', Freeman quotes Solon: 'When a man has risen too high, it is not easy to check him after; now is the time to take heed of everything.' Timeless words indeed!

also lectured British soldiers headed to the Mediterranean theatre of war on the terrain, customs and language of Greece, a country she had not merely read about but visited in the Thirties. During the cold war, when Freeman, passed over for promotion, had retired from teaching to devote herself to writing in a world confronted with yet another totalitarian menace, she returned to her inspirational theme, publishing *Fighting Words from the Greeks for Today's Struggle* (1952). Perhaps her most highly regarded layman-oriented work from this period is *Greek City-States* (1950), in which, notes scholar Eleanor Irwin, Freeman uses her 'uncanny eye for settings, as is often seen in her mysteries', to bring 'the city-states to life'. Freeman explicitly drew on her interests in both classicism and crime in her much-admired book *The Murder of Herodes and Other Trials from the Athenian Law Courts* (1946), which was effusively praised by the late Jacques Barzun, another distinguished academic mystery fancier, as 'a superb book for the [crime] connoisseur'.

In spite of her classical background, Kathleen Freeman derived her 'Mary Fitt' pseudonym – which she also employed to publish juvenile fiction, including a series of books about an intrepid young girl named Annabella – not from ancient Greece but from Elizabethan England, Eleanor Irwin has hypothesized, for the name bears resemblance to that of Mary Fitton, the English gentlewoman and maid of honour who is a candidate for the 'Dark Lady' of Shakespeare's queer-inflected sonnets. Irwin points out that Freeman's 'earliest literary publications were highly personal reflections on relationships in sonnet form'. The name also lends itself to a pun – 'Miss Fitt' – which it is likely the author deliberately intended, given her droll wit and nonconformity.

While Kathleen Freeman's first four detective novels, which appeared in 1936 and 1937, are stand-alones, her fifth essay in the form, *Sky-Rocket* (1938), introduces her burly, pipe-smoking, green-eyed, red-moustached series police detective, Superintendent Mallett, who is somewhat reminiscent of Agatha Christie's occasional sleuth

Superintendent Battle. The two men not only share similar builds but have similarly symbolic surnames.

Joined initially by acerbic police surgeon Dr Jones and later by the imaginative Dr Dudley 'Dodo' Fitzbrown – the latter of whom, introduced in *Expected Death* (1938), soon supersedes Jones – Superintendent Mallett would dominate Mary Fitt's mystery output over the next two decades. Only after Freeman's heart condition grew perilously grave in 1954 does it seem that the author's interest in Mallett and Fitzbrown dwindled, with the pair appearing in only two of the five novels published between 1956 and 1960. Similarly diminished in her final years was Freeman's involvement with the activities of the Detection Club, into which she initially had thrown herself with considerable zeal. In the first half of the decade she had attended club dinners with her beloved life partner, Dr Liliane Marie Catherine Clopet, persuaded Welsh polymath Bertrand Russell, an omnivorous detective-fiction reader, to speak at one of the dinners, and wrote a BBC radio play, *A Death in the Blackout* (in which Dr Fitzbrown appears), with the proceeds from the play going to the club.

Presumably Kathleen Freeman met Liliane Clopet at the University College of South Wales and Monmouthshire, where Clopet registered as a student in 1919. Precisely when the couple began cohabiting is unclear, but by 1929 Freeman had dedicated the first of what would be many books to Clopet ('For L.M.C.C.'), and by the Thirties the pair resided at Lark's Rise, the jointly owned house – including a surgery for Clopet and her patients – that the couple had built in St Mellons, a Cardiff suburb. In the author's biography on the back of her Penguin mystery reprints, Freeman noted that a friend had described the home where she lived as 'your Italian-blue house', though she elaborated: 'It is not Italian, but it is blue – sky-blue.' There Freeman would pass away and Clopet would reside for many years afterwards.

Born on 13 December 1901 in Berwick-upon-Tweed in Northumberland, Liliane Clopet was one of three children of native Frenchman Aristide Bernard Clopet, a master mariner, and his English wife

Charlotte Towerson, a farmer's daughter. Although Aristide became a naturalized British citizen, the Clopets maintained close connections with France. In 1942, during the Second World War, Liliane's only brother, Karl Victor Clopet – a master mariner like his father who for a dozen years had run a salvage tug in French Morocco – was smuggled by Allied forces from Casablanca to London, where he provided details of Moroccan ports, beaches and coastal defences, which were crucially important to the victory of the United States over Vichy French forces at the ensuing Battle of Port Lyautey.

Even more heroically (albeit tragically), Liliane's cousin Evelyne Clopet served with the French Resistance and was executed by the Nazis in 1944, after British forces had parachuted her into France; at her death she was only twenty-two years old. In 1956, under another pseudonym (Caroline Cory), Kathleen Freeman published a novel set in wartime France, *Doctor Underground*, in which she drew on Evelyne's experiences. A couple of years earlier, Liliane Clopet herself had published a pseudonymous novel, *Doctor Dear*, in which she depicted a female physician's struggles with sexism among her colleagues and patients.

Kathleen Freeman, who was rather masculine-looking in both her youth and middle age (boyish in her twenties, she grew stouter over the years, wearing her hair short and donning heavy tweeds), produced no issue and at her death left her entire estate, valued at over £300,000 in today's money, to Liliane Clopet. In a letter to another correspondent she avowed: 'My books are my children and I love them dearly.' Admittedly, Freeman shared custody of her mysteries with that queer Miss Fitt, but surely she loved her criminally inclined offspring, too. I have no doubt that the author would be pleased to see these books back in print again after the passage of so many years. Readers of vintage mysteries, now eager to embrace the stylish and sophisticated country-house detective novels and psychological suspense tales of an earlier era, will doubtless be pleased as well.

CURTIS EVANS

Death on Herons' Mere

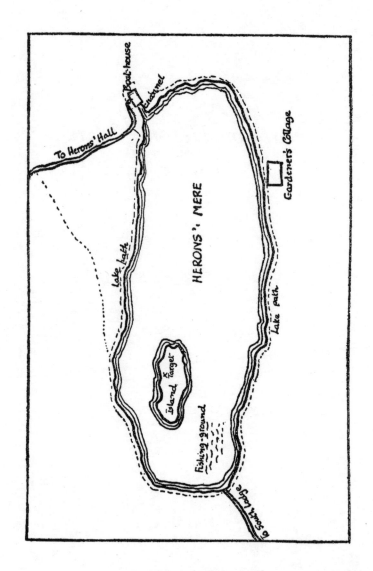

PLAN OF HERONS' MERE

FOR
L. M. C. C.

I t was the half-hour before dinner. In the immense drawing-room of Herons' Hall, Simon Gabb's guests waited without impatience for the summons to dine.

The room was warm. Simon's sherry was good, and so were his cigarettes and cigars. The guests sat in a widely-drawn semicircle, the centre of which was the fire: Simon apart in his leather chair on the right-hand side of the fire; Polly, his wife, deep in conversation with the newly-married young Mrs Olivier, whom she had pinned down on the settee for a talk about furniture; Jessica, Simon's daughter, yawning over a magazine; Basil, his younger son, and Pauline, Basil's wife, separate and silent, Basil because he was thinking of her, Pauline because there was no one near enough to talk to except him; and completing the semicircle, on another deep settee, James Gabb, Simon's brother, and Hubert Olivier the lawyer.

'You know,' James was saying confidentially to Hubert – though the distance between them and the other guests made a lowering of the voice unnecessary – 'I'm not at all sure Simon did the right thing in buying this great place.'

'The right thing?' echoed Hubert, giving the phrase a mocking twist, as if that were the last consideration that need apply. 'What makes you think so?'

'For himself, I mean,' said James, ignoring Hubert's misinterpretation. He glanced across at his brother sitting in his leather chair with his whisky and soda beside him, gazing into the fire, as much alone as if he were in his study 'at home,' as James automatically called it, meaning Simon's previous residence.

'I don't see why,' said Hubert Olivier in the richly-modulated voice which gave him so much pleasure: 'It's the finest property in the county, and it was going dirt cheap. Yet no one would look at it, because no one but Mr Gabb could have afforded to run the place. It had been on the market for nearly two years when Mr Gabb bought it, and already it was going to rack and ruin. Personally, I like to see these old places being kept up.'

James eyed him shrewdly. 'Oh yes. And your firm handled the deal. I can well understand—'

Hubert lifted a pained white hand. 'My brother William,' he corrected.

'Oh yes, your brother's the solicitor. But it was you who put the business in his way. Don't tell me you didn't get your pickings!'

Hubert did not deign to answer. He disliked James Gabb, and was not much interested in him as a possible client. Simon was the quarry, and he was pleased to see how well Madeleine seemed to be getting on with Mrs Simon. But still, one never knew. Simon and James seemed to be on good terms, and the families were much interwoven. It would not do to quarrel with James.

'No; what I meant was,' James was proceeding, 'this place is too big for Simon. We were born in a back street in Birmingham. Well, one's ideas change, and neither of us would want to go back there, even for our own sakes, much less now we've got children who've been brought up quite differently from ourselves. But buying this place was going too far.' He stared across the room, past the circle of heads, to the great windows that ran from floor to ceiling. It was still light enough to see the view, down over the terraced lawns and flower-beds to the lake that shimmered palely in the watery sunset, and the dark woods behind the lake. 'It makes one feel small, sometimes, and that's not good for a man like Simon, who's always had to fight his way in the world.'

Olivier laughed patronizingly. 'I don't suppose he would agree with you.'

'Perhaps not,' said James. 'He's stubborn. But all the same, when he looks round at a set like this, all sitting primly in their places, ten yards from the fire, he must laugh sometimes. He must know they'd sooner be bunched up all together in the sort of room they're used to, which would go about eight times into this one.' He sat forward, hands on knees. 'Look at 'em: do they look at home?' He leaned back. 'No, and they never will. In time they'll get to hate the place. 'Tisn't made for them.' He rounded on Hubert. 'Was it your brother,' he asked bluntly, 'or you, who advised him to buy the place just as it stood – furniture, pictures, everything?'

'It was a great bargain.' Hubert glanced round the room. 'The dealers would have been glad if he had turned down the fittings, believe me. He would have had to furnish the place anyway. He saved thousands.'

'Yes, but all these pictures, miniatures, knick-knacks and what-not—' James waved a hand. 'They belong to someone else still. He's paid for them, but they're not his. He's living in a house of ghosts.'

Hubert said no more. A moment or two later he rose and crossed the room to talk to Simon Gabb.

James called out heartily to Pauline:

'Well, my dear, and how's the boy?'

'Very well, thank you,' said Pauline stiffly. Her bored expression did not change. Basil watched her broodingly. He thought what a fool he had been to imagine that motherhood would change her. She was bored with the baby too, because it was his. She was beautiful, stupid, shallow, cold-hearted, untouchable – the rich spoilt daughter of rich common parents, like his own. 'Our parents are better than we are,' he thought. 'My father has talent, genius perhaps. He founded the great business on which we all live. My father is a master of men and of circumstance: if anyone got across his path, they would be removed. As for a woman:

could anyone see Simon Gabb altering a single item of his daily routine to please his wife? And yet doubtless he loved her, and she obviously doted on him. Whereas I,' thought Basil, 'am my father's employee, industrious, dependable, dependant. And as a husband, I am a joke, though so far a joke that only I have seen.' He clenched his fists. 'But one of these days, I'll make them all change their tune…'

Madeleine Olivier had left Mrs Gabb's side, and moved across to Pauline; for Mrs James Gabb had now come in, and was enthusiastically welcomed by Polly. The two ladies had much to say to each other. Madeleine therefore made her escape, and sat down beside Pauline. She and Pauline were old school friends.

Pauline, Madeleine thought, looked bored: more bored than ever, for her expression had never been very animated. It was clear that she was not very happy with Basil. Even the baby seemed to have made no difference; it had added to Pauline's air of discontent. What was the matter? Madeleine wondered. Did Pauline find her position unsatisfactory, in spite of the wealth and the power of the family into which she had married? Perhaps the trouble lay just there: Pauline had stepped into the second place, by marrying the younger son; and the second place was not by any means her rôle. Not that she, or any sensible girl, would have preferred to marry Giles…

Mrs Simon Gabb drew Mrs James Gabb down on to the soft settee. Mrs Simon Gabb was soft, plump and fair, covered with jewellery, yet breathless and unsophisticated in manner. Mrs James Gabb – Janet – was tall and large-boned and dark, little inclined to smile, much less laugh; but the two called each other sisters, and were in frequent consultation. Janet leaned towards Polly anxiously, anticipating misfortune.

'They may come at any minute,' Polly was saying in her breathless way. She applied her ivory fan to her pursed-up lips, and glanced behind her, over the back of the settee, out towards the setting sun. 'Of course I said, the moment I knew he'd met them, "Bring them here".'

'Don't you think you're foolish?' said Janet lugubriously.

'Oh no, no, I don't see why,' said Polly. 'The children have always brought everyone home, you know. Simon and I have always encouraged them. There's no harm when everything is frank and open, is there?' Her words tumbled out somewhat disconnectedly, and she kept bouncing round to look out of the great window.

'I don't know about that.' Janet's gloom did not lift.

'But,' said Polly, suddenly appealing to her, 'what can I do, my dear? You know what Giles is. The slightest word from me – from anyone – of course, his father wouldn't...' She glanced fearfully round, and leaned forward. 'Every day this week. Fishing on the lake. Shooting. Walking.' Her mouth turned down pathetically. Her pretence that all was well had dissolved before Janet's prognostication of evil.

'With the girl?' Janet's tone implied that all was lost.

'Sometimes with the girl, sometimes all of them. So I'm told. I haven't met them. I didn't think it necessary to call – and they've never called on me. Of course, the position was rather difficult.'

'Not at all,' snapped Janet. 'If any calling was done, they should have called on you. The mistake you made was in letting the South Lodge to them at all. It was bound to make things awkward, after their being here.' She surveyed the big room, in the corners of which the shadows were gathering. 'How many of them are there? Where had they been in the meantime? Who looks after them? Both the parents are dead, aren't they?'

'Yes. There's an aunt, a Mrs Charleroy, Colonel Laforte's sister. I believe she used to look after them when their father was abroad. They've only been at the South Lodge a couple of months, you know. Where were they before? My dear, I don't know. I gather they were very poor after the Colonel died; they couldn't sell the Hall, you see. Then, when we bought it, I'm told the first thing they did was to rush off to the south of France for a holiday. Then they asked if they could come here. What could we say? We didn't want the South Lodge, since Basil and Pauline had decided on the other.'

By now, Polly was quite out of breath. Janet studied her. Janet's hands, somewhat red, were spread out on the green taffeta of her dinner-frock like lobsters on lettuce leaves.

'How many of them are there?' she asked again.

Polly reflected. 'There's the girl,' she said, 'and a younger brother, and I believe a cousin, this Mrs Charleroy's son. I got this from Sims: Giles never tells me anything. He spends all his time with them. He never goes near the works. Basil has to do everything. Luckily, Basil is so reliable, otherwise I don't know what Simon would do.'

'And Simon? What does he say?' asked Janet sharply.

'Nothing.'

'Nothing? That's not like Simon. He's always been pretty strict with the boys – too strict, James and I said. James expects obedience, but he's not always shaking the cane under their noses. Yet Harry's not spoilt, and Giles is. And now: away for a week, you say, and Simon says nothing?'

'Nothing at all.'

'Then there's going to be a big row one of these days, you mark my words. So that's the reason why Giles will hardly look at Lucy.' Lucy was Janet's daughter.

'Reason?' Polly was taken by surprise.

'Yes: this girl. You'll have to take a line, Polly, that is, unless you no longer want it – you and Simon. Lucy will break her heart, but no matter. She can find someone else.' Janet sniffed. 'It's all very well for the girl: naturally she wants to get back her old home. A very clever move, I must say. But do you really want Giles to bring home a penniless adventuress? – for that's all she'll be, in spite of the name.'

Polly wriggled a little, and sniffed at her silver-topped bottle of opopanax, which lay, with other trinkets, on the round inlaid table beside her. 'I don't think it's come to that,' she said deprecatingly. 'Personally

I was thankful Simon said nothing. I'm sure, this time, it's wise.' She glanced round, fearfully yet admiringly, at her husband, who was leaning back telling a magisterial anecdote to the deferential Hubert.

Simon was proud of his position on the bench. He forgot that Hubert was a lawyer, as he jabbed at him with his gold-rimmed spectacles. 'Punish the crime,' he was saying, 'punish the crime immediately – or not at all.'

'But sir,' Hubert was saying in his silky tones, 'that would often mean taking the law into one's own hands; and you, as a magistrate, wouldn't advocate that?' To a sensitive ear, his tone was ironical, even insolent; but there was no sensitive ear present, except perhaps Basil's, and he was not listening.

Simon replaced his gold-rimmed spectacles on to his nose, and gave Hubert a look so direct and lively that Hubert was afraid for a moment lest his sarcasm had been too plain. But the fear was groundless.

'As a magistrate,' said Simon, 'I can't admit it. But I can assure you, as a man—. Well, that's the price we pay for respectability. Have a cigar. Have some more sherry.' He got up, decanter in hand, and began a tour of the circle.

Polly and Janet didn't even see him. Basil shook his head; but Simon had already passed him by, as he had passed over his daughter Jessica also. He paused before Pauline and Madeleine. As he filled up their glasses, his shrewd little eyes rested benevolently on them, and his face, much wrinkled, creased into smiles. The handsome well-built girl with the mass of golden curls all over her head was the daughter of his old friend Wilkinson the glass-manufacturer, and a most suitable wife for Basil. The other one, the flimsy pretty one, was only old Dr Parkes' youngest daughter, and married to a man who was courting Simon for favours. Nevertheless, as they sat there in their dinner-frocks, one in blue, one in pink, he saw them merely as two charming creatures, equal because of the ornamental quality which they shared.

'How's the boy?' he said to Pauline, and when she had answered, 'How are they getting on with that boiler-job at the Lodge? I sent a couple of men over yesterday.'

Pauline shrugged her shoulders. 'Thank you, yes, I know,' she said listlessly. 'But it wasn't much use, as Basil wasn't there, and I had no idea what was wanted. So I had to tell them to come again, one evening when there's a chance he may be in. The trouble is, I never know when he will be in, lately.'

Simon caught the note of reproach, and it seemed to him very natural and proper. 'I know, I know, my dear,' he said kindly. 'Basil has been hard put to it, like the rest of us. And I'm afraid things aren't going to get easier for a while. No, not for a long while. Still, we must see what we can do.'

He turned away. Her remarks had reminded him of his real life, to which this was a brief interlude; and a shadow crossed his face. His wrinkles returned to their normal hard lines, as he carried the decanter across to his brother James.

Pauline sneered: 'Like the rest of us! Except dear Giles, of course! If he did his share, Basil wouldn't need to work like an employee, while Giles draws his allowance and does nothing. If Giles stayed away altogether, it wouldn't be so bad; but he turns up whenever he feels like it, interferes with everything, and then goes off as he's doing now, for weeks at a time.'

Madeleine studied her. 'I gather he's going about with the people who used to live here.'

Pauline nodded.

'There's a girl, isn't there?' probed Madeleine carefully.

Pauline tossed her head. 'I believe so.'

'Yes, I thought there was. Hubert's brother acted for them over the sale of the Hall. I wonder what she's like. Have you seen her?'

'No,' said Pauline, 'though Basil's mother seems to think they may all burst in on us at any moment. I believe she has told Giles he can bring them here.'

'Well, why shouldn't she?' Madeleine knew the answer from Pauline's point of view, but she was interested to see how far Pauline was prepared to put it into words. 'It's time Giles got married.'

But all Pauline would say was, 'Do you think so?', and the curl of her lip expressed deep certitude to the contrary.

'Oh, come,' said Madeleine. 'All that must be six or seven years ago. He must be quite cured by now. It was only overwork, wasn't it? I thought you were all trying to marry him off to Lucy. If there's any taint in the family, the last thing they'd want would be to let cousins marry.'

'There was never any fear of that,' retorted Pauline. 'The mothers would like it, and so would Lucy; but not Giles.'

Madeleine changed the subject. 'Why are they so busy at the works?' she said curiously. 'I heard Father say the other day that Gabb's were taking on new men all the time. It's something big, isn't it?'

Pauline looked burdened with secrecy, and also embarrassed; for she remembered very well from her schooldays how difficult it was to keep anything secret from Madeleine Parkes.

'It's a Government contract,' she said. Madeleine forbore to press her further; for she believed she knew as much about it as Pauline.

Simon sat down beside his brother James, and turned towards him so that he could prop his elbow on the back of the settee, and his head on his hand.

'How is it going?' said James.

'All right,' said Simon. They spoke to each other in undertones, with the least possible movement of the lips, as if there were always someone near at hand who might be trying to overhear their conversation.

'You're going on with it?' said James.

'Of course. Why not? If things develop as they are doing, it'll be compulsory for everybody in our line sooner or later; so why not now?'

'But suppose nothing comes of it? You'll have converted all your plant and be left with it on your hands. Better stick to road-nails and beacons.' James gave a quiet laugh.

Simon rolled on to his side, a little closer to James. 'Things are pretty quiet with you, aren't they?'

James frowned. 'Average, for the time of year.'

Simon nodded. 'I wish you'd come in on this – or if you won't do that, come along and give me a hand. Just for a while, you know, until the thing gets under way.' He leaned closer still. 'The fact is, Jim, this new business is a big responsibility. I need help – someone I can trust.'

'You've got Basil,' said James gruffly, and added as an afterthought, 'and Giles.'

'Basil's a good lad,' said Simon, 'but he can't do everything.'

There was a silence.

'All right,' said James at last. 'I'll look in occasionally.' He tapped Simon's knee. 'What's on your mind?'

The brothers stared closely at each other for a second. Simon was the first to look away. He glanced round the room, and turned back to James: 'Come into my study after dinner, and I'll tell you.' Then he picked up his decanter and trotted back across the room to his place beside the fire.

Mrs Simon Gabb bounced round on her settee for the twentieth time. 'There they are!' she cried, interrupting Janet's discourse.

This time, everybody heard, and followed her gaze through the window. The dusk was falling, and the light had now almost left the surface of the lake, which was turning grey, like the skies above it. Along the terrace, past the window, a little procession was passing: four figures carrying fishing-tackle, silhouetted against the lake and the sky. In front, the long loping stride of Giles could be recognized; he carried a shot-gun as well as his rod. The other three, a girl dressed in slacks, and two young men, followed Giles in single file.

Mrs Gabb jumped up. 'I'll just go and see.'

Janet exclaimed, 'Surely they're not coming in like that!' But Polly was already at the door.

Twenty minutes later, the same odd procession, slightly altered in appearance, filed into the drawing-room, and stood on the hearth-rug, confronting the semicircle of critical eyes.

2

Polly came running across the tiled hall just as the door closed behind the visitors. She wished to greet them, to intercept them on the threshold. She felt that if she welcomed them warmly, as her son's friends, this return to their old home would be less painful to them; and mixed with this kindly thought there was – though she was scarcely aware of it – a feeling that they must be propitiated. They were like ghosts who come back to their old haunts and may be harmless or may turn malevolent; she felt that she alone could forestall them, nullify their power of hurting the present, actual occupants.

The little party stood in the middle of the hall in a row, as if waiting for someone to give them permission to proceed. Giles himself made one of them: he too faced his mother as she came tripping forward with outstretched hand. All four looked forlorn and alien in their strange clothes: Giles and the two young men in oilskins and waders, the girl in her slacks and big boots and sou'wester; all dripping with rain, and smelling of fish and mud from the lake. Polly, coming straight from the warm luxurious room, was a little taken aback at the sight of them. She stopped within a few yards of them, dreading the coming clasp of clammy hands; and her housewifely eye noted the wet, muddy footsteps, though it was no longer her business to remove them or even to see that they were removed. She glanced uncertainly at Giles.

Giles looked even paler and darker than usual. His day's sport appeared to have tired him. His hair, smoothly brushed back as a rule, was tousled and wet, and his features looked pinched and sharp.

'Arden,' he said in a thin tired voice to the girl, 'this is my mother. Mother, this is Arden Laforte.'

Mrs Gabb stepped forward, over-anxious, and nearly collided with Arden, who likewise had stepped forward. Somehow their hands met, and Mrs Gabb, glancing up, was relieved to see under the down-turned brim of the sou'-wester two smiling grey eyes. Arden had a charming smile.

'And this,' went on Giles sourly, 'is Billy Laforte.'

Billy Laforte followed his sister. He was younger and chubbier, and he too had grey eyes: but his were round and frank, and less conspicuous than his wide smile. He shook Mrs Gabb's hand so heartily that her many rings ground against one another and bit into her flesh. The pain made her stammer a little as she gasped:

'I – I'm so glad to see you.'

The last of the three awaited his turn. 'This is Royce Charleroy,' Giles's incisive voice continued. As Royce presented himself, Arden murmured, still standing beside Mrs Gabb, 'My cousin.'

'How do you do?' said Royce. He too, to Mrs Gabb's surprise, looked perfectly amiable, and not in the least put out by the situation. No one could have told that this smiling trio had ever set foot inside Herons' Hall before. Only Giles looked bitter, as he stood aside watching: bitter and impatient, as if he wished this farce would end.

'Well,' said Mrs Gabb to Arden, 'you'd like to wash, I expect. Come up to my room.' She could not help casting a glance at the muddy Wellingtons.

Arden smiled. She looked round for somewhere to sit down. The high-backed oak settle stood where it always had stood, against the wall. 'May I?' said Arden. The other two, encouraged, followed her. They seated themselves in a row, and struggled out of their fishing-clothes. Soon the floor in front of them was littered with waders, mackintoshes and boots. Three fishing-rods leaned against the panelled wall, and fishing-baskets and wallets were dangling from hooks near by.

Giles watched them sourly for a minute; then he slouched away, carrying his gun, his rod and his other impedimenta, and disappeared through a door. The three on the settle laughed and chatted to each other. Royce had to kneel before Arden and help her to pull off her Wellingtons. It was, for a moment, a family party, at which Mrs Gabb was beginning to feel an outsider. But Arden, realizing the position, jumped up as soon as she had been freed from her boots.

'I'm ready, Mrs Gabb,' she said cheerfully, preparing to step out of the chaos of discarded garments and follow Mrs Gabb upstairs.

Mrs Gabb eyed her, surprised. She was tall and beautifully built, slender, with wide shoulders, narrow hips and an extremely small waist. Her height and slenderness were emphasized by her dark well-cut clothes. Her head was small, and her hair golden; in spite of her excursion in wind and rain, she looked neat and well-groomed. She had tied round her head a piece of scarlet cloth, which had kept her hair unruffled. Mrs Gabb's eyes travelled down to her feet.

'But my dear, your feet!' she said. 'Let me get you a pair of slippers.'

Arden looked down at her feet. Her hands were in her pockets, and she leaned over, smiling, looking down as if the two feet clad in thick knitted stockings, sticking out from her trouser-legs, didn't quite belong to her.

'It's all right, thank you,' she said in her soft pleasant voice. 'I've brought a pair of slippers.' And she pulled out from each trouser-pocket a scarlet slipper of soft kid, folded small. She put them on quickly, and gave a little laugh. 'I thought of your carpets,' she said, with a glance towards the drawing-room. The naturalness of 'your' was perfect, un-spoilt by the slightest emphasis; yet Mrs Gabb noticed it, for she remembered the pale buff Chinese carpet on to which Arden would soon be stepping again, after nearly three years.

'I expect Giles will be back in a minute,' she said to the two young men. 'But of course you know your way about.' She waved vaguely towards the cloak-room.

They nodded back, with bright unembarrassed smiles. 'Oh, we shall be all right, thank you.'

Mrs Gabb led the way upstairs, past the sporting prints, the foxes' masks and the twenty-pound stuffed pike in its glass case; past the oil paintings on the landing walls, and the sinister-looking coat of mail that stood in a corner of the corridor and seemed to grin at her through its visor; past the Sheraton cabinet filled with Sèvres and Swansea china, that marked the approach to the ladies' sphere of influence in the house.

'Come into my room,' she said, tripping along ahead of Arden until she reached the massive carved door that led into one of the front bedrooms. She held the door open to admit Arden, and then tripped across to the windows. From here the aspect was the same as from the drawing-room. It was almost dark outside, yet still the lake shimmered faintly in the distance. There was no wind, and a few wreaths of mist were creeping out from among the trees across the trim lawns of sea-washed turf, and over the flower-beds that by day were bright with scarlet and pink begonias.

Arden entered, and stood looking round vaguely, not in the least as though she recognized the room or anything in it. The room was very large. She stood half-way between the door and the window, too far from the window to be able to see anything but the lowering sky, yet not looking to right or left or behind; not looking at the twin beds that seemed much too small to hold real people, or at the dressing-table with its array of silver and cut glass, or at the escritoire on which a clean neat blotting-pad hopefully awaited the indiscretions of its new owner. Arden merely stood there smiling, and her scarlet slippers, pointed and curled at the toes, struck a violent note of contrast with the Prussian blue of the carpet.

Polly pulled at the curtain cords, and the great velvet curtains, Prussian blue like the carpet, swung softly into place, interposing their darkness between the room and the fading landscape. She pressed the switch of the dressing-table lamp:

'Come, my dear. Here are brushes and combs. Please use anything you want. Here is the bathroom.' She hurried here and there, turning on lights, setting out towels. Arden, having washed her hands—and Polly, hovering about her, noticed that her hands were long and slim and not useless-looking, though what they were used for she could not have said for certain: certainly not for housework – Arden came out from the bathroom, and sitting down before the low dressing-table, began to comb her hair and rearrange it under the red band. And now she seemed perfectly at home, though she refrained from touching any of Polly's silver brushes and combs, and used a small comb of her own, from one of her pockets. She took her time, too. Polly even heard her humming a little tune as she pushed the scarlet band down on to her hair again, making the smooth hair above it look like a golden skull-cap.

Polly glanced at the tiny diamond-encrusted watch that dangled against her bosom: it was long past dinner-time. And there were still the introductions to be made – so many people! One could not hurry these things. She liked meals to be punctual. She forgot that it was no longer her affair if dishes had to be kept hot without being ruined, because people would not come to the table when told.

At last Arden rose.

'I'm ready,' she said again, with the same sweet smile. And Mrs Gabb, relieved, ran out of the room ahead of her, past the Sheraton cabinet and the sinister coat-of-mail, and the pike and the foxes' masks and the rows of sporting prints, to where Royce and Billy, smiling and at their ease, and Giles, entirely unsmiling, awaited them.

3

Giles, casting a displeased look round the semicircle in the drawing-room, stood with his three friends on the hearth-rug; and the three newcomers also surveyed the company with pleasant friendly smiles. Arden smiled amiably at no one in particular. Her hands were deep in her trousers-pockets, and she balanced herself on her heels and toes, rocking a little with enjoyment as the warmth of the fire began to penetrate. Billy smiled round at all indiscriminately. Royce, scrutinizing the company in more leisurely fashion, appeared not very much interested, until his eyes fell on Pauline. His face lit up at once, and he seemed about to go over to her; but Pauline, who had been staring at him in astonishment and with a touch of dismay, dropped her eyes and avoided his special greeting. Mr Gabb came forward.

'Father, this is Miss Laforte,' said Giles irritably, casting a look of hatred round the circle, and pausing to direct a specially venomous look at his Aunt Janet. 'She used to live here, you know,' he blurted out suddenly in louder tones, somewhat to his own surprise. And he rounded again on Aunt Janet, whose eyes were riveted to Arden's scarlet slippers.

Simon came forward hospitably. He was much shorter than Arden, but he did not lack dignity, and it was clear that he was the master of this house no less than of the great works of which the blast-furnaces reddened the skies twenty miles away. He shook hands with Arden and with the two young men; then, leaving the latter to find their own places, he shepherded Arden to the seat of honour beside himself. Hubert Olivier rose as she approached, and bowed exaggeratedly, but

Arden did not appear to see him. She settled herself down in the chair offered to her, accepted sherry and an Egyptian cigarette, and gave Simon her whole attention.

'Were you successful?' said Simon.

'Yes, thank you. Giles and I caught a pike each.'

'Shoot anything?' Simon jerked the words out at his son, who was standing behind Arden's chair.

'No. We saw a skein of geese, but of course they were well out of range.' Giles became animated for a moment. 'I tried a shot, but—'

'They took no notice at all,' Arden laughed. 'They just flew straight on, completely uninterested.' The look she threw up at Giles was malicious and provocative, though her tone was mild.

'Are you good at shooting, Miss Laforte?' asked Simon indulgently.

Giles gave a contemptuous snort. 'She's the best shot I know.'

Simon laughed. 'Well, you young people are welcome. I tell you, Miss Laforte, every morning before breakfast I take a walk, winter and summer – always have done, from a boy. And all I know about your lake is, it takes me just forty minutes to walk to the boat-house and back, by the terrace and the avenue of horse-chestnuts. As for walking round it, I guess I'll never have time.'

'You've never been on it either?' smiled Arden.

'No. Never even put my head into the boat-house.'

'You must come with us some time,' said Arden, bending on him a look which made him feel younger. He had quite forgotten that the lake, and the boats, and the pike, and the wild geese flying over, were his, not hers, to enjoy or destroy.

Royce strolled across to Pauline.

By now, Madeleine had vacated the chair beside her and had rejoined her husband. They were both getting a little resentful that dinner was delayed for so long because of these intruders; and Hubert had his own private cause for discontent.

'If they couldn't come properly dressed,' whispered Madeleine, 'they shouldn't have come at all.' She moved indignantly on her settee, so that the pink flounces of her georgette skirt billowed out like the ruffled feathers of a bird. Hubert murmured agreement; but he still watched the scarlet slippers opposite, out of the corner of his eye.

'Good evening,' said Royce, sinking into the chair beside Pauline. 'What a pleasant surprise! I thought you lived at the North Lodge.'

'I do,' said Pauline.

'I mean,' said Royce, 'I didn't know you visited here.'

'Didn't you?' said Pauline, not very brilliantly; but she was not quite sure whether she wished to tell him so soon who she was and why their acquaintanceship could not continue. It was one thing to say good-day to the young man with the gun when he saluted her so pleasantly on the woodland path, another thing to talk to him here in her father-in-law's drawing-room. Basil's brooding eyes would soon be upon her, and there would be, on the way home, the usual spate of questions: 'Where did you meet him? You never told me! Why didn't you tell me, if there's no harm in it?' And yet she did not want to say to this young man, 'I am the wife of that sullen-looking man over there. I have a baby, undoubtedly his, six months old. Therefore——' Here he was beside her, her cavalier of the woods, looking, in his old tweed suit, more distinguished than Basil or Hubert or any of these half-baked males could ever manage to look in a dinner-jacket. Pauline was a snob, and a romantic. She was pleased to learn that her admirer was not the gamekeeper, but the nephew of Colonel Sir Charles Laforte.

Royce meanwhile was thinking that in her way Pauline was very good-looking. She had high cheek-bones and a pointed chin; she was probably rather stupid, outside the limited range of her own immediate interests, but remarkably wide-awake within them. She was, he diagnosed, bored stiff with her present company, including her husband; for Royce knew quite well, and had known since the first day he met her, who she was. She was longing for a love-affair, but too shrewd to risk her comfortable position for love. Yet she had within her unsuspected possibilities of volcanic eruption. It therefore behoved one to approach warily, and be ready to leap away at the first stirring of the depths.

Pauline looked down from her higher chair on to the young man so negligently dressed, lounging beside her; and suddenly she had the absurd unaccountable feeling that she was the ephemeral guest, and he the inmate of the house. He seemed to belong. And yet, what right had he to make her feel an outsider? A wave of strong feeling, that she mistook for annoyance, rushed over her. She turned to say something unpleasant that would put him in his place, and caught the full impact of his lazy, laughing gaze. Pauline stared back at him, with parted lips. For the first time in her life she felt weak at the knees.

Billy crossed the floor and sat down beside Jessica.

'Hullo!' he said.

Jessica, engrossed in the magazine, tore herself from it with difficulty, and stared.

'What are *you* doing here?'

'Bless my soul!' said Billy. 'Haven't you been listening? I'm an honoured guest. We've been out on the lake all day. I say!' He wriggled forward eagerly. 'Why don't you come with us sometimes? I'll teach you to spin for pike. It's good fun. You'd like it. You're bound to be bored here.'

'Thank you,' said Jessica scornfully, 'I hate killing things.'

Billy said good-humouredly, 'You eat lamb and mint sauce, I suppose?'

'Yes,' said Jessica fiercely, 'but I wish I didn't.'

'But that,' began Billy, 'is quite illogical—'

'I know it is!' She almost stamped her foot. Jessica was dark, like Giles, but otherwise there was no point of resemblance between her and the rest of the family. Her black eyes flashed fire. 'I can't bear myself for not being a vegetarian; and yet I couldn't bear myself any better if I were. To me, it's murder to kill animals – just as much murder as to kill a human being; but I let it be done for me every day, though I couldn't do it myself. I'd starve rather than kill a lamb or a calf. In fact, I sometimes think it would be much easier to kill a human being – some human beings.' She brooded for a moment with drawn brows.

Billy wriggled forward still further and rubbed his hands together. 'Ah, now you're talking!' he said ecstatically. 'Now who would you start on? Anybody here?' He looked round the circle expectantly. 'Don't forget to let me know if I can help you in any way. I'm quite a good shot – and I know all the deep pools in the mere. A sack weighted with a couple of big stones—'

Jessica laughed. 'Oh, shut up!' She still looked at him suspiciously; but she was no longer bored. 'Are you staying to dinner?'

'Naturally.'

Jessica was pleased.

4

It was while they were dining that the storm began.

The evening had been unusually calm, with a ground mist, and a young moon obscured by the motionless film of milk-white cloud. Then suddenly a little wind arose. It moaned round the great windows and rattled the solid oak shutters inside; it even succeeded in stirring the heavy velvet curtains, though no draught penetrated past them into the room. The electric light in the massive hanging chandeliers wavered and flickered ominously. There was a sharp rattle of hail, like a handful of gravel thrown against the panes; and before the company had had time to do more than look round and make an astonished comment, a crash of thunder shook the house as if from the blast of a near high-explosive bomb.

'Good heavens, we're struck!' said Hubert. All looked towards the ceiling, as if expecting it to collapse or open to admit a thunderbolt.

'Don't worry,' said Billy to Jessica, patting her knee under the table. 'We were struck several times when we lived here. My father once had the telephone receiver knocked clean out of his hand. After that, he had the chimneys simply plastered with lightning conductors. You're perfectly safe.' He pressed her hand.

Jessica withdrew her hand. 'I hate thunder,' she said. 'I'm afraid of it, and ashamed of myself for being afraid.'

'Oh, there's nothing to be ashamed of,' said Billy cheerfully. 'It's a reflex. But it's silly to be afraid of thunder. By the time you hear the crash, the danger's over. Sound travels so much slower than light, so if you were going to be killed, you'd be dead long before you heard the thunder.'

Again the lights dimmed. Jessica seized his arm. The second thunder-clap was more violent than the first. After a terrifying crash, it reverberated away into the distance in threatening growls.

'Gosh!' said Polly, reverting to her natural dialect. Everyone waited. Everything was at a standstill. The servants ceased to serve. The diners ceased dining. The electric lights brightened, flickered, and went out; the glass pendants hanging from the chandeliers vibrated and tinkled as the thunder crashed again. Billy put his arm round Jessica's waist. She said nothing, but he heard her breathing quicken.

'Don't be afraid,' he said. 'It's only a fuse.'

There was a call for candles, and the butler's suave voice saying, 'Yes, madam; in a moment, madam.' One by one, candlesticks and silver candelabra were brought and set about the room. On the table they placed two three-branched candelabra with tall tapering pale-pink candles. Giles, sitting beside Arden, saw her look up at them with parted lips and an odd ecstatic smile. Then, glancing from her to Royce, and then to Billy, he saw that they, too, were watching her. He also saw the looks that passed between the three of them, when Arden became aware of their scrutiny.

Jessica, feeling that Billy's attention had momentarily left her, said, 'What are you looking at? Don't you like candles? We've never had them before.'

'No, of course not,' said Billy absently. Then, turning to her again: 'You see, when we were here, we never had anything else in the dining-room.'

They had returned to the drawing-room. The storm, the candle-light, the whole unusual experience, had thawed the company and dissolved the stiff semicircle. Simon and James had gone off for their conference in the study. Hubert, Polly, Madeleine and Janet had settled down to a game of bridge beside the fire. Billy and Jessica had wandered off to play billiards. Arden sat in the window-seat, and cast down her eyes at the carpet, while Giles devoured her with his gaze. Royce and Pauline sat uncomfortably apart and aware of each other, under the sulky wardenship of Basil. And all the time, torrential rain beat against the windows, drummed on the sills, streamed from every spout and gully.

'Mrs Gabb,' came Arden's soft voice at last, 'I think we must be going now.'

'Oh, but my dear!' Mrs Gabb turned, exposing her hand and annoying her partner. 'You can't possibly go home to-night. Can she?' She appealed to the company.

Janet sniffed. Madeleine shrugged her shoulders. Hubert gave an elaborate sigh and ostentatiously studied his hand. But Polly, unheeding, flung down her cards and ran across to Arden.

'It really wouldn't be safe – would it, Giles? The lake path is most dangerous, I'm sure, especially in the dark – and so slippery! We have plenty of room here – plenty of room. Why, my dear, who knows? – one of the trees might fall down on you, after all that thunder and lightning!'

Arden said mildly, 'I really think we ought to go.'

'If you're thinking of your aunt, my dear, we can telephone. Oh no, of course, the telephone is out of order. Well, I'm sure she won't expect you on a night like this.' Polly, who would on no account have been left alone in any house, even one of a row in a crowded street, for five minutes at night, cheerfully awarded Mrs Charleroy great merit for her unselfish courage in the cause of the children's safety.

'Oh, I'm not worrying about Aunt Helen,' said Arden in her unemphatic, soft voice. 'She won't mind.'

'Then you'll stay!' Polly jumped up, delighted as always at gaining her point, though a moment later she might have forgotten even what it was. She ran to the bell-push beside the fire. 'Oh!' she said, remembering that probably it too was out of order.

'There's a bell-cord over there,' said Arden to Giles. 'I expect it still works. They always used to.' Giles made for the corner near the window, and pulled. Polly came back to Arden.

'Is there any special room you'd prefer?' she said, almost anxiously. 'Don't hesitate to mention it, my dear. It's no trouble at all.'

Arden looked up at her. 'Oh, please!' she murmured, waving the suggestion away. And unaccountably she blushed.

Polly went off to superintend the arrangements.

'That was silly of me, wasn't it?' said Arden to Giles.

'You know best,' said Giles. 'You know if you can stand it.'

Arden ignored the intensity of his solicitude. She answered as if irrelevantly, 'Your mother's a sweet woman. I shouldn't like to hurt her feelings.'

'Basil,' called out Hubert, 'come and take your mother's hand.'

Basil shook his head.

'Then perhaps you'd care to?' said Hubert to Royce.

Royce got up from the easy chair in which he had been lounging. 'With pleasure.' He left Pauline and Basil to hate each other in the shadows.

Nobody spoke for a while. The fire glowed, the rain beat relentlessly against the great windows, the bridge-players concentrated on the inter- rupted game. There came a murmur of voices outside. Polly re-entered.

'It's all arranged!' she cried, delighted. 'And Pauline, I've had your room put ready too. You can't walk back to-night. There *is* a tree down across the drive, and everywhere's streaming with water. Janet! Harry and Lucy are here! They've had to leave the car in the drive, because of the elm tree. *You* won't be able to get home, either!' She clapped her hands and gave a little skip of pleasure. 'Oh, what a lovely party! The house is almost full, for the first time!'

Simon leaned back in his old leather chair in the study. It was his own, brought from his den at home.

'So that's how it is,' he said with a sigh. 'If I could wake up one morning and find the answer – something simple I'd overlooked – or better still, find it was all a mistake, I'd give ten thousand pounds to the hospital as a thank-offering. As it is—' He shook his head.

'Are you sure?' said James. 'A leakage may have occurred, but perhaps it was an accident, or not from Gabb's at all.'

'I try to hope so. But they don't seem to be in any doubt. And if it is from us – well, no one knew about this new thing except Giles, and the foreman. As for Challoner, he'd never speak. He'd let himself be torn in pieces first. And as for me, I don't know myself exactly what the lad's doing; and if I did' – a faint smile creased the wrinkles at the corners of his eyes – 'I'm no talker, even in my sleep.'

'Basil?' queried James.

'No. He hadn't been told, either – not exactly, that is. Basil's on the administrative side, as you know; Giles would never have thought of consulting him. When the proper time came, he would have been told too, but that wouldn't have been until we began seriously considering production. In any case, Basil's not mechanically minded – not like Giles. Giles is a genius at it, when he cares to give his mind to it. But with him, it's all fits and starts.'

'But Simon,' said James, shocked, 'you don't mean to say you suspect Giles of – well, of parting with information about his own invention? Why should he?' James scraped his throat. 'It's not as if he – well – needed money or anything of that kind.'

Simon thought for a while. 'It wouldn't be that,' he said at last. 'It would be some cranky idea he'd got, about benefiting the human race, or something. He's moody sometimes – always has been. We've had arguments – quarrels, you might call them – about the business. Sometimes he's interested. He's got an exact mind, and the chemistry and the engineering and mathematical side of it appeal to him. At other times he'll fling out something about engines of destruction, and piling up weapons meant to kill innocent people, and so forth; and when he's in *that* mood, there's no holding him. He'll go off for a week or more, and fish or shoot until he's got it out of his system – as he's doing now. He's a queer lad.' Simon spoke fondly. A touch of genius, like our father.'

'Father never could make ends meet, for all his cleverness,' objected James. 'It's steadiness you want, if you're to do any good in life. Where would you be when Giles runs amok, if you hadn't got Basil to rely on?' He sighed. 'Ah well, well! I wish my son were half as dependable as yours. Harry's a wild rascal. I don't know what to make of him.' In James's tones, as in Simon's, there was fondness and pride.

The two fathers were silent, thinking of their sons.

'What about this girl?' said James suddenly.

'Eh?' said Simon, coming out of his reverie. 'What girl?'

'The girl Giles brought in to dinner to-night. You don't think he could have talked to her, or let something slip accidentally?'

'No, no, of course not,' said Simon irritably. And then, 'What made you think of it? What difference would it make if he did? The girl wouldn't understand enough to repeat, anyway.'

'I don't know about that,' said James. 'He has drawings that can be stolen, or borrowed, no doubt. Remember, too, she has a brother. They've all lived abroad, haven't they? They have foreign connections. And they've no special reason to be fond of you and your family.'

'Why not?' snapped Simon. 'I paid them a fair price for the place.'

'No, you didn't,' said James bluntly. 'You paid them the lowest price you could. And even if you had paid them what it was worth, they still wouldn't see all of you as anything but the family who had supplanted them. It's only natural, on both sides.'

Simon smacked the arms of his chair, and rose. 'Well, you know now why I want a bit of help from you, for the next few weeks, Jim, until Giles gets back. And if you can spot any leakage, anything that seems suspicious, anyone who isn't absolutely above suspicion, I'll be very grateful to you. I'd rather it were you than the police.'

James shook his head doubtfully. 'You wouldn't be grateful if—'

Simon laid a hand on his shoulder. 'Jim,' he said, 'if one of my sons were proved to have sold, or even given away, a secret of military importance to a foreign Power, or any foreign agent, I give you my word as an Englishman, I'd shoot him with my own hands.'

5

'Which room are you in?' said Billy. 'I'm in Uncle Fred's old room. You can still see the marks on the wall where he used to put his feet up in front of the fire. He always had a fire in his bedroom, do you remember? It smells a bit damp, though, now, and a great chunk of soot has come down the chimney.'

'I'm at the other end of the corridor,' said Royce. 'And to tell you the truth, I don't think it was ever one of the best guest-rooms. It seems to be a home of lost causes. For instance, Arden, there's a frightful photo of you on the mantelpiece, with your hair in long cork-screws and a big sash round your waist and your toes pointed out. One can almost see your drawers.'

They were sprawling across the bed in the room assigned to Arden, while she, in pyjamas and dressing-gown, sat in front of the mirror brushing her short hair back from her forehead.

'No, Royce dear, you couldn't,' she said, without turning round. 'That would be my grandmother. Drawers went out of sight long before my time.'

'I said "almost,"' corrected Royce solemnly. 'I spoke metaphorically only. I mean you looked a priggish little piece, and I should have liked to bite you. Perhaps I did. Tell me, Arden, did I ever bite you when I was a little boy? Not one tiny nip? Not one tug at the cork-screws?'

'So far as I remember,' said Arden, 'the first time your mother brought you here was to Aunt Margaret's wedding. You wore a satin suit with very short trousers and a wide lace collar. On your golden curls you wore a huge picture hat with a beautiful white ostrich feather. All was purest white. I remember you sat in a corner and sulked, because you were not allowed to get married yourself – to Aunt Margaret.'

Billy gave a whinny of joy. 'An ostrich feather!' he squealed, and rolled on the bed. 'There must be a photo of it somewhere. Let's make a tour of the house and look. I'm sure they wouldn't mind. After all, it can't interest them, can it?'

'S-sh!' said Arden. She glanced at the door.

'Why?' said Billy. 'Is there anyone else in this corridor? I thought it was deserted.'

'Oh, we were early upstairs.'

'There's no one next door to me,' said Billy, 'on either side. I'm over yonder, next to the bathroom. I say, Arden, I do think she might have offered us our old rooms, don't you? Royce can't complain; he always was a beastly visitor, really. But you and I – well, we're used to our own rooms. We can't be expected to sleep properly anywhere else. It would serve her right if we went sleep-walking, and—'

Royce cut in. 'Now that's a moot point. Wasn't it perhaps an even nicer sense of delicacy: she didn't want to remind you? You see what I mean. She therefore treats you as guests merely, just like the others. Personally I think she was right. If I were a hostess, that's exactly what I would do.'

'Well, I wouldn't,' said Billy loudly. 'I would either have grasped the bull by the horns—asked us point-blank which our old rooms were, and put us in them, even if I'd had to turn someone else out; or I'd have given us the best rooms in the house.'

'S-sh!' said Arden again. She got up, having brushed her hair till it shone like electrum. 'Go away now. I want to sleep.' She crossed over to the mantelpiece, where a candle burned between two glass jars of pickled minnows. 'Giles and I are going on the lake again to-morrow, fairly early.'

'H'm,' said Royce. 'Tiring work, catching pike – and other fish.'

Arden shot him a look of displeasure, as she took the candlestick and carried it to the bedside table.

'No, but honestly,' Billy was saying, 'all this pretence and awkwardness about our having lived here before seem to me absurd. After all, old Simon Gabb made his money and we lost ours. So why shouldn't he and his family have our house, if they're a virile young race and we're an effete one, as the Nazis would say? I think he's a fine old boy, and Mrs Gabb's a jolly good sort; and Giles is a good sort too. And Jessica – Jessica's a peach, let me tell you. But Basil – no. I can't say I really take to Basil.'

'Neither does Royce – do you?' murmured Arden maliciously, as she passed him by.

Royce turned to watch her. He was oblivious of Billy's presence. 'Tell me,' he said, 'Arden, are you really going to marry Giles?' He tried to keep the tremor of seriousness out of his voice, and failed. Billy, aware of the change of atmosphere, stared at him in surprise, then in curiosity.

'He hasn't asked me yet,' said Arden.

'Oh, but he will do, have no fear – to-morrow, on the lake, when you are trailing your bait so prettily. The little minnow comes spinning through the water; the silly pike makes his rush. He struggles a bit. You play him. Soon he's in your landing-net. You knock him on the head with a stone, and he knows nothing more.' He gave a laugh. 'You do it so beautifully, Arden! One simply can't believe it hurts the fish at all. In fact, one thinks fish have no feelings.'

The cousins confronted each other like enemies: Arden still holding her candle, Royce defying her, pretending to be cynical and amused. Billy, realizing that this scene was not meant to be witnessed, muttered some unheeded excuse and crept away.

Royce paused, as if he expected an answer; but Arden was silent. He plunged on:

'Of course, I see your point of view. It is the quickest way to get back the old homestead, I suppose, with the necessary income for its upkeep this time. But be careful of that fellow. He looks to me a dark horse, and one with none too pleasant a temper. Once you've landed him, you'll find the game is over. No more trailing your bait, Arden, when he's in the boat. No more—'

Arden took a half-step towards him. The candle lit up her face.

'Royce,' she said in a very low voice, 'please get out of here.'

He stared at her, then turned on his heel. She said after him:

'And you might remember, before you go any further with Pauline, that Basil is Giles's brother.'

He swung round, and came back to her. He grasped her by the wrist of the hand that hung limply at her side. 'Arden—'

There was a rap at the door. Arden looked round. Royce did not release her wrist, and she made no attempt to free herself. Billy's round head appeared in the doorway.

'I say, Arden,' he said, pretending to see nothing odd, 'Giles is here. He wants to speak to you for a moment.'

Royce dropped her wrist, but not before both of them had seen Giles's dark profile through the half-open door, and heard his rather tired voice saying:

'It doesn't matter. I merely came to say, Arden, don't get up early to-morrow. I shall have to go down to the boat-house first, to do one or two things. I think we'd better call it off. The lake may be too choppy. Good night.'

With long loping strides he was gone.

Royce stood watching Arden, defiant yet appealing. 'I'm not going to apologize,' he said.

Arden gazed at him, implacable. 'Why should you?' she said, turning away. 'You haven't done any harm.' She set the candle down on the bedside table. 'You see, Royce, I lied to you just now. Giles asked me to marry him this afternoon, and I agreed. So go ahead: make a fool of yourself with your Pauline. But remember: you and Basil will be cousins by marriage very soon.'

Royce stared at her stupidly. 'How soon?'

'We shall get married by special licence, next week probably. It's a secret, of course: that is to say, his father and mother don't yet know. But don't imagine you can interfere, Royce, by telling them. You see, either they won't oppose it, in which case what you say won't affect them; or they will, and we shall ignore them. But meanwhile, you will have made an enemy. I don't advise you to. Giles is an ill person to cross.'

'Oh, Arden!' Royce had given up all pretence of nonchalance. 'Don't do it, for God's sake! Can't you see the fellow's – well, perhaps not mad, but dangerous somehow? Please don't do it, Arden! Look here, I know you think nothing of me; but I'll get a job, I'll make money somehow and buy this place back for you, if that's what you want. Arden, I know you've never taken me seriously, but I am serious over you, really I am!'

'Dear me!' said Arden. 'And you've just discovered it? What a flop for poor Pauline!'

'Oh, to hell with Pauline!' Royce made a movement towards her, but changed his mind. 'I didn't think, before. I mean, we've always been together, and nothing's been serious. I thought we were all playing. If I'd known—'

Arden smiled indulgently. 'Go to bed, Royce,' she said. 'Don't say anything you'd be sorry for in the morning. Just think: I might take you at your word, and where would you be then? In a bowler hat and pin-striped trousers, with a train to catch every morning and a little house to come home to every night. Don't worry: you've got years of fun ahead of you yet, thanks to me. You should be grateful. Good night.'

Royce went away.

6

Next morning, after the rain, the air was sweet and clear. The begonias had muddy faces, and the trim lawns were thick with drifts of fallen leaves; but the raindrops had spun a spangled web across the grass, and birds sang in the welcome sunshine. The sky was blue, and the waters of the lake danced glintingly, now that the last wreaths of mist had trailed away.

Simon Gabb picked his way carefully along the drive, among the fallen leaves and branches. He snuffed up the air with deep delight, heavy as it was with the scent of leaf-mould. He was later than usual, this morning, with his walk; but then it was Sunday, and everyone seemed to be still sleeping. Perhaps, he thought, there would be time to walk round the lake before breakfast.

The beauty of the place he had bought almost without examining it struck him for the first time. He had bought it because it was a bargain. His ears had been too long attuned to the sounds of men's voices, machinery roaring, typewriters tapping; his eyes to indoor sights; his mind to complicated yet limited thoughts. In his daily walks hitherto, he might have been treading on pavement. But last night's storm had done something to him: had cleared his brain. Nothing seemed of importance except to savour the bright morning. Where, for instance, were those ridiculous suspicions he had been entertaining, and had so foolishly confided to James?

He stooped to pick up a bright horse-chestnut, newly-emerged from its white-lined prickly coat; and then, remembering that he had no one for whom to save them, he threw it down again. His own sons were grown up, and the first grandchild was still a baby... He was half-way to the lake now; it shimmered invitingly. He understood its lure for these young people. Giles, now: was it not possible that Giles's queer outbursts, when he would not go near the works for several weeks together, were due to some surging rush of desire in him for simple things, the antithesis of all that his father's vast enterprises represented: merely for the open air, the sky, the water, the pleasures of hunting, the search for a mate? Once, soon after he had joined the firm, he had had what was euphemistically called a nervous breakdown. They sent him away into the country, and he came back cured. But there was no doubt: Basil was dependable, steady, unimaginative, useful, never springing a surprise, pleasant or unpleasant; while in Giles there was still an explosive force, that might be genius, or might bring disaster.

He turned aside from the broad path he was following, that led straight to the boat-house, and took a smaller track towards the edge of the lake. The waters lapped among the reeds. There was an island at one end, covered with trees and shrubs, hazel and willow and alders that overhung the water. He noticed a moorhen among the surface weeds. So the lake was full of pike, was it? And he had bought all this, mansion and grounds and lake and all that therein was. He turned to give an appraising glance at the long frontage of Herons' Hall with its great windows, its terraced lawn and beds of many-coloured flowers. Hard to leave such a place, if you had been brought up in it. He spared a passing thought for the three young people, Giles's friends, who had dined with them last night. However, they had little to complain of: they had the best of the lodges, at a very small rental. He could see the red tiles of its gabled roof among the trees on the opposite bank. Basil had had his choice of the two lodges, but he had chosen the North Lodge, perhaps to be nearer the main road. Basil would always put his work first, of that one could be sure.

Was that girl going to be Giles's choice? It would be odd, Simon reflected. He had no views on the matter. The lad had never shown the slightest interest in women before, though he was now, Simon thought, twenty-seven, or was it twenty-eight? That had been one of the things wrong with him, his unnatural avoidance of women, his preference for lonely walks, his long brooding silences even in company. The mothers, Polly and Janet, would not be pleased at this new development. Simon's face creased in a smile. He knew that they planned to marry off his niece Lucy to his elder son Giles; and that it would be most suitable, even he could not deny. Lucy was a lively spirited young thing, just the right sort of companion for Giles in his moroseness, and she was said to be sweet on him. But such suitable things seldom materialize. And if Giles chose to prefer someone as unlike any of the women in his family as that tall good-looking young woman with the red band on her hair, Simon would raise not a finger to prevent it. He would be badgered to do so; but he would refuse.

He thought it time to turn back. His appetite was sharpened by the walk, and he could almost smell the kidneys-on-toast that awaited him. He walked along the lake edge, towards the boat-house. There was just time to have a look inside. It seemed that he possessed, without ever having seen it, an excellently-built boat-house containing two rowing-boats, a motor-boat and a canoe. There was a channel, formed from an inlet of the lake, and edged with concrete; it led to double doors opening over the water, and behind these were the boats under cover. At the side was another smaller door.

Simon walked along the concrete edge of the channel. The double doors were closed; but the side door was ajar. He opened it and peeped inside.

A rush of cold air met him; and for a moment, while his eyes adjusted themselves to the dim green light inside, he could distinguish nothing except the bar of sunshine that lay across the opening below the double doors, and the brown prows of a couple of rowing-boats.

A larger shape loomed behind in the shadows; and then as the shape became the outline of the motor-boat, he could see a dark form huddled forward on one of the seats.

Hardly knowing what he did, he released the heavy iron bar which was attached to one of the double doors and which hooked into a staple in the concrete wall. It fell with a crash into the shallow water, as the door swung slowly open. Simon turned, fear knocking at his heart.

Seated in the motor-boat, leaning forward limply with his hands hanging down, was his son Giles. Between his knees a sporting gun was braced; and its muzzle, pressing against his chest, was the only thing that supported the body in that sitting position. Blood had trickled from a wound in his forehead. Simon saw his white marble-like profile, the dark tumbled hair, the dark ill-shaven chin, and knew that Giles was dead.

7

An hour later, silence hung over Herons' Hall.

Simon Gabb and his brother James were closeted in Simon's study, awaiting the return of the doctor, who with Hubert Olivier had gone down to the boat-house. Simon had wanted to go too; but Dr Fitzbrown, after a glance at his white face and trembling hand, had forbidden it.

Simon and James did not talk. Simon sat at his desk, stabbing the blotting-pad with an old rusty pen. James walked round the room, looking at the books, trying to remember that he must not indulge his confirmed habit of whistling, trying also to keep his hands off his tobacco-pouch and his thoughts off his pipe. Simon was a non-smoker. It would never occur to him to say 'Smoke if you want to,' and James could see that it would not do to begin, or even ask permission. So he fidgeted, occasionally going to the window; but Simon did not look up, or speak, or move.

Upstairs, maids with preternaturally solemn faces carried cups of tea and toast to bedroom doors. 'Mister Giles has shot himself': the news had been whispered round. Nobody in the house dared to say, yet, what he or she thought; but there were meaning nods as the news was passed on, from housekeeper to butler, from butler to cook, from cook to parlourmaid. Outside, comment was a little freer: Willis the chauffeur said to Morgan the head gardener, 'He always was a gloomy blighter,' and the head gardener gave a grunt of acquiescence. Morgan had been for twenty years with the late

Colonel Sir Charles Laforte; and this family so far, except for the old man, Simon Gabb himself, had hardly impinged on his consciousness. Still, he had been beginning to be aware of Mister Giles, who had passed him most mornings lately, coming back from the lake or the woods with his gun under his arm. He had also become aware that Mister Giles had lately been calling a good deal at the South Lodge in the evenings; for Morgan spent his evenings in loving care of Mrs Charleroy's small garden.

He pushed back his cap from his grizzled short-cropped head, rubbed his head with an earthy hand, and said slowly: 'It's funny: I saw him on the lake early this morning.'

'You did?' said Willis eagerly. 'What time?'

'When I got up. About six, maybe, just before sunrise. He was paddling the canoe in the middle of the lake. I didn't think much of it at the time. He was a queer sort of chap, and always up early about the place. If I'd known he was going to shoot himself—'

He shook his head, for he himself did not know what he would have done if he had known that Giles was going to shoot himself; but he savoured the significance of that moment in retrospect. It would last him all week, as he moved about the kitchen-garden arranging for the clearance of the old kidney beans, the tying up of raspberry canes, and the planting of winter onions.

Polly lay on her bed, drinking tea and dabbing her eyes. Janet, bolt upright beside her, tried to think of words of comfort; but none came. To her, suicide was a supremely wicked act; and she could not console Polly when she knew perfectly well that Giles had disgraced himself, not only in this world but in the next. He would arrive there not as an honourable soldier, one who has fought the good fight, but as a man convicted of cowardice, and worse still, of dishonesty; for his life had been lent to him only, and he had squandered it and thrown it away. She saw him exactly as she would see an embezzling solicitor or a defaulting banker, who having got his accounts into a hopeless muddle, flees the country, leaving his shame to be borne by innocent relatives. Even she did not relish the prospect of having to explain to her friends the circumstances of her nephew's suicide. And why had he done it? That was the question. She did not doubt that worse revelations were to follow.

'I'm sure that girl had something to do with it,' sobbed Polly. 'I felt as soon as I saw her, no good would come of it.'

'You didn't show it at the time, then,' said Janet bluntly. 'You welcomed her as if she'd been his fiancée already. And that though you knew he was practically engaged to Lucy.'

Polly sat up and reached for her smelling-salts. 'My dear, what could I do?' She sniffed at the bottle, and her tears flowed. 'He told me he wanted to bring them: and he almost warned me—'

'You gave in to him a great deal too much,' censured Janet. 'Whoever heard of a son warning his mother?'

Polly, unable to cope with her, lay down again, weeping. She had not, in truth, been very fond of her son Giles. He had always rebuffed her, made her feel silly, as soon as he was old enough to be independent of her physical care. She did not understand him; she feared him for his cleverness, and his desire for solitude seemed to her morbid. Basil listened to her, Giles never; in fact, for years past they had been complete strangers. Therefore her grief was not of that aching kind that realizes helplessly a loss, irremediable and lifelong. Nevertheless, her distress was genuine: she liked fun and laughter, joy, plenty of company, an easy-going normal everyday life; and now, this black shadow lay on the house and stilled the laughter, drove out the fun, altered everything, and would continue to do so for as long as one could look ahead. If she could have articulated the feelings that moved her to weeping, she would have said, 'How cruel of Giles!'

'Have you seen Lucy?' she said faintly. 'Is she still here?'

'I don't know,' said Lucy's mother sternly.

'She will take it so badly! I do hope Harry has taken her home.'

'She must bear it as best she can,' retorted Janet. 'We all must. No one can help her. We all have to bear such things alone.'

Dr Fitzbrown and Hubert Olivier came slowly away from the boat-house. Fitzbrown had pulled back the folding door of the boat-house and dropped the iron hook into its staple; then he had shut the side door and dropped the Yale key into his pocket.

'Keep to the steps,' he said to Olivier. 'There may be footprints.'

'But are you really sure about this business?' said Olivier as they reached the path.

'Perfectly. Do you know anything about him? Your brother is the family solicitor, you say. Who's the old man's successor, now this one's gone?'

'There's a younger brother, Basil; married, with a young child.'

'Any quarrel between them?'

Olivier glanced at him sharply.

'Sorry,' said Fitzbrown with a laugh, which rather shocked Hubert. 'I'm not the police doctor, so I've no right to ask questions. But Mallett, the superintendent here, is a great friend of mine, and I've been associated with him and Jones – that's the police surgeon – in a good many cases. However, keep your answers for them, if you prefer. It's more orthodox.'

Hubert decided to propitiate him. 'The brothers had no quarrel that I know of,' he said. 'They were most unlike in every way, but they didn't quarrel. They just had very little to do with one another.'

'Giles was unmarried.'

'Yes. But he showed signs of changing that. His *inamorata* – presumably – was there to dinner last night. In fact, she spent the night there, she and her brother and her – cousin, I think he is.'

Fitzbrown shot a look at Olivier from under his thick dark eyebrows. Fitzbrown was a tall raw-boned young man, with an abrupt somewhat commanding manner. The look was suspicious: he was thinking, 'This suave-toned fellow is putting on an act of studied ignorance.' And he made a mental note to draw Mallett's attention to Olivier as a born liar. Hubert was continuing:

'Miss Laforte is the daughter of the previous owner.'

'Oh – ah!' Fitzbrown was interested. 'I remember – old Colonel Laforte. My father used to attend him, when he was at home. Became a baronet rather late in life, didn't he? and lost all his money.'

Hubert nodded. 'They now live in the South Lodge over there, beyond the lake.'

'What, the old Colonel? I thought he had died, years ago.'

'Three years ago,' said Hubert. 'I meant his children, and his sister and his sister's son.'

Fitzbrown noticed that Hubert was no longer vague about the relationship. 'So this poor chap was courting Miss Laforte. And' – Fitzbrown nodded back at the boat-house – 'that means she won't come back into the family property after all.'

'I suppose so.'

'Then we can safely assume she had no hand in it.'

'I suppose so,' said Hubert again. He resented this questionnaire to which he was being subjected. What right had a young country practitioner with shiny clothes and a shabby little car to put him, the great – well, prospectively great – Hubert Olivier into the witness-box? Yet he could find no means of evading Fitzbrown's questions without antagonizing him.

'Well now, keep all you've seen under your hat,' said Fitzbrown irreverently, as they reached the steps of the house. 'No one must know of this except his father, until the police get here.'

Fitzbrown came across the room to where Simon Gabb sat at his desk. Simon raised his eyes as they entered; but he did not get up.

'Sir,' said Fitzbrown, 'I want to speak to you alone.'

Simon said, through scarcely opened lips, 'My brother. You can say what you like in front of him.'

'All the same,' said Fitzbrown firmly, 'I want to speak to you alone. I'm sure Mr Gabb won't mind.'

Simon said nothing. When James and Olivier had gone, Fitzbrown said gently, 'Mr Gabb, you must prepare your mind for a very great shock – perhaps greater than the one you've had already.' He leaned forward across the desk, and said in low clear tones, 'Mr Gabb, your son did not commit suicide. He was murdered.'

Simon raised his great head, and fixed his solemn eyes on Fitzbrown's face, as if seeing him for the first time. The look of dull indifference gradually passed, like a mist clearing away from the surface of the lake; and as the realization of what Fitzbrown had said sank in, the look of helpless grief passed also. He jerked to his feet, and the chair on which he had been sitting rolled away behind him on its castors.

'Murdered? Do you mean that?'

'Yes, sir,' said Fitzbrown, putting out a hand, ready to grasp Simon's elbow. But Simon needed no support.

'You mean he didn't shoot himself?' A queer gleam, one might almost have said, of joy, came into his eyes. He glanced to left and right, as if making sure of his position in space, and verifying that he was awake.

'No. The sporting gun you found between his knees couldn't possibly have shot him. The police will easily prove it to you, but it's obvious. It would have blown half his head away, for one thing, and the shot would have been all over the place. Have you ever, seen a rabbit shot at point-blank range? It's—' Fitzbrown had been going to say 'uneatable,' but he choked off the word, and was relieved to see that Simon had not been pained at the reference. 'Anyway, Mr Gabb, you can take it from me, he didn't do it himself.'

He followed Simon's gaze, out of the window, towards the lake; and he was not altogether surprised to see that though Simon's eyes were wet with tears, yet he was smiling.

'Poor boy!' he was saying. 'My poor lad! You're right – of course you're right. I ought to have seen. I did see. But I was so sure— Thank God for that, at any rate.'

He sat down suddenly, and broke down completely for a few minutes, sobbing with his head on his wrists. Fitzbrown came round to his side, and put a hand on his shoulder, patting it absently, for he was used to seeing men cry, and knew that this happened oftener than is usually supposed. His skilled eye took in the broad shoulders, the large head, the long powerful-looking arms, the short legs; and he thought, 'Wrong diet in youth. Vitamin D deficiency. But heavy manual work. And a good brain.'

When Simon recovered, he looked up unselfconsciously, and the moment he had dried his eyes and blown his nose, he gave Fitzbrown a sharp shrewd look of appraisement.

'Now, doctor,' he said, evidently satisfied with his scrutiny, 'let's get to business. The first thing is to telephone the police.' He handed to Fitzbrown the receiver from the desk-telephone. 'Will you get on with it? I shall go and break the news to my brother and my wife.' At the door he turned: 'Tell the police,' he said solemnly, 'to spare no effort and no expense. Everything I can do will be done. All my time will be theirs. They must find the murderer, even if they find him in the very centre of my home.'

8

Mrs Charleroy listened to their tale attentively. She was a tall fair handsome woman with a long thin nose, long thin hands and feet, and sceptical amused green eyes. Her manner as a rule was languid; but the three of them, she and Billy and Arden, had been shaken out of their usual manners, and were confronting one another with serious and anxious looks.

'Well, you can't help it, Arden dear,' she said. 'You did your best to be gentle, I'm sure.'

Arden looked away. Her lips trembled. She was very pale. Billy broke in:

'So we didn't even wait to say good-bye. We just crept out of the house, and we saw no one. The place was as quiet as a tomb. If the maid hadn't told Arden, we might have been there still, or come bursting out of our rooms and singing in the bathroom.'

'I think you did very wisely to come away,' said Mrs Charleroy soothingly.

'But what time did Royce come in, then?' said Billy, puzzled. 'And when did he leave? It's not like old Royce to get up at crack of dawn on a Sunday morning.'

'I don't quite know, dear,' said Mrs Charleroy. 'I went to bed early, and left the key under the mat for you all. I thought you probably wouldn't come home while the storm was raging, and I even thought of ringing you up to tell you nor to, but I remembered it wasn't safe to phone during a storm.'

'The phone was out of order last night,' said Billy, 'or we would have rung you. It's all right this morning, though. We heard them ringing up for the doctor as we left.' His eyes grew serious again. 'I say! I wonder if old Royce knows.'

Arden turned as if about to say something, and then bit her lip.

'Oh, I expect he does, dear,' said Mrs Charleroy. 'If you heard about it before you left, you can be sure he did too. I daresay he felt as you did – that it would be kinder to leave without seeing anybody. Strangers aren't wanted at such a time.'

'Yes, but,' persisted Billy, 'why didn't he come and call us?' He caught Arden's look, but refused to heed it. 'Oh, I know you and he had a bit of a squabble last night, Arden,' he said bluntly, 'but old Royce wouldn't go off without telling us, just for a little thing like that. He'd have fetched me, anyway, and I'd have fetched you. And where is he now?' he said, looking round.

Mrs Charleroy also looked round rather helplessly, as if Billy expected her to produce Royce from under a settee or behind a china-cabinet, and she was unhappily not able to oblige him. They were sitting in the southward-facing room which she used in the mornings. It was a charming room, looking out on to a small formal garden with stone paths, climbing roses on poles, and flower-beds. The roses still kept their flowers, in spite of the storm: robust Gloire de Dijon blooms ramped over an archway, and shell-like Ophelias continued to grace their long almost thornless stems. The garden was shut in and sheltered; one could not see the big house or the lake from here.

'He went out, I think,' she said. 'Winifred gave him his breakfast very early, as soon as he came down. I believe he told her he was going for a walk.'

'But how—'

At that moment they heard a step outside, and Royce entered. He looked pale and drawn.

'Oh, hullo!' he said, harshly and defiantly. 'I see you've heard the news.' He came forward. 'Make room for me, will you? We must hold our own *post mortem*.'

'Royce, dear,' said Mrs Charleroy deprecatingly. She managed to convey to him with a look that he ought to say something consolatory to Arden.

'Oh yes,' he said aloud. 'Of course, Arden, I'm frightfully sorry and all that. You must feel very cut up about it, just when everything was all settled. I mean, please forget anything unpleasant I said last night. I was talking like a fool. And anyhow, one can't – I mean, even if one weren't altogether sorry for your sake, one couldn't say so, could one? I do quite realize what a frightful shock it must be to you.'

He floundered on, while his mother watched him with pained indulgence. Arden turned, and when he finished, she said in her usual quiet tones:

'I'm sorry I misled you, Royce. We both were a little – beside ourselves, last night.' She addressed herself to her aunt: 'You see, I told Royce a lie. I *said* I had told him a lie earlier on – but it was the second statement that was really the lie.' She turned back to Royce again. 'This really is the truth, this time: Giles did propose to me on the lake yesterday afternoon, but I didn't accept him. I tried to refuse him. He wouldn't take "no" for a final answer, so I said – stupidly, but really, I meant to be kind and do it by stages, and he was so very violent—' She covered her eyes with her hand for a minute, and her voice shook. Then she went on calmly: 'I said I'd think about it. You see, he threatened to kill himself if I really meant "no." We were in the middle of the lake, in the deepest part, and I didn't know what he'd do—'

'Go on,' said Billy. He explained to his aunt: 'They – Giles and Arden were in one boat, and Royce and I in the other. We kept out of their way, of course.'

Arden continued: 'Well, he agreed to that, and I was so relieved, I agreed to go back to the house for dinner as we had arranged, though it was the last thing in the world I wanted. For one thing, I wanted to come home and dress, but he said it was too late, and there was a storm coming up, and it didn't matter anyhow. So I let him have his own way, and there we were, plunged into the middle of the family, looking like gypsies. It was funny, going back there and seeing it almost exactly as it used to be, furniture and all, and yet to have to face a party of complete strangers, and know we were intruders.'

'Pooh!' said Billy. 'We got on very well, I thought. And anyway, Arden, they weren't all strangers. Hubert Olivier was there.'

Arden's voice grew strained. 'I knew Giles was watching me all evening, and it bothered me. Then, after you left me—' Her glance took in Billy and Royce. 'They came to say good night to me,' she said to her aunt, 'and Royce and I did have a few words about Giles, and I said, more in fun than anything else, that Giles had proposed to me and I had accepted him.'

'I see,' said Mrs Charleroy, nodding sympathetically; she was watching, not Arden, but her son.

'Then,' broke in Billy again, 'Giles came and asked me if I knew where you were. I said I thought you were in your room. He asked me to tap on the door for him, and find out. So I did. I didn't know you were still there,' he said to Royce apologetically.

'It doesn't matter,' said Royce, looking down.

'Well, you see,' Billy hurried on eagerly to his aunt, 'when Giles saw Royce was there, he just cut in and said it didn't matter: all he wanted was to tell her not to get up early in the morning. Then he went off. He didn't seem put out at all.'

Royce jerked up his head. 'So all that stuff you told me,' he said to Arden, 'about getting married next week by special licence, and how you'd go through with it even if his people objected, and how Giles was "an ill man to cross," were all lies? How do you manage it?' He turned away bitterly.

'Oh, Royce,' said Arden contritely, 'I only repeated all the things he had said to me. I didn't invent any of it, really. That's what I always do when I tell a lie: I take something that's really happened, and—'

'Oh, shut up;' shouted Royce suddenly. He held his temples between his two fists, and his down-bent face was red, with fury or some other overpowering emotion. All the time, his mother watched him, and sketched out in her mind the heart-to-heart talk she would inflict on him in private afterwards.

'So you see,' said Arden, ignoring his outburst, 'I feel responsible for what's happened. In a way, that is. And yet I don't see what else I could have done. The only thing he wanted was— impossible. But all the same, I wish it hadn't been because of me.'

Royce glanced up at her as if a new idea had struck him. He was jerked out of his surmising by Billy:

'But I say: when did you clear out? Why didn't you come for me?"

Royce looked up, startled. 'I left last night,' he said, 'quite soon after I saw you.'

'Last night? Then you didn't sleep there? By Jove, I looked into your room this morning, and I noticed your bed was made, but I thought they must have made it as soon as you had gone. I never realized you hadn't slept there at all.' He came back to the point. 'Why did you leave, at that unearthly hour? It was still pouring with rain, wasn't it?'

Mrs Charleroy saw the muscles at the corners of Royce's jaw tighten: so that was a question he had dreaded!

'I'll tell you,' said Royce grimly. 'When I went along the corridor after leaving you, Arden, I found Giles waiting for me at the head of the stairs. We had a row. I could have knocked him flying down the stairs, but I remembered he was shortly to become my cousin by marriage, or so I thought, and I refrained. He called me some pretty names, for one who hoped to be my relative; and it developed into a kind of competition between us. I was saying with dignity that I was about to remove myself from under his roof and I hoped never to darken his doorstep either in the immediate or the remote future. He was ordering me to get to hell out of there. I got out, therefore.'

'What time was that, dear?' said Mrs Charleroy.

'Oh, about eleven, I suppose.'

'Then you didn't come straight home? I think I would have heard you. I went to bed early, but I was reading until – oh, it must have been nearly midnight.'

'No, Mother, I didn't,' said Royce curtly. 'I went for a walk. I was in a hell of a rage, and I wanted to cool off.'

'And what time *did* you come in?' insisted his mother.

'Oh, I don't know.' His worried look had returned. 'Some time in the small hours, I suppose.'

'Which way did you go?' said Billy curiously. 'You couldn't have spent the whole night walking round the lake, surely.'

'I walked in the other direction, along the drive towards the main road.'

'Plenty of branches lying around, weren't there?' said Billy, 'after the storm? I thought I heard someone say there was a tree down.'

'I don't know. I didn't notice. I walked out past the North Lodge and on to the main road. I suppose I got nearly to Chode. Then I turned back.'

'Who told you about Giles, then?' said Billy.

'Morgan.'

'Morgan?'

'Yes, Morgan!' Royce was getting angry again. 'I met him just now, when I went out after breakfast. He said "Mister Giles has shot himself." I came back here at once— What are you staring at me like that for? Do you think *I'm* telling lies?'

'Oh no, of course not,' said Billy. 'I thought you meant Morgan had told you when you got back first thing this morning. But of course he couldn't have. He wouldn't be about in the small hours. So you've only just heard?'

There was a tap at the door.

'Oh madam!' Winifred, disturbed out of her usual chilly politeness, hurried forward. 'Oh madam, Morgan's been here, and he says Willis says they are saying the doctor says Mister Giles didn't shoot himself – he was murdered! They've rung up Chode for the police!'

'Murdered!' gasped Arden.

Mrs Charleroy half-rose from her chair; but she never took her eyes off Royce. 'What *can* he have done last night,' she thought, 'that he wants to conceal?' But the word 'murder,' though it was ringing in her ears, never occurred to her.

'Call Morgan back,' she said to Winifred. 'Send him here. I'd like to see him. Children, go away now, please. I'll tell you what Morgan says later. Don't talk to anyone about this. You were all there last night, and you may be asked some questions. So keep what you know for the police.'

9

A s Superintendent Mallet, with the Police Surgeon, Dr Jones, followed Dr Fitzbrown along the path to the boat-house, he said:

'Do you know anything about these people, Fitzbrown? The Gabbs, I mean.'

'Suppose you tell me what you know first,' said Fitzbrown, 'and I'll see if I can add anything. If I know you, you have them on your files already.'

'Well,' admitted Mallet, 'I did jot down a few things when they came here. I like to keep a record of the families in my district – any important changes and so on.' He pulled his red moustache. 'I *have* been accused of running a little Gestapo down there. But it's been useful, on more than one occasion.'

'Go on,' said Fitzbrown. The path along which they were walking was thick with mud after last night's rain, and on the grass verges, twigs and leaves lay piled against the wire netting at the bottom of the railings. The three men watched the ground, more in order to keep their footing than in the hope of finding clues; it was useless to look for footprints.

'I'm afraid there's nothing, this time, except what everyone knows. Mr Gabb bought this house from the heirs of the late owner, Colonel Sir Charles Laforte. I expect you knew the old Colonel, Fitzbrown?'

'I've seen him,' said Dr Fitzbrown. 'But I never had any dealings with him. He was abroad a good deal, wasn't he? Didn't he die out in the wilds of tropical Africa, a year or so ago?'

'That's right,' said Mallett. 'In the Sudan. He didn't die, though: he was killed. By a rhinoceros. I've got his obituary notice on my files. Aged fifty-eight. A great sportsman – one of the few who had succeeded in bagging, I forget the name of the beast; anyhow, some rare and nearly extinct animal.' He sighed. 'Wrote a book of big-game-hunting reminiscences, entitled *The Lure of the Spoor*. It's in the Chode Public Library. I looked into it one day. You know the sort of thing: "Below us, forty yards away, there was the elephant. It was a gift. I decided on the old ten-bore…," and so on. Five hundred pages. With illustrations. The Colonel standing behind a dead lion. The Colonel holding up a dead bustard. The Colonel sitting astride a dead buffalo. The Colonel surrounded by his native boys.'

'Not dead, I hope?' said Dr Jones.

'No. – What? No, of course not,' snapped Mallett. 'Well, anyway, you get the idea. The rhino, apparently, did not wait for the old ten-bore. He – or no, I believe it was a she, a cow as they call them – she just charged at the Colonel. I gather from his book, a rhinoceros has been known to charge a train. Well, she didn't like the look of the Colonel, and – as she can't write her reminiscences, we shall never know the rest.'

Fitzbrown laughed. '"Photo of rhinoceros sitting on dead Colonel." What a pity!'

Dr Jones, trudging behind, cut in: 'Yes, but all that has nothing to do with this affair. That's the late owner. What about the present?'

'Simon Gabb,' said Mallett thoughtfully. 'Yes, of course. He's the head of Gabb's iron and steel works at Broxeter. Formerly principally engaged on cast-iron goods of a special kind; but also has, as a side-line, a very efficient small-arms factory. Used to manufacture sporting rifles, but rumour says that recently they've secured a Government contract for military types. Simon Gabb has two sons and a daughter. His brother James has a hardware stores in the town. James is comfortably off; and Simon is a millionaire. He's also a J.P., and I know him quite well in that capacity.' Mallett turned to Fitzbrown. 'Well? Can you add anything?'

'Nothing, I'm afraid,' said Fitzbrown, 'except that the Laforte-Gabb connection didn't cease with the buying of the property. Sir Charles's two children and their aunt – his sister – and her son live in the South Lodge over there. And Giles Gabb was courting Miss Laforte. The three of them – brother, sister and cousin – spent last night at Herons' Hall, because of the storm.'

'Oho!' said Mallett. 'Ah yes, I remember now: the Colonel's sister, Mrs Charleroy. She used to visit here a good deal, in fact she used to take charge, latterly, when he left England. She had expectations from her brother; but luckily for her, her own husband left her enough to live on, for the old man died penniless, to everybody's surprise. I suppose they all live on her money now, and what they got for Herons' Hall.'

'I gather,' said Fitzbrown, 'they moved into the Lodge a couple of months ago. I wonder what made them all come back here?'

They approached the short slope leading to the boat-house door. Mallett paused at the top to take a look round, while Fitzbrown descended four concrete steps and fitted the Yale key into the lock. The morning mist had dispersed; the whole of the lake, and the small island, were visible, and on the opposite bank of the lake, Morgan the gardener's cottage. Above the trees at the further end, the red pointed roof of the South Lodge appeared. A slight breeze had arisen, and as Fitzbrown opened the side door, from the dark cold interior of the boat-house the plashing of water on the bows of the boats sounded gently and hollowly.

'There you are, Mallett,' said Fitzbrown, standing aside. Mallett entered. He had to turn his large form sideways to get through the door, and he moved crabwise along the narrow concrete ledge inside, holding his raincoat tightly round him. After a minute, his voice, magnified and hollow-sounding, came out to them:

'All right, Bob.' Dr Jones, short and stout, likewise edged his way through the door into the cavern.

'Do you want light?' called Fitzbrown. 'Shall I open the double doors?'

'A little,' said Jones. Fitzbrown pulled the great hooked bar out of its staple in the wall, and let the near door swing open a short way. A shaft of bright light penetrated into the cavern, revealing the huddled body of Giles still propped up by the gun on which his chest leaned, the down-sunk head, the white sharp-featured profile. Jones was already in the motor-boat, kneeling on one knee beside the body, examining the wound in the forehead by the light of his torch. After a while, he moved round to the other side, stepping carefully over the butt of the gun that rested on the floor of the boat. Mallett meanwhile was examining the boat's engine.

Jones shut off the torch, stepped over the gun again, and climbed out on to the ledge. 'You're quite right,' he said to Fitzbrown. 'This man has had a bullet through his brain. It went in at the temple and came out behind the ear.'

'Came out?' said Fitzbrown. 'Then we ought to be able to find it. It couldn't have got out of the boat-house.' He looked at the concrete wall opposite. 'I didn't know they went though a man's skull quite so easily.'

'Depends on the bullet,' said Jones, 'and the muzzle-velocity of the gun, and the distance from which the shot was fired. These modern stream-lined bullets have a penetrating power that would surprise you; in fact, that's one of their drawbacks for sportsmen. They can go right through a large animal and do little harm, provided they don't pass through a vital part. Whoever did this man in must have stalked him carefully to get what sportsmen call " the brain shot."'

Fitzbrown stepped into one of the rowing-boats and from it into the second, and so out on to the opposite ledge.

'Then it must have left a mark on this wall,' he said, playing a torch over the concrete surface, 'and ricochetted off into the water.' He ran the palm of his hand over the concrete. 'I'm in a direct line with him now.'

Mallett looked up. 'You can spare yourself the trouble,' he said. 'He wasn't shot in here.' He turned to Jones. 'You mentioned stalking.

Have you any opinion as to the distance from which the shot was fired?'

Jones shook his head. 'None, except that when sportsmen try for the "brain shot," they like to get as close as possible: say not more than about forty yards.'

'Naturally. You think as I do, then, he wasn't shot in here?'

'Well—' Jones reflected. 'He can't have been in that position if he was shot from anywhere in here.'

'Why not?' Mallett watched him attentively.

'Because the direction of the shot is *across* the boat-house, from where you are standing to where Fitzbrown is standing. Well, that's impossible, because even if a man could stand there without this fellow Gabb's knowledge – which is ridiculous unless he was unconscious already – he wouldn't have elbow-room in which to aim his rifle. The muzzle would be beyond Gabb's nose.'

'Quite so,' said Mallett, rubbing his large red hands on a large red handkerchief. 'Add to that, that this motor-boat obviously hasn't been in use for years: there's no oil or petrol, and the engine's all rusted up.'

'Couldn't he have been tinkering with it?' said Fitzbrown.

'Look at his hands,' retorted Mallett. 'And where are his tools? If he had come here to tinker with the engine, he'd at least have brought a spanner. And he'd hardly do so without bringing enough juice to try her with.'

'True,' said Fitzbrown. 'Then what do you think? Did someone shoot him and then hide the body in here? Rather risky, wouldn't it be?'

Mallett edged his way back along the ledge towards the side door. Heavily yet carefully he planted a large foot in the centre of one of the rowing-boats, and played his torch about on the floor. He bent down.

'Ha!' he said. He picked up a dead match and a cigarette end. 'There may be more, but this is enough. It's just as I thought: he was using this boat when he went on the lake this morning.'

'They were out yesterday,' objected Fitzbrown. 'It may be left over from then.'

'I don't think so,' said Mallett. 'This cigarette-end looks too fresh and new. However, we'll get this boat outside into the daylight presently and see what else we can find. Meanwhile, what I'm suggesting is— Throw the double doors right open. We'll see if it works.'

Fitzbrown disconnected the iron bar on his side, and together he and Jones pushed the double doors outwards, flooding the boat-house with light. From where they stood, there was now a clear channel about six feet wide and twenty yards long, edged with concrete, and debouching into the lake itself.

'I suggest,' said Mallett, 'that Gabb was coming in from his trip. He rowed as far as those reeds there, and he would then ship oars and drift along this channel straight into the boat-house. As he drifted, he'd look to right and left, over his shoulders, to see he didn't foul the quay or the doors. I'd say at a guess that your stalker was standing or kneeling in the shadows at the back of the boat-house. He let Gabb drift in as near as he dared, and as Gabb drifted up to the double doors, he got him through the head. Gabb fell forward, the boat floated in, and there you were!'

He had climbed out of the rowing-boat, and Fitzbrown rejoined them both on the nearer quay. 'What about the bullet?' said Fitzbrown.

'If I'm right, you'll never find it. It would land somewhere in the mud of the channel. If he used one of the stream-lined type, he may have chosen it purposely, knowing that if he could get within close range the bullet would go through the fellow's head and get lost.'

'H'm,' said Jones. 'But surely a man who could handle a rifle as confidently as that wouldn't expect us to be taken in by the wound? He's staged it to look like a shot-gun suicide. That presupposes he thinks the police are complete fools.'

'Well, well,' said Mallett, 'many of us are. Anyway, if we can't find the bullet we can't be sure of the rifle, can we? And that's a snag at the outset. We can't look for the owner of a gun whose make, calibre, type, et cetera, we don't know. Of course I'll have the channel and the approaches to it dredged for the bullet; but it'll require a stupendous bit of luck to find it.'

'And the cartridges?' queried Jones.

'We can search. But I think he'll have got rid of those all right. You're dealing with a pretty determined criminal,' Mallett continued, studying the corpse with his head on one side. 'He didn't stalk: he lay in ambush. That's all right, Jones. You can close the door.' He turned away.

'But I say!' said Fitzbrown, 'why, having shot Gabb, didn't he leave well alone? Why did he go to the trouble of lifting the body from the rowing-boat into the motor-boat? It must have been difficult, and dangerous too.'

Mallett came back. 'Yes. I'd been wondering that, too. To drag a dead man out of this boat, along the ledge, and put him into that one, would be a bit of a feat.' He stood and considered. 'He had decided, as you say, to stage a suicide. That means, gun between knees, head pressed against gun. He'd have a clear picture of that in his mind. Now the seat of the rowing-boat is very low. It's just possible he quite failed to prop the corpse up in a sitting position, with the gun as a buttress, in this boat. But the seat of the motor-boat is the height of a chair. Even so, he failed to get the head in the right position; but he fixed the barrel into his chest, where his clothes prevented it from slipping. We'll have photos taken before they remove him. Then we can examine the shot-gun, though I doubt if it'll tell us much. We'll find one, perhaps both, barrels fired; but Gabb may have fired them himself. The murderer would look into the breech, and shoot or not shoot as required.'

'Shall I look?' said Jones.

'No. Finger-prints. Though I doubt if he'll have left any.' They filed out, and Fitzbrown closed the side door. 'Now to find out the material times,' said Mallett as they climbed the four concrete steps, 'and have a look at the inmates. Jones, will you go ahead and make the arrange-ments? You can have the body now; but leave a man on guard, and pack the gun yourself. Tell them to dredge the channel for the bullet. If they find it, you'd better deal with that too. Let me know the type of rifle the moment you're able.' And as Jones slithered off along the muddy path, 'Oh, and I say! Get me that copy of the Colonel's reminiscences out of the Public Library. I'd like to read it again.'

10

Simon was alone when Mallett and Fitzbrown entered his study. He was seated at his desk, with his spectacles on, and he looked up over the tops of them with his magisterial air.

'Ah, Mallett,' he said, half-standing up and leaning out over the broad desk with outstretched hand, 'how are you?' His tones were firm and resonant, and he had regained his air of command. 'I'm glad to see you, glad this terrible business will be in your hands. I know I can trust you to lay my son's murderer by the heels, if any man could.'

'H'm. Ha.' Mallett puffed a little at this praise, and pulled at his red moustache, as soon as Mr Gabb released his hand. 'Glad to be of service, if I can. But remember, sir,—' He pulled up a chair and sat down on the opposite side of the flat desk, confronting Simon. 'If you want to call in experts, or you'd rather have these investigations conducted by a C.I.D. man, don't hesitate to say.' And he glared somewhat defiantly across at Simon. Fitzbrown, standing behind him, blinked apprehensively.

Simon looked at Mallett over his glasses. 'Superintendent,' he said, 'if I thought that to call in outside help would further this business in any way, I shouldn't hesitate. But I have complete confidence in you. You know this place. You know more about us than any outsider could do. Go right ahead. Pull the place to pieces – but find the murderer of my son.'

'Ah,' Mallett sat back, content. He did not thank Simon for his confidence; he merely ceased to look aggressive, and became business-like. 'Now, sir: I want a complete list of the people who spent the night in this house, when they arrived, when they left, and anything else that they said or did during their stay which struck you at all. I shall probably want to interview some of them. Can you give me a room here?'

'A room?' Simon gave a bitter laugh. 'Help yourself, Superintendent. There are about thirty rooms on the ground floor, and forty-five bedrooms on the upper floors. At present I suppose about a quarter of them are in use, if that. You can have any room you please, except the ones my wife and I are using, and the staff.'

'Right,' said Mallett. 'I'll look around.' He glanced round the room they were in. 'I take it this is the library?'

'Yes. Sir Charles Laforte's library. I took it over as my study – or office, I should say. Not that the books are of much interest to me; but the room he called his study was a bit too overpowering. So I let my son Giles have it and took over this place.' He gazed round at the dark shelves, and up at the lofty ceiling. 'Though I don't really know that it's much easier to work in. However, I don't spend much time here.' He sighed.

Mallett recalled him. 'If you'll let me have that list, Mr Gabb, I'll copy down the names and times. And another thing: I want to know, if you can tell me, which of those present last night could use a rifle. Dr Jones has not only confirmed Dr Fitzbrown's opinion that it wasn't any shot-gun that killed your son; he has also ascertained that the shot was fired by someone who had every confidence in his aim. So—' He took out his pencil and note-book.

'Well,' said Simon thoughtfully, 'let me see. There were myself and my wife, of course. I got home at about one-thirty, as it was Saturday. I played a round of golf in the afternoon, and came in to tea. There were people coming to dinner, so I had a little rest and read the paper before changing for dinner. That was my day. Then there was my son Basil. He came home with me in the car from the works, and got out at the North Lodge, where he lives. I didn't see him again till evening, when he and his wife were in the drawing-room with the others, waiting for dinner.'

'They left after dinner?' said Mallett.

'No. My wife insisted on their staying the night, because of the storm. But I haven't seen either of them since, so I don't know exactly when they left. I went just now to break the news to my poor wife – but she hadn't seen Basil, either. She was prostrate, of course, but I gathered that Basil had heard the news and gone home to his wife.'

'His wife left before him, then?'

'I suppose so. I don't know. She'd certainly leave early, because of the baby. But you'd better ask her, Superintendent.'

'I will. Go on, Mr Gabb.'

'Then there was my son Giles. I don't know exactly how he spent the day, but I understood he had been out on the lake most of the day with those young people he brought home. They were pike-fishing. They came in to dinner rather late, between eight o'clock and half-past, I suppose.'

'Did you notice anything unusual about your son?'

'No, nothing special. He had been spending a good deal of time with his new friends, and he seemed anxious that we should make them welcome. Of course both his mother and I did that. He looked a little pale and tired, but not more so than he often does.'

'No signs of agitation, fear, or anything like that?'

'None. I thought he was very much engrossed with this Miss Laforte, but I was quite pleased to see that.'

'And they too stayed the night?'

'Yes, because of the storm. There were three of them. There was Miss Laforte, the daughter of the late owner, a very pretty girl, quite a lady. I quite took to her. Then there was a young fellow, her brother; and another young man, who, I think they said, was the son of my tenant at the South Lodge, Mrs Charleroy. She's the sister of the late owner. You know her, Mallett, I dare say.'

Mallett nodded. 'Well, now to go back a minute, Mr Gabb. You must excuse the question: but which members of your family can handle a rifle?'

Simon stared a moment, then gave a short laugh. 'I'm afraid that's not going to help you much, Mallett. You know my business, and you know that as a side-line Gabb's have been manufacturing sporting guns for the last twenty years. I used to consider myself a pretty good shot in my time, though my hand and eye aren't so steady as they used to be. It was I who founded the Broxeter Rifle Club in 1902. I was the President for many years, and as soon as my two boys grew big enough to hold a gun, they joined too. Giles and Basil were both crack shots before they were sixteen. Giles took a great interest in the mechanical side, and I had hopes he might do something out of the ordinary, until he overworked and had that breakdown six years ago. Since then we've had to watch him carefully, and he's been more erratic, though just as keen when he did decide to work. Now Basil – he never was mechanically-minded. He was all for the administrative side, and very good he is at it. I don't know what I'd do without him. But Giles – he might have had genius.'

Simon's face was flushed a little as he spoke of his lost hopes. Mallett paused a moment before asking gently:

'Do I understand that Giles had done little work of any importance since this illness you speak of?'

'Oh no!' Simon's face lit up for a minute; then the light faded as he realized what had happened. 'Until we came here, Superintendent, he hadn't done anything much, although we had every reason to believe he was cured. Of course, he occasionally had fits of silence or brooding, when no one could talk to him, and then he'd go off by himself for long country walks. In fact, when I bought this place I thought it would be ideal for him; he was so fond of the open air, and interested in these country sports. When we came here, he was all right. He had begun to work on his mechanics again. At that time, we were negotiating for this contract for military rifles, and Giles seemed to think he'd be able to work out some improvements, if he were given the time, and plenty of room for his experiments. He wouldn't tell me the exact nature of his experiments, but I gathered they had to do with securing a flatter trajectory, greater accuracy at longer range. Everybody's exploring the same avenue; but I know Giles, and I had hopes that something would come of it, something that would be to the advantage of the nation, as well as our firm.'

'What happened after he came here? Did he stop working?'

'No,' said Simon. 'For a while he worked harder than ever. As I told you, I gave him Sir Charles's old study. He used to spend whole days there without a break. He wouldn't let anyone inside when he was in this mood. They had to leave his meals on a tray outside. One day, though, his mother did get in – he used to lock the door, but she caught him unawares for once – and she found him knee-deep in papers. She told me his desk was covered with calculations, and he had quite a wild look as he turned and saw her. She asked him what he was doing, and he said he was inventing a gun that would kill the man who used it, when he was least expecting it.'

'He was joking, of course,' said Mallett.

'Oh, yes, he was joking, if you can call the sort of thing a man says when he's at the end of his tether a joke. After that he had a sort of relapse. But it was very brief, and as soon as he'd recovered physically, he came back to the works. Since then, he's alternated between working hard and going off on his own, sometimes for a day or two, sometimes for a week or more.'

'And the brothers: were they on good terms?'

'Eh?' Simon gave Mallett a straight look over his glasses. 'Oh yes, quite good, quite good,' he said abruptly, 'considering the difference in temperament.'

Mallett registered, by means of a hieroglyph invented by himself, 'Not altogether true.' Mallett could write orthodox shorthand, but he had also a system of grading answers, which no one but himself could read.

'Thank you,' he said absently. 'Now for the other names, please.'

'My brother James,' continued Simon, checking them off on his fingers, 'and his wife. They were brought here in time for dinner by their son Harry, my nephew. He was to come and fetch them home; but once again the storm interfered. Harry arrived on foot shortly before eleven, with his sister Lucy. He said he'd had to leave the car half-way up the drive, as there was an elm-tree across it. Of course they stayed the night. We considered they'd had a very lucky escape, and we wouldn't have dreamt of letting them go again. I don't know if the children are still here, but James and Janet are. James will be glad to see you and help you in any way, Superintendent; and Janet – she's standing by my poor wife for the present.'

'Any others?'

'Yes: Mr Olivier and his wife. You know him, Mallett. He's the brother of the Broxeter solicitor, and a barrister himself. His wife's a sort of friend of the family. She was in school with Pauline, my son Basil's wife, and often visits them at the Lodge. She's been married to Olivier about six months, I believe: a nice girl. A good deal younger than her husband, I should say.'

'Not much good asking you if any of these can handle a rifle, I suppose,' said Mallett, putting up his book. 'It would have been easier to ask who can't.'

'Well, my wife can't, for one,' said Simon, smiling. 'And I doubt if my brother's wife, competent as she is in most things, has had much experience with rifles. But I'll warrant she'd make shift to use one if necessary. Harry's an old member of the Rifle Club, like my own boys. My brother James isn't much of a shot, though naturally he's not without some experience, as I've been so long in the business. But he's kept busy with his shop, and he doesn't much care for that sort of thing.'

'And the other ladies?'

'Eh? Oh yes, of course. I don't know about Pauline, but I've never heard that she could, unless perhaps she's done a bit of grouse-shooting with her father on the moors some time. As for Mrs Olivier, I've no idea. And my daughter Jessica—'

Mallett looked up. 'Your daughter?'

'Yes. Er – did I forget to say she was there? I'm so used to seeing her about the place, it never occurred to me to mention her specially.' Mallett noticed the slight hurry in his speech, and though he did not bring out his note-book again, he mentally added Jessica's name with a hieroglyph opposite it. Simon was continuing: 'Jessica can shoot straight, as straight as the boys; but she's not much interested. She's been away at school a lot, and since she came home, she's done nothing much that I can see except sit about reading books, and rush out to play tennis, and so forth. She's got her own friends. – That's the whole lot of them, so far as I know.'

'And you know of no reason why anyone should want to get rid of your son – silence him, for instance? Nobody outside this household, or in it, who had any grudge against him?'

'Not so far as I know.' Simon seemed to hesitate, and Mallett noticed this. But he evidently changed his mind, if he had been going to add anything; and Mallett decided to press him no further for the present.

'And now,' he said, 'if you're ready, Mr Gabb, I'd like to take a look over your son's study.'

Simon was about to answer when there was a knock on the door, and a tall good-looking young man with fair crinkled hair and bright blue eyes burst into the room.

'What's the matter, Harry?' said Simon, annoyed. 'Can't you see I'm busy with the Superintendent?'

'Sorry, Uncle,' said Harry breathlessly, 'but I think it's very important both you and the Superintendent should know this. Father thought so too.' He glanced back, but James had not followed his son into the room.

Simon said coldly: 'Very well, if it's important.' It was clear to Mallett that Harry Gabb was not a great favourite with his uncle.

Harry, looking a little dashed, withdrew a couple of paces. He said again: 'I'm sorry, Uncle, terribly sorry, about poor Giles, I mean. I've seen Aunt Polly, and I forgot I hadn't seen you.' He came forward again. 'It'll take me a minute or two to explain. Shall we sit down?' His confident manner reasserted itself, and he waved them all to chairs. When no one accepted his invitation, he sat down himself, on Simon's desk.

'I wouldn't have thought much about this,' he said, 'except for what has happened. You know, Uncle, Lucy and I got here between half-past ten and eleven last night. We were supposed to pick up my mother and father and drive them home. We'd been out to dinner ourselves in Broxeter, and we didn't leave till after ten, when the storm had abated a bit. It was still raining in torrents, and I thought they'd probably spend the night here, but Lucy seemed to think we ought to come. I tried to phone, but you were cut off—'

'Yes, yes, all right,' said Simon testily. 'We know all that. You got as far as the fallen elm, and walked to the house, and you spent the night here. Well? What then?'

'Just this, Uncle: we spent the night here all right, but only by a most amazing contretemps. You see, you heard Aunt Polly ask us to stay, and you heard me agree. But then you went off to bed – you remember? – and soon afterwards so did she. I was still in the drawing-room, having a last night-cap – it was getting on for midnight by now – when my sister came into the room. I thought she'd gone to bed ages ago. She had been crying, and was in a furious rage. She said I must take her home at once: she wasn't going to stay here another minute. Of course I told her not to be a fool. She said if I wouldn't take her, she'd drive the car herself.' He threw out his hands with a deprecatory smile. 'What could I do? It so happened that I was driving a new car, a Jaguar Eight, which even I wasn't used to; and I knew she'd never be able to handle it on a night like that, in pouring rain, a car she'd never seen before.' He threw back his head, revealing splendid white teeth, and laughed. 'Lucy's not exactly a Malcolm Campbell at the best of times; but to let her go, in her state of mind, would have been murder.' He stared round. 'Oh, sorry! Sorry, Uncle! I mean—'

'Yes, yes,' said Simon testily again. 'Come to the point, lad.'

Harry proceeded more soberly. 'I asked her what was wrong. She wouldn't say much, but I gathered that she considered Giles had – well, let her down.'

Simon frowned. 'What do you mean?'

'Well – excuse me, Uncle, I'm afraid you'll consider this irrelevant, but I don't. It seems that when she was going upstairs to bed, she heard Giles's voice and another – a man's – at the head of the stairs. They were quarrelling, violently. Giles ordered the fellow to clear out; and he said nothing would suit him better. It only lasted a few seconds, she said, but Giles's fury was terrific. She said she knew by the sound of his voice. By the way, she didn't tell me this at first, but I'm telling it back to you in the right order. All she'd say to me at first was that Giles had insulted her.'

'Insulted her?' Simon's scowl deepened.

'Well, that was how she put it, Uncle. You know she was – well, expecting to marry Giles. She made all the running, I admit; but Giles never actually discouraged her. He let her think—'

'He did nothing of the kind,' said Simon contemptuously. 'All of you pack of fools encouraged her. And now you blame Giles because he wasn't willing to fulfil a promise he never made.'

Harry seemed about to retort angrily, but he controlled himself. 'All right, Uncle: have it your own way. Anyhow, after this other fellow had bolted off down the stairs, Lucy came forward. Damned silly, as I told her, to tackle a fellow in a rage; but there you are: you know what fools women can be.' He was about to give another hearty laugh, but this time the general lack of response checked him. 'What happened, I don't quite know. This was the part she told me first, or rather, I dragged it out of her, and she was crying too much to be very clear. But it seemed that she'd heard enough to realize that the quarrel was over this new flame of Giles's, and she went up to him and tackled him about it, and got what you'd expect, a flea in her ear. Giles simply told her that if he married anyone it would be this Laforte girl, and that he hadn't the slightest use for anyone else. He also added that if *she* wouldn't marry him, it would be of no interest to Lucy, because he'd blow his brains out. That was why, this morning when I first heard, I thought—' He turned to Mallett. 'My theory is that this fellow he turned out of the house heard him say that, and banked on our all taking it for suicide. I should arrest him on suspicion, if I were you, Superintendent. He'll do a bunk if you don't.'

'Thanks,' said Mallett. 'But I haven't quite completed my evidence. Now suppose you tell as what happened next. You agreed to take your sister home?'

'Yes, I did, in the end. We started out, to get back to the car, along the drive. It was an awful night. The rain was still streaming down. You can imagine how I felt, therefore, when we came to the fallen elm-tree, climbed over it somehow – and found my car had gone!'

'Gone?' Mallett drew out his note-book.

'Yes, gone!' said Harry, admiring the effect of his surprise.

'Sure no one had moved it – out of the way, for instance?'

'Out of the way? Why should they? The drive was blocked, anyhow. Still, I couldn't quite believe it myself, so I walked to the end of the drive, as far as the North Lodge where Basil lives, to see if by any chance it had been moved and parked elsewhere. I even went and looked through the window of his garage, in case anyone had had the kind thought of putting my nice new car away out of the wet. But no: Basil's own car was there; but not mine. I trudged back to where Lucy was waiting by the elm, and we had no alternative but to creep back to the house and go to bed. By this time – it was now nearly one – we were both soaking wet and in the worst of bad tempers. I tried to ring up Chode Police Station about my car, but the phone was still not working. So that was that—until this morning.'

'You rang up Chode this morning?' said Mallett. 'What time? It must have been after I left.'

'No,' said Harry. 'I rang up Broxeter. I thought by now the car thieves would have got farther afield, and Broxeter could handle it better. Then I went and had breakfast. Just as I was finishing – Basil was there too, I remember – Olivier came in and told us about poor Giles. Basil went off at once. I hung about, and as no one came, at last I thought I'd go and get a breath of fresh air: have a look at the elm-tree that was down, and perhaps meet the boy with the papers. You'll probably think I was drunk the night before, and I should too if Lucy hadn't been with me; but—' He got off the table and stepped back, to deliver his second surprise in the most telling manner possible: '– the car was standing there, with its bonnet almost touching the elm-tree, just as I had left it!'

Fitzbrown spoke for the first time. 'Someone had moved it the night before. You didn't look far enough.'

Harry turned to him blandly. 'You think so? Well, how far do you think I should have looked exactly? Twenty miles, for instance?'

They all stared.

'– For twenty-odd miles was what would have been required,' went on Harry triumphantly. 'My car had been taken for a ride. She does about fifteen miles to the gallon, and there were nearly three gallons less petrol in her this morning than when I parked her there last night.'

Mallett flipped open his note-book. 'The number?'

Harry gave it. 'And what's more,' he said, 'I found this beside it in the drive.' He took out of his pocket a small irregular-shaped block, and laid it on the table. Coated as it was with mud, for a moment Mallett did not recognize what it was. He picked it up, and saw that it was the heel of a woman's evening slipper. He grunted.

'We'll look into the matter,' he said. 'You needn't stay, I'll send for you if you're needed.' As he spoke, the telephone on Simon's desk rang. Mallett picked up the receiver.

'Hullo! Yes. Superintendent Mallett of Chode speaking. Eh? Oh yes, he's here; but you can give me the message.' He wrote down on his pad: '"Swan Bridge Inn." Yes, I know it: twenty-two miles on the other side of Chode. Down by the river.' He listened for some minutes, grunting and nodding. 'Thanks. By the way, you needn't bother any further: the car's been returned. Yes, returned. Thanks. Same to you.' He replaced the receiver.

'Your car was traced to the Swan Bridge Inn near Stickle-brook,' said Mallett. 'I don't know if you know it?'

'Well,' said Harry, 'as a matter of fact, I do.'

Mallett nodded. 'It's a lonely spot,' he said to Simon. 'Or rather, it used to be: one of these quiet little country inns which suddenly blossom forth into a rendezvous for people with big cars and nothing better to do. There's a cocktail bar for the winter, and a "picturesque beer-garden" for the summer, Your car was seen arriving there,' he said to Harry, 'last night at eleven-fifty. A man and a woman went up to the pub, which was half-closed and half-open, that is to say, a few people were still in the smoke-room, though *of course*,' emphasized Mallett, 'the sales of drink were over. They were admitted, and – according to the landlord – asked for drinks, which were *of course* refused. They then asked for, and were served with, ham sandwiches and ginger ale. They left about half-past twelve. That's all. Now: who were they?'

'That's your affair,' said Harry, looking rather startled at the sudden question, emphasized by the wagging of Mallett's red forefinger under his nose. 'That's your job, not mine.'

'Sure you didn't change your mind,' said Mallett, 'and turn back – with or without your sister?'

'Oh, really, I say!' Harry protested feebly, not sure whether to take Mallett seriously and be indignant, or to laugh it off.

'That's all right,' said Mallett grimly. 'The landlord will soon pick you out if it was. Fitzbrown, can you spare the time to get that landlord here for me? Tell them to send a police car to fetch him. I want him here this afternoon. Now, Mr Gabb, will you show me your son's study?'

'By Jove!' said Mallett, stopping on the threshold, and blocking the entrance with his large bulk. 'You say the Colonel called it his study? "Museum" would have been better.' He stepped inside, and Simon followed.

The room was octagonal, and nearly as large as the library. There was a desk, and some book-shelves. But on each of the eight walls, mounted on a polished wooden shield, was an exceedingly lifelike animal's head. Mallett walked round looking at them and reading the plaques underneath, which gave in gilt lettering the animal's name, and the date and place of its decease. First he stopped before a magnificent antelope-like creature with upright scimitar-shaped horns, so long that they almost touched the ceiling; its white face with the chestnut blaze above the nose, and the slanting eyes, gazed down sadly as if it were thinking. 'Well, well! How odd, and how unkind! But I suppose he didn't understand.' Mallett peered at the lettering, and read aloud: 'White Oryx, Wadi Hawa, November, 1911.'

He turned to Simon: 'Like living with a ghost, eh? I'm not a fanciful man, but I couldn't stand it.'

He moved along to the next panel, where a smaller head with double backward-curving horns gazed into the distance, like one who absent-mindedly listens, with only half an ear, but with infinite politeness, to a conversation going on in his presence. '"Addra Gazelle,"' read Mallett. '"Libyan Desert, February, 1927."' He passed on. '"Abyssinian Duiker. *Cephalophus grimmi abyssinicus.* Local name *Um-Dig-Dig*."

Well, one can understand why Latin didn't survive. *Um-Dig-Dig* was good enough for the Abyssinians.' He moved round, stopping at each panel, and commenting on name or face or place: '"Giant Eland. Addax. Kudu. Ariel." That's odd. Ah, here's his real name: *Gazella Saemerringi saemerringi*. That'd keep him on the ground. "Tora Hartebeest, Isabella Gazelle."'

'I begin to understand,' said Mallett as he came back to Simon, 'why he couldn't pay his rates. This sort of thing costs money: guns, licences, upkeep of expedition, wages of native boys, getting the spoils home when you've killed them.' He glanced over his shoulder to the sad-looking White Oryx again. 'You know, I'd say that for a sensitive man, such as your son seems to have been, this was the very worst room in the house. Look at those eyes! They're glass, of course, but everything has been done to restore the appearance of life; and the taxidermist is very expert nowadays. And in this particular room, you can't escape them: eight pairs of eyes centring on you. It would get on one's nerves in no time at all, if one had any.'

'I know,' said Simon apologetically. 'There were a lot more when we came here. I bought the place furniture and all, and these heads were on all the walls, even the dining-room; up the stairs, on the landings, everywhere. One kept coming upon them in the most unlikely places.' He coughed. 'My wife and daughter said they must go. So I offered them to the Broxeter Museum. They took all the African ones except these. They didn't want the foxes' masks and the fish in glass cases; but as soon as we can find someone to take them, they'll go too.'

'And why didn't the Museum take these?' said Mallett. 'I don't pretend to know much about big-game hunting, but I have an idea that these are the pick of his collection. That's why he put them here where he could see them while he wrote his reminiscences.'

'I know,' said Simon again. 'But when we told Giles, he astonished us by refusing to let us move them.' Simon became animated as he explained. 'His mother argued with him, and I remember he and Jessica had quite a battle over it. But he simply said he wanted them left here. He said they were a help to him in his work. And that was all we could get out of him.'

'H'm,' said Mallett. 'Ambiguous, eh?'

'Yes,' nodded Simon, 'ambiguous. However, we let him have his own way. His mother wanted to get rid of them while he was out one day, but I said no, it would only annoy him. We had got rather into the habit of considering his whims.'

'Naturally.' Mallett looked round. 'Well now, let's have a look at the arsenal, now we've studied the natural history museum.' He turned to the gun-rack that ran along two of the walls. 'Are these the late Colonel's? Or are they some of your own?'

Simon went up to them. 'Both. Some of them were there already. Some of them have been put here by Giles. This one—' He pulled out a heavy-looking double-barrelled rifle, and looked along it. 'This is an obsolete pattern, even for sporting purposes. You find them abroad sometimes in very hot climates, because they fire black powder, that is, the old "gun-powder," made of nitrate, charcoal and sulphur, that was in use from earliest times till the present day. Its advantage is indifference to heat; its disadvantage, smoke. As for the gun—' He placed it back in the stand. 'Imagine carrying that over rough ground, in tropical heat! It's an effort even to get it up to your shoulder.'

'What's it called?' said Mallett, interested.

'That's a double-barrelled 10-bore Paradox,' said Simon. 'And believe me, at fifty yards it'd knock down an elephant.'

'"The old 10-bore"!' exclaimed Mallett, delighted. 'So that's it! So he didn't have it with him when he met the lady rhino, or he might be here to-day. – What's this?'

'Oh, that's just a curiosity,' said Simon, passing it by. 'An old muzzle-loading flint-lock. They're just museum pieces now, of course.' He moved along the rack. 'Now here are some of the regular sporting rifles. Here's a medium-bore .45 Martini. And here's another medium-bore:

a Gibbs magazine. Both of these are pretty formidable. Here's a light shot-gun, 28-bore for the ladies; and this—'

The old man was lost in the fascination of handling these products of the gun-makers' art. He stroked the barrel of one, looked into the sight of another, broke the breech of a third. Mallett recalled him, reluctantly, for Simon Gabb had knowledge which he desired; but now there was no time. There so rarely is time, he thought regretfully, to consider anything in detail for its own sake.

'You know the uses of all these different guns,' he said. 'Yet you don't shoot game yourself, even locally?'

'Not now. I used to when I was younger and had more time.'

'And you've never been to the tropics – never seen a lion outside a zoo; yet you know the exact type that will best kill an elephant, a hippopotamus, or any of these antelopes and gazelles?'

'Yes, or even a man,' remarked Simon grimly. 'It's my job to know that, though not to do it.'

'That's what I'm coming to, Mr Gabb. Now tell me: you know the sporting jargon. You know what sportsmen mean when they speak of the "the brain shot."' He went carefully, anxious to spare Simon's feelings.

Simon nodded.

'It's my present theory that someone – an expert shot – lay in wait for your son inside the boat-house, and shot him through the head as the boat drifted in. Now if you had to choose, what rifle would you take for such a shot?'

Simon stroked his chin. 'It's a difficult question.'

'I'm sure it is. But you see, I've got to get a line on the gun used, if I can. The bullet is not yet recovered, and probably never will be. It's like looking for a needle in a haystack. Still, what you say may help us a little. My colleague Dr Jones, who knows something of ballistics, suggests a small-bore rifle of some sort, or an H.V. Express. Can you add anything?'

'H'm,' reflected Simon.

'Suppose I were a customer,' urged Mallett, 'out to shoot, not an elephant but something smaller and thinner-skinned: an antelope, or a man? What would you advise him?'

'Well, of course,' said Simon slowly, 'the most obvious choice would be a military pattern, wouldn't it? They're designed for the job, though they are used for big-game hunting as well. Our own .303 magazine, for instance. I don't meet the sporting fraternity myself. We only sell wholesale. But I know from the buyers what goes on, and I'm told that for a brain shot, or as a matter of fact, a heart or lung or other anatomically fatal shot, the connoisseurs nowadays choose a very small bore, such as the Mauser .275 or the Austrian Mannlicher .256 and its derivatives.'

'Do you manufacture such a rifle?'

'Not yet. We've not gone in for any smaller calibre than the .303 hitherto. But we were thinking of doing so. In fact— He stopped suddenly, as if confronted with a train of thought which he did not care to follow up.

'What?'

Simon came to himself. 'I was going to say, it was such a gun we'd recently been working on, at the request of the Government. I needn't tell you, Superintendent, the trend is all towards smaller and smaller calibres, thinner and thinner bullets, higher velocity, flatter trajectories, all giving greater range and more penetrative power.' He was talking rapidly, as if to cover up the unspoken thought. 'My engineers, like those of other firms, would give a lot to be in the vanguard of these developments.'

Mallett watched him shrewdly. 'And that was also what was occupying your son, Mr Gabb?'

Simon blinked rapidly. 'I think so. I think so.'

Mallett waved a hand at the gun-rack. 'Is there such a rifle among this lot?'

Simon peered. 'No. I don't see one. These are all large- or medium-bore.'

'But if your son was experimenting with a small-bore rifle, he must have had one here?'

'Why, yes. I suppose he would. Except that of course his work was still mostly in the calculation stage, I believe.'

'Have you ever seen a small-bore rifle here, either on this rack or elsewhere in the house?'

'I don't remember doing so. We have them at the works. He may have brought one home. I fancy he had a Mannlicher at one time, and used to experiment with it at a target.'

'Where is the target?'

'I believe there used to be one on the island in the lake. It was an old one, used by the Colonel for practice when he was at home. It gave a two hundred yards range from the opposite shore. Giles found it one day when he disembarked there, and set it up again.' He turned to face Mallett squarely. 'What are you getting at, Superintendent? My son didn't shoot himself, you know!'

'No, Mr Gabb. But I'm thinking that someone had observed him and thought what a good idea it would be to use him as a moving target. Perhaps the gun was taken from here, and the killer intended to use it to suggest suicide; but for some reason – perhaps because he was disturbed – he failed to complete the picture. He must have thought he had plenty of time, because he troubled to lift the body from the rowing-boat into the motor-boat, which was a mistake to begin with; then he hadn't time to arrange the body with the rifle as a prop, but only time to prop it up with the shot-gun. Or perhaps he lost his head, and thought it better to use Giles's own shot-gun and confuse the issue by getting rid of the gun that really shot him. If he did, we shall find it. You can't get rid of a gun so easily as all that, as you'll be the first to agree.'

Simon's heavy eyes flickered. 'No. If your reasoning's right, you'll find the gun hidden somewhere. No one would dare to be seen carrying it away.'

Mallett nodded. 'We'll search the reeds and dredge the lake if necessary. Now, Mr Gabb: can I have the keys of this desk?' He tried the lid. 'Ah! Never mind, it's not locked, I see. That's odd. Is this the only place where he kept his papers?'

'So far as I know, yes,' said Simon, staring.

'Presumably these calculations of his had some value.'

'They were highly confidential, I can assure you. He had access to data which no eye but myself had been allowed to see; and his own results, if he'd lived to complete them, would have been, one might almost say, of national importance.'

Mallett pulled out a sheaf of papers, some tied together neatly in bundles, others single leaves; some covered with figures, others containing a few words scribbled in pencil.

'Then you'd better look after them,' he said. 'Will you take this lot and go through them carefully? They seem to be figures that would convey nothing to me. Let me know if you consider them important, and if so, lock them up yourself in your own safe. I'll go through the rest.'

Half an hour later, Mallett was still sitting in the octagonal room. His lunch had been brought to him there, and he had found on the bookshelf a copy of Colonel Laforte's *Lure of the Spoor*. As he read it, his coffee grew cold. It had evidently been studied closely by at any rate one previous reader. There were slips of paper marking certain passages, and paragraphs scored in the margin. One sentence of the preface was so heavily underlined that the pencil had almost dug a hole through the paper. It read:

'But for all true sportsmen, the eternal code abides: Be fair. Kill moderately, *in order that the world's Big Game may survive to give Sport to Those Who Come After.*'

And elsewhere, underneath a photograph of 'White Rhino, shot by Lord Beganbury,' the caption was likewise underlined: '*Very rare and local and strictly preserved.*'

Mallett went all through the book, savouring the hatred of the reader. Everywhere that the author had mentioned an animal as being 'very rare,' the words were underlined. Sometimes the hunter spoke of his quarry as 'very beautiful' also; this too was picked out with exclamation-marks and underlining. In the book, Mallett also found photographs of some of the animals whose heads looked down on him from the walls: The Addax, 'a great prize,' living in far-distant waterless country, 'among the least accessible of species,' and the Addra, 'one of the biggest and most beautiful of African gazelles'; the Bongo, 'very rare and elusive forest-dwelling beast,' and the Kuda, likewise 'rare.' But what made him sit up suddenly in his swivel-chair was a photograph near the end: a group of Sudan natives, the author's porters, and in the centre a little English girl of about ten, and a little English boy of about eight. 'Group of Nyam porters, photographed after our return, with my small son and daughter. Inset: Giant Eland, the highly successful result of our expedition.' Underneath, in inverted commas, were the words: '*Quality, not quantity*,' and these, of course, had been heavily underlined by the censorious reader. 'My small son and daughter.' So the Colonel had blooded his family young! And these were the two, now a young man and a young woman of – he noted the date of the expedition – about nineteen and twenty-one respectively. Very interesting. Mallett's desire to interview the young Lafortes increased.

Lastly, he turned to the frontispiece. It was a reproduction, in colour, of a water-colour sketch of 'Abyssinia: a wild escarpment, haunt of the Ibex. Reproduced by kind permission of my sister, Mrs Bruce Charleroy.'

The telephone rang on Simon's desk. 'Dr Jones speaking. Is Superintendent Mallett there?'

Mallet was fetched. 'Hullo, Jones. But the way, you needn't bother to get that book out of the Library. There's one here. Very instructive indeed.'

'I know,' said Jones. 'I've been reading the library copy.'

There was a significant pause. 'And the result of the p.m.?' said Mallett.

'Nothing fresh to report. Confirms what we thought.'

'Can you give a time of death?'

'Taking all things together, five to six hours before our first examination,' said Dr Jones. 'That is, between five-thirty and six-thirty a.m.'

'Nothing more?'

'Yes. Just an idea. Don't you think the only possible reason a man would go to the trouble of moving a body from one boat into another is, he wanted to use the first boat himself?'

12

A s Mallett ran down the steps of Herons' Hall, he met Fitzbrown coming up. Fitzbrown turned and joined him.

'Well,' said Mallett, 'any news?'

'A few scraps,' said Fitzbrown. 'Coleman and I have been dealing with these people as best we could while you've been having lunch. There seem to be numbers of them standing about waiting – I might almost say hoping to have the honour of an interview with you. They want to get away, you know, to their homes.'

He spoke with mild reproach that did not seem to penetrate to Mallett's conscience. Mallett was in a hurry. Fitzbrown, long-legged as he was, had to bestir himself to keep up with the big Superintendent, whose coat flapped out behind him as he took the way past the front of Heron's Hall, and so to the path leading down to the boat-house. Fitzbrown spoke more acidly:

'I hope you enjoyed your quiet time. I could see you through the window. You appeared to be reading.'

'That's right,' said Mallett complacently. 'Jones has been reading too, the same book. We agree about it entirely.' He chuckled: and Fitzbrown, now a few steps behind him in the narrow muddy footpath, regarded his broad back with a mixture of annoyance and surprise. Conversation became difficult, then impossible, as they approached the slope to the boat-house.

A policeman stood on guard. As Mallett and the doctor approached, he stepped down to the boat-house side door, and opened it with the

Yale key. Again Mallett peered in eagerly, blocking the entrance with his large bulk. He played the beam of his torch on to the two rowing-boats which day side by side, their prows almost touching the double doors. After a moment he stepped back:

'Open these doors,' he said to the policeman. The double doors swung slowly open, flooding the concrete chamber with light. Mallett took Fitzbrown by the arm.

'I want to settle the matter of the boats,' he said, and now there was no trace of raillery in his manner.

'The boats?' said Fitzbrown.

'Yes. We found Gabb's body in the motor-boat. But the motor-boat is out of commission, hasn't been used for years. It was therefore merely serving as a repository for the body. But why should a man who has just shot another man go to the trouble of lugging his body from one boat to the other? We thought of a tentative answer, but it wasn't really satisfactory, as I felt at the time. Jones rang me up just now with the obvious answer: the killer wanted to use Giles's boat himself.'

'Yes?' said Fitzbrown dubiously. 'But—' He peered into the boat-house. 'Why would the killer want to do that? It isn't usual, I imagine, when you've just shot a man, to take a pleasant row on the lake, fishing or duck-shooting or what not.'

'Leave that for the minute,' said Mallett. 'That's what we've got to find out. Meanwhile, Jones's reasoning is sound; in fact, it's right beyond question.'

'I don't know about that.' Fitzbrown stared at the sunlit water lapping against the brown pointed boats. 'There are two boats here. Why shouldn't he use the second? It's not padlocked – merely tied.' He stepped across from one boat to the other, to examine the rope that moored it to a ring in the wall. 'We know this boat's sound. They were using both boats yesterday, when Giles and the Lafortes went fishing.'

'Quite so,' said Mallett. 'And therefore we are led to the inevitable conclusion that when the killer shot Giles, the second boat was not there. If it had been he would have used it, and saved himself trouble and time wasted in moving Giles's body. We are postulating, of course, that he had some urgent reason still unknown to us for taking a boat out on to the lake after he had shot Giles.'

Fitzbrown, from the opposite ledge, looked up with real interest. 'By Jove, Mallett, I believe you've got on to something there!' He bent over the second boat, scrutinizing the seats and inner surface.

'Yes,' said Mallett. 'It opens up possibilities. For instance perhaps it was urgently necessary to the killer that he should follow, or pursue, whoever was on the lake already.'

'Or,' said Fitzbrown, absorbed in his examination, 'perhaps the killer was the man in the second boat—and the person who took Giles's boat was someone who saw the whole thing from in here and then went after him.'

Mallett shook his head. 'I don't think so. Gabb's boat was approaching the boat-house, in all probability, when he was shot; and if he had been shot from the lake side, that is, by someone in the second boat, the shooting would have to have been done from in front, so that the killer would have been face to face with the victim. Gabb would have been bound to see him, and he was a pretty good shot himself. He could have defended himself. He had his shot-gun.'

'But,' said Fitzbrown, 'suppose Gabb was shot when he was rowing away from the boat-house, and not on his return? He could then have been shot from behind, by a man behind him in the second boat.'

'In that case,' said Mallett, 'Gabb's boat would have been facing the wrong way. The killer would have had to turn it round and tow it back to the boat-house. And even if he had risked doing so, what possible reason can you suggest why he then should have gone to the trouble of lifting Giles from the rowing-boat into the motor-boat?'

'I see what you mean,' said Fitzbrown. 'Well, can we find out which boat Giles took, and which the killer?'

'Perhaps,' said Mallet. 'But it doesn't matter very much, unless the killer left something behind, and he doesn't seem to have been so obliging. We can probably assume that Giles took the nearer boat. It would be the obvious thing to do. However –'– he stepped heavily into the nearer boat himself, and sat down – 'there's one thing certain: if the killer took a boat, he wanted to cross the water; and the only reason why he should cross water would be to get to somewhere on the other side. Jump in, Fitzbrown, and take an oar. We're going to do the same.'

Fitzbrown protested. 'Can't we walk? There's a path all round the lake, you know.'

'But not across to the island,' said Mallett. 'That's where the killer wanted to go, otherwise as you say he would have walked; and that's where we're going now.'

13

Jessica sat on a stile half-way up the hill behind the South Lodge, and watched Billy toiling up the slope towards her. Behind her, covering the crown of the hill, was a wood of birch and beech and hazel, with a narrow path winding through it; before her, the grassy slope stretched down to a deep lane. The view from the hill was wonderful in the after noon sunshine: the lake, rippling gently under the westerly breeze, gave back in softer, more manifold tones the blue of the sky. The island, a mass of dark green foliage, dipped its alders into the water. Beyond the lake, across park land, lay the long façade of Herons' Hall; even from here, Jessica could see the brilliant splashes of colour that the beds of begonias made in the trim surface of the lawns. But the landscape might have been painted in sepia for all the pleasure that her face showed.

Billy struggled up the last few yards, and stood before her, panting.

'Hullo! I'm so glad I saw you. I've been looking out for you all morning, but I thought you must be indoors, and I didn't like to come and ask for you.' He sat down on a large boulder beside the stile, and pushed his hair back from his forehead. 'Then I happened to go into our garden just now, and I looked up and saw you sitting up here. Have you been here long?'

Jessica did not answer. He chattered on:

'Aunt Helen is being rather awful to-day. She seems to think we must all stick about the house in case the police descend on us… I suppose it's even worse at your place… He gave her a side-long glance to see how she was taking things, and noticed the pallor that threw into relief her dark eyebrows and dark hair. So far as he could see, she had not stirred or responded in any way. She still sat gazing into the distance, just as she had been doing before he came. He jumped up, and threw an arm round her impulsively.

'I say, Jessica, don't take it so hard! It's an awful business, but – well – the poor chap didn't feel anything, you know. He probably knew nothing about it. Instantaneous death really is the best, I assure you. It's been proved: fellows who've been sand-bagged and knocked out – they wake up later and haven't the slightest idea what's happened to them. If they'd been killed, they wouldn't have known. I myself once fell out of a window on to my head; and one minute I'd been admiring the scenery, the next minute, as it were, there I was in bed in the hospital surrounded by nurses admiring *me*.'

Jessica moved a little along the stile, out of reach of his encircling arm. 'Don't waste your sympathy on me,' she said in a strained voice. 'I don't either need it or deserve it. I'm not grieving for Giles. I never liked him. Nobody did.'

Billy jumped up on to the stile beside her. 'Oh, come!' he said, still watching her solicitously. 'Somebody must have. Remember the old song: "Everybody's loved by someone, Everybody knows that's true." It's about a little orphan boy. We once had a governess who used to sing it. It ends like this: "I seem to be the only one that nobody loves at all".' He laughed, mimicking the governess, and put his arm round Jessica's waist again.

Jessica smiled, in spite of herself; and then, annoyed with herself for smiling, frowned more deeply.

'It's true!' she said vehemently, 'He hadn't a friend in the world. He never talked to any of us. Most people were afraid of him. He couldn't have got anyone to listen to him if he had talked.'

'Surely his father and mother—' began Billy.

'Oh, they!' said Jessica scornfully. '*She's* too silly to understand anybody or anything. And he – well, to my mind, of course, he's too old and set in his ways to realize the separate existence of anyone under forty. I bet he never thought of Giles except as someone who would run the firm when he died, and carry on the name of Gabb. And what a name!'

'I suppose,' said Billy, 'you're about ten years younger than Giles. You never knew Mr Gabb except as an oldish man. It was something like that with me and my father – though of course I idolized him when I was a kid.'

Jessica went on unheeding: 'And then there's that fathead Lucy. She knew Giles couldn't stand her. But there she goes this morning, with red eyes, trying to look like a young widow. It was the sight of her that drove me out of the place. And yet she must know he was mad on your sister.' She rounded on Billy. 'I suppose your sister disliked him too?'

'Well,' said Billy uncomfortably, 'I'm afraid she didn't like him well enough to marry him. She turned him down yesterday, or tried to.'

Jessica brooded. 'Isn't it funny this should happen the day after you three arrived? It seems like a fate, somehow – a sort of curse on the house, driving out the intruders.' She laughed mirthlessly. 'I'm glad I'm not one of them, anyway.'

Billy glanced at her, puzzled. 'You mean you're scarcely ever there?'

'I mean I don't belong!' she said fiercely.

'Oh, come!' said Billy again. 'Of course you belong! You're not going to be taken in by all that nonsense, old families and so on? My father spent all his money hunting and shooting; your father made his money by sheer brains and hard work. As I see it, he's more than entitled to take over our possessions. After all, my father never bothered to look after Herons' Hall. Your father has put it in order again. So why—'

'You don't understand,' said Jessica, brooding with her chin on her hands.

'Not quite,' said Billy patiently. 'Well, never mind. But tell me – it'll do you good to get it off your chest-why did *you* dislike poor Giles? I thought he wasn't a bad sort, you know. He was very decent to us and took us about a good deal. Of course I know, it was chiefly to get hold of Arden he did it, but still—'

Jessica interrupted violently. 'I hate all my family!'

'Why?'

'For a reason I can't tell you!'

'Oh, but you can! There's nothing you can't tell *me*.' He jumped down, and standing in front of her, took both her hands. 'Look here, if you're really hating them because you think they don't belong here, that's absurd. The moment I saw you, that day by the lake, I knew *you* belonged, anyway.' He smiled up at her. 'Listen, Jessica: if things had gone well with us, I suppose I'd have inherited Herons' Hall. Well, for the first time in my life, I wish I had – so that I could give it back to *you*.'

Jessica blushed, and her eyes filled with tears. 'You're sweet,' she said, 'But you don't understand. I'm not talking about Herons' Hall. I'm talking about myself, always myself. I'm horribly selfish. I hate myself too, if that's any satisfaction to you.'

Billy laughed. 'Oh, that puts everything all right! That includes the whole family! You forgot to mention that. I suppose it's because you've been away so much, at school and so on. And then when you came back – last July, wasn't it? – you had to live with them for the first time, and you found them just awful. Anyone would feel the same. You'll get over it.'

'No,' said Jessica, 'no, I never shall. It's something that can't be got over. One can't forgive people for having deceived one, used one for their own convenience, made a fool of one. Or else, if they have done just that, they should go on doing it. They should keep up the deceit for ever and ever, not suddenly let one know that all the previous years of one's life one has been living a lie! I hate lies – especially the lies one doesn't know one's telling! They're the worst of all.'

'"The lie in the soul,"' murmured Billy.

'What did you say?'

'Oh, it's only Plato. He says, you know, " to think falsely and have a false opinion in one's soul about the facts, to be ignorant, and to have and hold a lie therein, is the least acceptable of all things to every man: all loathe the lie above all things in such circumstances." It struck me so much at the time, I learnt it off by heart, though I didn't quite believe it.'

Jessica repeated slowly: '"To think falsely, to have a false opinion in one's soul about the facts." He might have added, especially when "the facts' concern oneself... And what about the people who put the lie into your soul? Does he tell you what they deserve? No, I suppose not.' She broke out vehemently again: 'I never wanted to be one of them! I don't like them, I never did! And yet I could never say so. You can't say, even to yourself, can you? – "I hate my father and mother, I hate my brothers, and my cousins and my aunt and my uncle." The words dry up in one. One's afraid – afraid some Nemesis will rise up and smite one. One's choked and muzzled by ideas of duty and the fifth commandment, by superstition and taboos. And so it all eats inwards, and what began as a mild dislike, a feeling of not being one of them, turns into an obsession that alters one. I used to dread going home for the holidays. I used to long to get away again. And yet always I thought the fault was mine. I used to lie awake and pray to be like other people, just normal and casual about them all. And all the time, I was tormenting myself about nothing! I could have said, "Poor old Mr and Mrs Gabb! They've done their best to be a father and mother to me, but I just can't feel that way about them, that's all. And as for Giles and Basil, well, they wouldn't have been my choice of brothers, but then I daresay they wouldn't have picked on me for a sister, either." And I should have made the best of all of them.'

Billy looked at her with dawning comprehension.

'You mean it really? You don't belong?'

Jessica nodded.

'And you don't know anything about your real family?'

'Very little. They've taken good care of that. It's too late to find out now, even if I wanted to. And what use would it be, anyway?'

'Do you mean to say you've only just been told?'

Jessica nodded. 'Would you like to know how? I'll tell you. One day, about a week after I got back from school for good, it was raining and I was bored. Oh, worse than bored – irritated and nervy and miserable, as I always was at home; and unable to imagine why. As a rule, when I came home to the Hall, I filled up my time playing tennis or whatever was going. I got into touch with any of my friends who lived round about, and I spent all the time I could avoiding the family. But this day I was at a loose end. Then I remembered the library. It was the day after I'd seen you for the first time – do you remember? – walking down by the lake with your dog, and I had our Rufus, and they both went after a rabbit. I knew who you were: one of my friends told me. And she also told me about your father, and how he had written a book about big-game hunting, and she thought there was a photo of you in it, as a little boy. So I went into the library to look for the book. I had seen it before, but hadn't taken much notice of it. It wasn't much in my line. But now I thought I'd like to read it.' She smiled suddenly and sweetly down at Billy.

'That was nice of you, darling,' said Billy, 'though I'm afraid I don't look my best in that picture. *It* stalked *me* all through my schooldays, until I wished the beastly book had been burnt in the market-place. But still, if it aroused your interest, I forgive all.'

'When I got there,' pursued Jessica, 'I couldn't find the book anywhere. And yet I felt sure I'd seen it, in a certain place on a certain shelf. Then I remembered the study. I thought there'd surely be a copy there, as it had been your father's study. I even thought perhaps Giles had taken the book along there. So I went to look. It never struck me that there was anything odd in my doing so. I had never been at home long enough to realize that Giles's new study was sacrosanct. The door wasn't locked, and I just walked in.'

'What's it like now?' said Billy. 'Has he got rid of those awful animals' heads? I hope so. I see they've removed most of them from the rest of the house, and a jolly good thing too!'

'No,' said Jessica. 'It's just the same. However, I didn't stop to look at them. I went straight to the bookshelf, and then, when I didn't see your father's book there, I turned to Giles's desk. It was littered with books and papers and drawings – and to my surprise, there in the middle of them all, open, was the book! And not only that: Giles had obviously been reading it, and marking it too. There was a pencil in the middle, just where he had left it, and in the margin there was a thick line, or several lines, drawn. I picked up the book and began looking through. On almost every page he had underlined something, or scored lines in the margin.'

'What kind of things?' said Billy.

'Oh, all the stuff about shooting rare animals, and what terrific sport it all is, and how the laity doesn't understand the importance of doing everything according to the correct code… I found the picture of you in the end, and I was gazing at it and wondering how it was that anybody brought up like that, to sit on dead animals and hear that sort of talk, could turn out to be so – so nice – when the door opened and Giles came in. I started as if I'd been caught burgling his desk, and I felt myself blushing in a ridiculous way.'

'Bless you!' said Billy ecstatically.

'I've never seen Giles look so furious. He came up to me and snatched the book out of my hand. He was not looking his best to begin with. If only he hadn't looked so unpleasant, he'd have been quite handsome, I've always thought. His profile was good and when his hair was brushed back—'

'Yes, yes,' said Billy impatiently. 'What did he do or say?'

'He said, " So it's you who come in here prying round and looking at my papers?" He was ghastly white, and his face looked pinched and worn, and he was unshaven. He wasn't properly dressed, either: he had only his shirt and trousers on, and I should imagine he'd been sleeping on the settee in the study. I said – I was as furious as he was, and I didn't mince my words – "Who gave you the right to speak to me like that? Surely if I want to borrow a book from here, I haven't got to ask your permission." He said, "You'll damned well keep out of here." I said, "I'll damned well go where I please. This is as much my home as yours." Of course, I didn't really mean I wanted to intrude on him in his study – heaven forbid! – but he had got me into such a rage that I was ready to say anything. And all this though we hardly ever spoke to each other as a rule. But there was something in his tone—"

'Go on,' said Billy, 'go on. You did quite right, of course. The Lafortes were behind you to a man. Go on.'

'Well, at that last remark of mine, a very queer look passed over his face: he relaxed, in a way, and yet I liked the look of him even less then than when he had snatched the book from me. He said with a sneer, "You think so?" I said, "I certainly do. Correct me if I'm mistaken." He said, "Well, of course, adoption is a legal process – but it remains a fiction essentially, doesn't it?' I said, "What do you mean?" He said, "I must say I think you're old enough to be told you aren't a blood relation of ours at all. I believe my father intends to tell you himself, now you've left school. They adopted you, eight years after Basil was born, because they wanted a daughter." He gave the kind of sneering laugh which was all he was capable of. "They didn't consult us at the time, of course. And now I'm afraid it's too late. But I'll thank you to remember that I'm the future master here."

'I threw the book down on the desk, on top of all his beastly papers, and sent them flying all over the floor. I rushed out of the room. I knew it was no use talking to Mrs Gabb – thank God I can call her that, now I'm released from having to say "Mother" – she would merely weep and bewail *her* misfortune in having brought someone so troublesome and ungrateful into the house when what she wanted was a good daughter, someone to comfort her in her old age… We've had rows before, and I could make a rough guess at what she'd say. I waited until old Simon came home; then I went to the library after dinner and tackled him.'

'And what did he say?'

Jessica laughed. 'He was busy with some other matter, writing letters and 'phoning and so on. At first he wanted to get rid of me; the idea was, "Don't bother me just now, my dear child; I'm doing something important." Then when insisted on telling him what I'd come for, he just pooh-poohed the whole thing. He said, "Your mother and I thought it best that no one should know until you came of age, then you'd grow up feeling one of the family. But of course if Giles has told you, you're old enough to realize." He seemed unable to grasp that I had anything to complain of: I'd always been well treated, hadn't I? They had sent me to the most expensive schools. And of course, I would always be well provided for. When I got married, he'd see I was "all right," as he called it.'

The scorn in Jessica's voice increased with every phrase. 'He finished up by saying, "I'm sure we've always treated you like a daughter." At that, I lost my temper entirely. I said, "Yes, and you thought fit to tell Giles and Basil who I was, before you told *me*." He said, "There's nothing to tell. Your father was a clerk in my office. He and your mother were both drowned in that pleasure-steamer that went down off the Isle of Man. His name was Mason. Is that such a great improvement on Gabb? Take it back if you like: it's all one to me." And he went back to his letters, or pretended to, in great dudgeon. Since then he's taken no notice of me at all — whereas before that, he used to say, "Well, Jessica?" when I came home from school, and "Here's a fiver for you, my girl," when I left. So you see what I meant when I said, all this business of Giles is no concern of mine, and I couldn't bear it if anyone thought it was and tried to offer me sympathy. If I stayed down there, I'd have to go about pretending to be sorry, because I wouldn't have the energy to explain to every fresh person I met, "He wasn't my brother at all."

I never liked him. For the last month, I've been hating him; and I can't suddenly stop doing so just because he's dead.'

Billy waited for a while. 'But you can,' he said gently.

'Can what?' Jessica spoke through the tears which she was trying to control.

'You can stop hating him, just because he's not your brother – just because you don't belong. You're free now. You can be detached therefore. Give up bothering about the Gabb family; they won't notice you or what you're doing, for the next fortnight or so. Stay away as much as you can. Come with me, and I'll show you the countryside. Forget about them. You can't help. If they cut up rusty, come and live with us. They can't stop you: they have no claim on you, and evidently they don't really need you.'

'Don't you think so?' said Jessica, drying her eyes. 'You see, the worst of it is, I feel they *have* a sort of claim on me, in spite of everything, because they've brought me up and spent money on me. Isn't that horrible? It shows how they've imposed their beastly commercial standards on me, after all.'

'Why did they adopt you in the first place?' said Billy curiously. 'Do you know?'

'Oh yes,' said Jessica, 'I know. It was as Giles said. Soon afterwards, I was told even more explicitly. You see, after the row I had with Simon, Polly – that's Mrs Gabb – rather avoided me. I knew she would. She hates trouble of any kind. But Aunt Janet – that's Uncle James's wife, Lucy's and Harry's mother – she took it upon herself to speak to me. She read me a sermon on ingratitude, which it appears is worst of all when it's found in orphans, and she informed me that Polly had wanted a daughter, " to look after her in her old age," once again. She would naturally have preferred a "real" daughter, but something happened to her when Basil was born, and it was impossible, so at last they adopted me. Janet told me I was a wicked ungrateful girl not to appreciate all that had been done for me. I told her to mind her own business. She said if she were " my father," she'd teach me a lesson, that is, disinherit me. She said how sad it was for them to see their costly experiment ending in failure. I said I agreed it was a bad bargain. And so on, and so on. Oh, it's been hateful! Not one of the family has been on speaking terms with me. I've longed to clear out, and haven't known how.'

She stepped from the stile, and smiled at Billy. 'Where shall we go?' she said. 'Let's go for a long walk. And then, perhaps, will you take me back to your house to tea? Do you think your aunt would mind?' She gazed round. 'Perhaps one day you'll take me on the lake, and over to the island. I used to envy you when I saw you all going off together. But it would never have occurred to Giles to ask me. Don't think I'm not sorry for him. I am, I am! I'm terribly sorry for anybody who's dead, on a day like this…'

They crossed the stile into the wood. Before he jumped down, Billy turned, to take a last look at the view.

'I say!' he called out to Jessica. 'Look at that!'

She came back, and they both looked down at the lake, towards the boat-house. A rowing-boat, heavily down astern, was slowly moving out of the channel. The oars, at every stroke, seemed to bring out a tangle of weeds, and for a time progress was arrested. Then slowly the boat got under way again, moving towards the island.

'It's the police,' said Billy, 'of that you can be sure. No one else would be allowed on the lake to-day. Oh well, they can't want us… One day, when all this is over, I'll teach you to spin for pike. You'll enjoy it. Oh yes, you will, no matter what you may think, if you're properly taught. You know, you've got hold of all the wrong ideas, where shooting and fishing are concerned…'

They disappeared, arguing, along the narrow winding path that led to the top of the hill, through the trees.

14

The boat moved slowly across the lake towards the island. Fitzbrown pulled vigorously, his raw-boned wrists sticking out a long way from his dark overcoat; but he could not overcome the resistance provided by Mallett's bulk. The boat was well down astern; but Mallett did not seem to notice this, or Fitzbrown's exertions. He sat as if enjoying a pleasure trip, gazing round him at the pretty scene.

First, Fitzbrown had had some difficulty in getting the boat out of the narrow channel into the lake. The channel was not wide enough to admit of a full sweep of the oars. Several times the policeman on duty at the boat-house had to come to the rescue and push the boat off from the side again. Then, when they left the channel and Fitzbrown attempted to pull away, the oars became entangled in the weeds of the lake bed, and the stern, weighed down by Mallett, grounded on the mud. Fitzbrown, using his oar as a punt-pole, again got them clear.

'You see,' said Mallett, 'the result of neglect. The previous owner wouldn't have allowed this channel to get silted up with mud and choked with weeds. Still, there are pretty hiding-places for pike among those reeds.'

'Yes, and for a rifle,' said Fitzbrown.

'Ah, yes,' said Mallett, 'we mustn't forget the rifle.' But he did not seem greatly interested, and he made no attempt to watch the water, though in places it was shallow enough to be transparent except when the mud was disturbed.

There was now no trace of mist. The lake rippled gently in the bright sunshine. They sky was blue, with large white clouds massed motionless on the horizon. In front of them lay the island, its alders and beeches and hazel scrub showing little sign of autumn colouring, though the trees on the parkland round the lake were already beginning to turn. In the distance, on its slight elevation, the long facade of Herons' Hall was visible, and the avenue of chestnuts leading beyond it to the North Lodge, which was out of sight. The island with its trees blocked the view of the South Lodge roof; but near the lake edge, Morgan the gardener's cottage commanded an excellent view of the scene. Fitzbrown jerked his head towards it.

'You'd better have a talk with that fellow,' he said. 'It seems he saw Gabb on the lake early this morning. He also may have heard shots, so he thinks, but he took no notice: he's much too used to shooting. Still, you might get some idea of the time Gabb was killed.'

'Do you question him at all?' said Mallett.

'No. He told the chauffeur, and the chauffeur told one of your men, who told me.'

'We'll go into it later,' promised Mallett. He was leaning forward now, as they approached the island, and his change of position made the boat move more quickly. Fitzbrown shipped his right-hand oar as they drew in under an overhanging alder; its horizontal trunk had obviously provided a useful place on which to fasten the mooring-rope. There was no landing-stage; but on the muddy shelving edge beside the alder, a few logs had been laid down to give foothold.

The island rose quite steeply out of the water. The place where they had landed seemed to be the only spot that resembled a shore, and even this in winter was probably submerged. The whole island was thickly wooded except for the space directly in front of them, where the trees and bushes had been cleared away to make room for the target. Mallett climbed up the slippery leaf-strewn path towards it, and examined it curiously.

'It was here in the time of the late Colonel,' he said to Fitzbrown, 'and I gather that Giles Gabb still used it for his experiments. He seems to have had no difficulty in finding the bull's-eye.' He turned to look across the water to the shore on the other side. 'About two hundred yards,' he nodded. 'But of course he could increase his range as much as he liked, by moving back all the time towards the house. He would want to do so by exact stages if he were experimenting with a military pattern. You couldn't have a better place. There's no danger to other people, as the ground rises up behind the target.' He turned back, and began examining the path and the ground near by.

'Several people have been here recently,' he said. 'I wonder why.'

'Well, surely,' said Fitzbrown, 'there's nothing odd in that. We know that they were out on the lake yesterday, and Giles was out this morning.'

'Yes,' said Mallett, still peering at the ground, 'but why should they come here? The party yesterday were fishing. They fished from their boats, not from the island: you couldn't cast from here, because of the trees. And as for Giles: why should he come over this morning? To inspect the target? But that would imply that he had been shooting and wanted to inspect his results. Yet he can't have been shooting from the shore this morning. He wouldn't have been able to see this target at two hundred yards.'

'I suppose not,' said Fitzbrown. 'Well, perhaps he came over to see if the target was all right after the storm.'

Mallett gave the iron frame-work on which the target hung a sharp shake. It did not stir.

Fitzbrown walked away from the clearing, up a narrow track leading towards the high centre of the island, through the trees and thick shrubs. The track was dim and hardly visible; whoever had used it lately had not bothered to keep it clear of entangling briars and brambles. Fitzbrown plunged onward and upward, helping himself along by means of the moss-covered boulders that lay on either side. He could no longer see the lake; and even when he reached the top, and sat down on a large flat rock to get his breath back, he found himself completely hemmed in by the thick growth of hazel, beech and alder, so that not a glint of water was visible. He shivered: the stone on which he was sitting struck chill, and even the sunshine could scarcely penetrate through the foliage above his head. At his feet was a thick drift of dead leaves piled up against the base of the rock...

A moment later, Mallett heard him calling, 'I say, Mallett! Come here a moment, will you?'

Mallett, detecting the excitement in his voice even at this distance, struggled up the steep path after him. He found Fitzbrown on his hands and knees, with a pile of dead leaves beside him.

'Look here!' he said, pointing to the space beneath the overhanging rock on which he had been sitting. 'It struck me that those leaves had been newly turned, not just blown there by the wind.'

Mallett looked. Then he too dropped on to his knees on the damp moss. Beneath the rock, now that Fitzbrown had removed the leaves, there was revealed a small chamber formed by two flat upright stones with a third laid against them. Mallett lifted the third stone away. Inside the cist was a box of brass-bound walnut, about two feet long and one foot broad. Mallett felt in his pockets and produced a bunch of miscellaneous keys.

'Probably there'll be something here that will fit,' he said. 'I know these old deed-boxes.'

The deed-box lay open before them. Mallett lifted the flaps upholstered in faded purple velvet that curled back at the corners through age and damp. The space beneath was empty except for a few paper-clips and rubber bands.

'Someone has been here before us,' said Mallett. 'However, it's not his secret that matters to us, but the fact that he had one, and chose to hide it here.'

'You think he kept the results of his experiments hidden away here?'

'Not a doubt of it. The desk in his study was unlocked. Anyone could have ransacked it. It therefore stood to reason that he didn't care; and if he didn't care, it was because he had, or thought he had, a safe place elsewhere.' Mallett, as he talked, had drawn out his pen-knife, and was carefully running it along all the joins in the interior of the deed-box. 'From all we hear of Giles Gabb, we gather that he was a very reserved, difficult, morose kind of fellow. Such men rarely have a good opinion of the rest of the world. They are suspicious, secretive. Giles had a secret, possibly a very important one, possibly important only in his own imagination. I can't gather yet from what I hear and observe whether he really was a genius on the verge of a discovery or whether his brain had gone agley after that breakdown of his. Anyway, for our present purpose it doesn't matter. He believed he had a secret which would result in the manufacture of an even more deadly rifle than the present military pattern. He was working at it all the time, calculating and experimenting...'

The pen-knife, running round the edge of a shallow pen-tray, struck against something metallic. Mallett, still talking, probed round the obstacle, this way and that, with the point of the blade.

'It was a kind of compulsion,' he continued, 'because actually he was a man who loathed killing. At least, he loathed the killing of animals for sport. I've seen the copy of the Colonel's memoirs that he found in his study, and if ever a reader managed to infuse hatred into his annotations of a book, that man was Giles.'

'Possibly that made him all the keener on inventing a weapon intended for men,' suggested Fitzbrown.

'Possibly. Anyhow, he carried on with the work – that is, until he was deflected by this new interest of his in the tenants of the South Lodge.'

'In Sir Charles Laforte's daughter,' said Fitzbrown.

'Yes. Now let me see: it's about two months since those people moved in. Giles's interest has been growing steadily, until at last it has swallowed up everything, even his work. Last week he gave up attempting to work, and spent the whole of his time with his friends.'

'Funny it should be the daughter of a man whose tastes he disliked so much,' said Fitzbrown. 'Though of course one has to remember that he himself spent quite a lot of his time shooting and fishing in this country.'

Mallett nodded. 'Giles's mind must have presented a pretty picture of conflicting forces, from a psychologist's point of view,' he said. 'And remember, a mind at odds with itself is very ready to conceive suspicions about others. Suppose that during the last week or so, Giles had reason to believe that his desk was being tampered with; and suppose he decided to transfer everything that mattered from there to here. Suppose whoever tampered with his desk had also discovered this hiding-place, and – hullo!'

The pen-knife, catching suddenly in an unseen notch, moved forward a quarter of an inch, and Mallett, gently levering, was able to lift the pen-tray on its hidden hinges. Tucked away in a corner of the space revealed there was a small note-book with a limp black cover, about three inches square.

'This is what the visitor didn't find,' said Mallett, lifting out the small book and flipping over the pages. A piece of transparent paper, closely folded, fell out; it was covered with figures and diagrams. The leaves of the book likewise were covered with a minute shorthand interspersed with figures and thumb-nail designs. Mallett put the note-book into an inner pocket, and pushed the deed-box back into its cist.

'We don't want to advertise the fact that we've found this hiding-place,' he said, as he replaced the stone and began banking the dead leaves against it. 'I don't think our thief is likely to risk coming back here again. Still, one never knows.'

They began the descent to the shore. Mallett, stumbling and sliding, reached the bottom safely, accompanied by a cascade of stones. But Fitzbrown, following less warily, slipped suddenly on the mossy track, and would have fallen if he had not flung out an arm and embraced one of the alders growing alongside. His hand encountered something hard on the other side of the tree-trunk. When he had recovered his balance, he went behind the tree to investigate. There, propped against it, with the butt end well hidden in the scrubby growth at the foot, and a wreath of ivy twisted round the barrel end, was a waterproof rifle-case. Fitzbrown pulled it out, laid it on the ground, and opened it. Inside was a small-bore rifle of a pattern which he did not recognize.

He gasped, as if he had been stung by a snake, and for the second time, in a voice pitched high with excitement, he recalled Superintendent Mallett from below.

15

Basil paced up and down the thickly-carpeted bedroom. Pauline, sitting in front of the mirror, gave all her attention to her face. Yet the hand with which she was so carefully applying cream trembled a little, and there were two bright angry spots on each cheek-bone.

'Don't expect me to protect you,' he was saying. 'In half an hour the whole world will know, including the police. In any case, you've left me no chance.' In spite of his fury, there was a note of dismal pleading in his tone that did not escape Pauline.

'Don't trouble yourself,' she said coolly, bending forward to gaze even more closely into the mirror. 'I shall deny nothing. I have nothing to deny.'

'Your lover won't thank you for that,' said Basil. 'Unless of course the whole thing is a put-up job between you, and he's counting on you to secure him an alibi.'

Pauline swung round. 'What exactly do you mean by that?' she said. Basil recoiled slightly, but he continued nevertheless, with a sneer:

'I see: you're his dupe, not his accomplice.' He sat down opposite to her. 'You don't understand the position, my dear Pauline. Giles did not commit suicide; he was murdered, this morning, in the small hours, or at any rate, before anyone else was up and about. You—well, you went off with this fellow. You won't tell me how or when, or what time it was when he left you.' The muscles at the corners of his jaws contracted as he tried to control himself; his voice was strained and harsh. 'But presumably he left you before daylight, before the servants were up or the gardeners about, or anyone else – myself, for instance – could come along. And Giles was shot this morning. So you see, even if you won't tell me, you'll have to tell the police, especially as your lover's skin may depend on it.'

Pauline waited for a moment or two. When she answered, her voice was cold and quiet. 'Basil,' she said, 'I suppose it's quite impossible for you to believe that he is not my lover, and that nothing occurred last night of which I need be ashamed. I shall tell the police exactly what happened, absolutely without regard to you—or him. By the way, what makes you think that he had anything to do with Giles's death – if Giles really was murdered, which I can't believe?'

Basil got up and came towards her. 'I'll tell you,' he said through his teeth, 'if you really don't know. I suppose it's vanity that makes women so blind, though I did think jealousy sharpened their wits, if nothing else could. That fellow is in love with his cousin, the girl Giles wanted to marry. Don't you believe it? Then I'll prove it to you. Last night, after you cleared out, I happened to open the door of my room. I heard voices. Giles was standing at the head of the stairs. Charleroy was on his way past him, downstairs. Giles was telling him to get out of the house, and Charleroy was pretending that that was his own idea too. They said enough for me to gather that Giles had caught Charleroy in his fiancée's room—'

'Who said she was his fiancée?' said Pauline sharply.

'I meant, Giles's fiancée,' retorted Basil. 'Did you think I meant Charleroy's? However, whether or not Giles had actually asked her to marry him is immaterial. It was perfectly clear to us all that he would. I know Giles. He is—' A spasm of recollection contracted Basil's forehead. 'He was no philanderer. It's not the custom, in our family. He meant to marry that girl, and you can depend on it, she wouldn't have said no. Isn't that what they came back here for – to worm their way back into Herons' Hall, one way or another? Depend upon it, that was the aunt's idea, if no one else's. And who should know of it better than Charleroy? She's his mother, isn't she? So he shot Giles – after he had used you as an alibi.'

Pauline looked shaken, yet defiant. 'I don't believe a word of it,' she said. 'You're making it up, to get me to tell you what actually happened last night. It's your beastly mean horrible curiosity, the thing that makes you watch me, whoever I speak to, whatever I do; the thing that makes you go sneaking round listening to other people's affairs, opening doors at the critical moment, overhearing things. Well, I'm sick of it. You can divorce me if you like, though you haven't any cause. Or you can give me a divorce. You will if you have any decency. I never was in love with you. I was a fool to marry you. And now I'm through with the whole business.'

'You think that fellow will marry you, perhaps?'

Pauline did not answer. She turned back to the mirror and continued her careful face-massage, as though Basil were no longer in the room.

'Don't worry,' said Basil. 'I shall never divorce you, nor give you a divorce. So you won't have the humiliation of being turned down by a murderer.'

Pauline turned round again. The expression on her face was vixenish, and it seemed likely that she would so far forget herself as to throw at her husband the large pot of cream she was holding. Basil, satisfied now and content to make a neat exit, was already half-way across the room. But Pauline's gesture was arrested by a tap on the door. Basil continued towards it, and pulled it open.

A maid, frightened yet agog, gazed from him to her, and back to him again.

'Please, sir, there's a policeman downstairs. He says will Madam kindly come along to the Hall as soon as possible? The Superintendent wishes to have a word with her.'

'Where is he?' said Basil. 'I'll speak to him.'

Pauline, ignoring him, called out: 'Tell the officer to say that I will see the Superintendent immediately.'

When Pauline arrived at the Hall, a policeman conducted her to what had been Giles's study. The guests of the night before seemed all to have departed. She caught sight of Hubert Olivier in earnest conversation with someone in the hall; but he had his back turned, and did not appear to see her. She marched past the various strangers, policemen and others, with head held high. As they reached the door, however, the policeman who was conducting her indicated her presence to another who stood on guard, and the latter shook his head.

Her escort gave her a chair. It seemed strange to be sitting there in the dark corridor of the house she knew so well, outside a door, as though she were a housekeeper waiting to be interviewed. She tapped her foot impatiently: she was not used to being kept waiting.

She had not long to wait. Suddenly the door opened, and Royce appeared. She stared at him, amazed. He looked utterly broken down, as if he had been crying. There was little left of the debonair young man who had smitten her fancy so violently when he had accosted her in the woods each morning: who had driven her last night, out along the dark road at sixty miles an hour in somebody else's car, and assured her that there was nothing to be afraid of... She hoped for a smile of recognition, at least; but his glazed look passed over her where she sat, as if he had never set eyes on her before, as if she were indeed the waiting applicant she had fancied herself. Before she had time to assimilate the shock of this surprise, she heard her name called.

'This way, please, madam.'

She recalled, with a brave effort, her fleeing dignity, and followed the officer to the door.

16

Pauline entered.

She had never been in Giles's study before, she now realized; and its aspect, caught hurriedly and confusedly as she moved towards the desk where Mallett sat, was somewhat overpowering. She seemed suddenly to have stepped out of the familiar house into a natural history museum, the sort of place which she would never voluntarily have entered either in search of instruction or amusement. The eyes of the animals that gazed down from the walls seemed fixed on her with a pity and understanding that she certainly would not have welcomed even from a fellow-creature; but she had no time to feel more than a certain resentful bewilderment, before she confronted the Superintendent.

He was writing, and did not look up for a moment. Beside his desk another man was standing. It was with an unpleasant shock that she recognized the proprietor of the Swan Bridge Inn.

Mallett glanced up from his writing at the innkeeper. The innkeeper nodded back. Mallett said, 'Right. You can go.'

Pauline, red with annoyance, waited while the man, with a last insolent stare, left the room, and Mallett waved her to a chair. Even then he kept her waiting, while he finished entering something into a note-book; and when he finally was ready to give her his attention, he began curtly and without preamble:

'You are Mrs Gabb?'

Pauline assented. She had now been married for over a year; but she doubted if fifty years would ever reconcile her to this ridiculous name. Basil's second name was Quentin. She had tried to persuade him to hyphenate this with his surname, and make her Mrs Quentin-Gabb; but Basil, so docile and devoted in the early months of their marriage, had nevertheless laughed and refused.

'Mrs Basil Gabb,' Mallett was saying.

Again, Pauline assented. Mallett laid down his pencil, and leaned back, studying her with an expression she did not relish, as if he were in a position to get what he wanted out of her, and had no intention of letting her off anything.

'Now, Mrs Gabb,' he began. 'Are you going to help the police? A murder has been committed, a cold-blooded treacherous murder of someone you know. We are out to find the murderer, no matter who he may turn out to be. Can we count on your assistance?'

Pauline said, 'Of course.' A faint curiosity arose in her. She wondered if they already suspected someone, and if so, who it could be. Until now, she had been too much preoccupied with her own affairs to grasp the real meaning of the news Basil had brought her that morning: it was not merely that Giles had been shot on Herons' Mere, but that someone had shot him, and that the murderer was still at large — might, for all she knew, be still in this very house, still accepted, still undetected, by all. But the police were busy weaving their web around him, wherever he might be... She added, and Mallett noticed the new interest in her look and tone:

'What do you want me to do?'

'I want you to answer my questions, without regard to your own feelings, or those of anyone else.' Mallett's voice, though authoritative, was not unkindly. Pauline said impulsively:

'Of course I will. I should like to. This is confidential, isn't it?'

'Yes. I may ask you for a more formal statement later, but if that becomes necessary, I shall let you know. Meanwhile, I'm merely asking for your assistance.' He paused: this was certainly the right line to take with the young woman; she was all eagerness, for the moment. But how long would the helpful mood last beneath a barrage of personal questions? He began:

'You were one of the party who dined here last night.'

'Yes.'

'And I take it that like the others you were asked to spend the night here – you and your husband – because of the storm.'

'Yes. I wanted to leave. We live quite near, at the North Lodge, as I suppose you know. But my mother-in-law thought it wasn't safe. Someone said there was a tree down in the drive. Actually, she loves to have people round her. So when I saw how keen she was, I agreed. It was raining very hard, and I knew the baby would be all right with his nurse. So it didn't matter really. So to please her—'

'And your husband? Did he think it was a good idea, too?'

'My husband.' Pauline's face lost its schoolgirl eagerness for a moment and grew obstinate, almost sullen-looking, as she remembered the long evening of alternate bickering and silence that she had had to endure before her exit. 'Well, no. He didn't want to stay. He doesn't like spending nights away from home.'

'I see,' said Mallett. It was obvious enough: Pauline's decision to stay, interpreted by the jealous husband as a wish to enjoy the company of the attractive young Charleroy; accusations on his part, obstinate determination on hers, leading to the climax… 'And yet, I believe, as it turned out, he was the one who actually stayed, but you left. How did that come about, Mrs Gabb?'

Pauline thought for a minute before answering. Mallett's green eyes were fixed immovably on her; his look had the compelling pressure of one who is relying upon you to do your part. She didn't want to betray anybody, and yet – she was no good at finesse. Lying is difficult: like playing cards, it requires a good memory as well as resourcefulness. Pauline, simple, impulsive and rather slow-witted, was never at her ease unless she could tell the truth. She answered:

'Well, Superintendent, you may as well know it: my husband and

I had a quarrel. We had been working up for it all evening. He said some things I didn't like, and I resented his insinuations; and so it went on all evening, until when we got to our room we were both determined to have it out.' She stopped, realizing that she could not for much longer keep Royce's name out of her story, yet unwilling to take the plunge. Mallett prompted her gently:

'Your husband is of a rather jealous temperament?'

'Yes. Oh, yes!' Pauline agreed gratefully. 'He can't help it, you know. It's his nature. But it's terribly trying for me. He really ruins everything because of it. And yet, till now, he's never had any cause.'

Mallett noticed the naïve 'till now,' of which Pauline seemed still quite unaware. He interrupted: 'Just one question, Mrs Gabb, before you proceed—and let me say I appreciate your frankness very much indeed. But tell me: had your husband ever any cause – or did he ever imagine he had cause – to be jealous of you and his brother Giles?'

Pauline looked up, in genuine astonishment. 'Of me and Giles?' she echoed. 'Oh no! Never! I assure you, Giles never looked at girls at all, not even at his cousin Lucy, whom he was supposed to be going to marry – until these new people came. As for Giles and me, I don't believe he ever gave me a thought; and certainly I never gave him one. It seems wicked to say so now in view of what's happened; but I rather disliked him. I was afraid of him, he was so abrupt and queer. We had nothing whatever in common, I assure you. Even Basil, I'm sure, never wasted a moment's suspicion on me and Giles.'

Her protestations were undoubtedly genuine. Mallett made in his note-book a hieroglyph which meant 'Question settled,' opposite the bracketed names of Giles and Pauline.

'Right,' he said. 'Well, you were saying: you and your husband had a quarrel after you reached your room. I gather he thought he had reason to connect your acceptance of your mother-in-law's invitation with one of the other guests?'

'Yes,' said Pauline bravely, tossing back her head. 'With Mr Charleroy. My husband accused me of having spent the evening flirting with him, which was absurd, as I pointed out, because he himself had taken good care we should hardly exchange a word. Then he said that flirtations could be carried on silently. At that, I realized that he was beyond reason, and I told him that if he said another word, I'd leave the house, storm or no storm. But he was too far gone to care. He taxed me with having met Mr Charleroy before, and told me not to lie to him, as I had been seen. When I said I had no intention of lying – that I had seen and spoken to Mr Charleroy twice or three times before in the grounds – he rounded on me for what he called my brazenness, as if I had admitted all he was accusing me of.'

Her breath came fast as she remembered this painful scene.

'You had met Mr Charleroy twice or three times before in the grounds?' prompted Mallett. 'That was all you knew of him before last evening?'

'Yes,' said Pauline vehemently, 'absolutely all. And what's more, I had no idea who he was. We had merely said 'Good morning" to each other. I tried to get Basil to understand this, but he was so absorbed in his theory that he hardly listened. When I saw that it was hopeless, I realized that there was only one way to bring him to his senses and prevent further trouble. You see, he was threatening to shoot Mr Charleroy, among other things. So I just said 'You've won,' and walked out of the room.'

'Did you see anyone – Mr Charleroy, for instance – before you left?'

'No. No one at all. At least, yes, I did: as I was leaving, I saw Harry and Lucy – my husband's cousins, you know – in the hall. I heard them say they'd had to leave their car in the drive, as there was a tree across it. However, I didn't let that stop me. I ran out into the rain, down the drive towards the North Lodge, where we live. My one idea was to get home before my husband and bolt the door. I thought it would do him good to follow me and find he couldn't get in, and have to go back to his mother's again.' Pauline laughed unkindly.

'And did he follow you?' said Mallett.

'I don't know. I ran down the drive, through the pouring rain. I was wearing a long frock and thin shoes, and I had nothing but a little fur cape round my shoulders. I realized as soon as I got outside that everything I wore would be ruined, and I should be soaked to the skin. However, I pulled the cape up over my hair and ran as best I could, with my head down. Suddenly I found my way absolutely barred by the huge elm-tree that had fallen. I didn't know what to do. The trunk was right across the drive, and the branches made it terribly difficult to get near, even if I could have scrambled over in my long frock without help. And I was afraid that if I left the drive and tried to find my way round it, I should be wading ankle-deep in mud and water. I was standing there wondering what to do – determined not to go back, and yet unable to see how on earth I could get past – when I heard footsteps… Of course, Superintendent, you'll probably not believe what I'm going to tell you. You'll think, either that it was all arranged between us, or else, even if I didn't know, Mr Charleroy must have followed me. I thought so myself at first, but I found out later, he hadn't.' She gave Mallett one of her defiant looks. 'It was just a coincidence, though that can never be proved.'

'Well, at least I accept your own *bona fides*, Mrs Gabb,' said Mallett gallantly. 'As for Charleroy, he can speak for himself. I don't doubt you were very glad to accept help from any quarter.'

'I thought, when I heard the footsteps, it was my husband,' said Pauline, 'and really I was so uncomfortable by then, I would have been glad to see even him. Mr Charleroy seemed surprised to see me there; but when I said I wanted to get past the tree and home, he didn't argue. He merely told me to follow him and do as he said. He had a torch; and somehow, by breaking the branches off and leading me on step by step, he managed to get me over. In the process, though, I lost the heel of one of my slippers; and there was still another quarter of a mile to walk to the Lodge. On the other side of the tree, there was Harry's car.'

'Providential,' murmured Mallett.

'That was just what Mr Charleroy said. He told me to get in, and he'd drive me the rest of the way. I was rather doubtful, but it seemed the easiest way. He turned the car, and in a minute or two we were outside the Lodge. – You may think me foolish, but I couldn't let him go off like that, after he'd helped me. We sat there talking for a few minutes; then we realized that we were both rather wet. So I asked him to come in for a minute and have a drink and get warm.'

'What about your husband?' said Mallett.

'By that time, I didn't care. I mean, if he had made a scene in his mother's house, among all those strangers, it would have been dreadful; but in our own house he could do as he liked for all I cared.'

'And Charleroy accepted your invitation?'

'Yes, rather reluctantly. There seemed to be something on his mind. He said he didn't want to go indoors again so soon: he had been setting out for a long walk. But he realized that whereas he was wearing an oilskin and was comparatively dry, I was completely bedraggled; so he agreed. We went in. The servants – that is, the maid and the nurse – had gone to bed. He mixed himself a whisky and soda, and I made up the fire. Then suddenly he suggested that we should borrow Harry's car and go for a drive.'

'H'm,' said Mallett. 'The suggestion came from him?'

'Naturally,' said Pauline, with heightened colour.

'Quite so, quite so,' Mallett soothed her. 'So you changed your clothes and went?'

'Yes, I did. I saw no reason why I shouldn't do something unexpected, for a change. My husband was always making mountains out of molehills; so I thought, if he did come back, he'd have something to think about for once… We went out and got into the car. Mr Charleroy drove at a furious speed. I was rather frightened: the roads were so wet and slippery, and I knew he was driving a strange car. He hardly spoke a word, and I had no idea where we were going. I was afraid to talk, in case I distracted his attention. However, we arrived at the Swan Bridge Inn, just before midnight. We stayed half an hour or so. Then I said I ought to be going back. I was a little sorry I had come, by now, especially as Mr Charleroy seemed to be worried about something.'

'What made you think that?' said Mallett.

'Well, he would be very bright for a few minutes, then he would suddenly stop talking and withdraw into himself, as if he were brooding on something that annoyed him. Then he got very irritable because the landlord wouldn't give him anything but soft drinks – that man I saw going out just now. In the end, the landlord beckoned to him, and they went off together, and presently Mr Charleroy came back smelling rather strongly of whisky. However, he was much more cheerful again, and when I suggested we'd better go home, he seemed quite willing. I was a little nervous about letting him drive me home in his condition—'

'Was he drunk?'

'No, not drunk: just excited and elated, not quite steady enough to be trusted with a powerful car...'

'And did you gather at all what had been worrying him?'

'Well, yes, Superintendent, I did. – Ought I to tell you this, really? It doesn't seem fair.'

'Murder isn't a pretty thing, either.'

Pauline gazed at him, shocked. 'Oh, but you don't mean to say you think Mr Charleroy did it? Why, he's only a boy!'

'I think nothing, Mrs Gabb. I merely collect evidence, at this stage. If Mr Charleroy were a murderer, you wouldn't want to protect him, I'm sure. If he is innocent, then the more we know of his movements, the better for him, – especially as he himself doesn't seem to want to talk.' He leaned forward. 'Frankly, I think he was holding back because he wanted to protect *you*. But you can talk where he can't, and so you can release him from his obligations, as he considers them. Do you see?'

Pauline looked down at her hands. 'Yes, I see.' She looked up hopefully, a new idea dawning. 'I suppose you wouldn't let me have a word with him first?'

Mallett smiled, sadly and kindly, and shook his head. 'I'm afraid I can't do that. – Come now, don't be too distressed. That was what I meant when I asked you to put away your personal feelings. Tell me just what happened, and leave me to sort out what's important to this case, and what's not. I gather he didn't drive you straight home after all? Well, never mind that. Let's suppose you had trouble with the car: you had to change a wheel, or do some other repair that took time. All I want to know for the present is: how long did it take? Or in other words, what time did you get home, and what time did Charleroy leave you? Did he bring you back to your house, to begin with?'

'Yes, he did. He drove me to the door. Then he drove on, up the drive. He said he'd leave the car exactly where we found it, and perhaps no one would know, though of course the petrol had gone down considerably.'

'And the time?'

'It was early-before daybreak. Not later than five, I think.'

'Not later than five,' repeated Mallett thoughtfully. 'And your husband? Was he there?'

'No. To my surprise, he was not. Whether he came in and went away again, I don't know, and he won't tell me. But I think he may have done, from the way he behaved when he came back this morning; or perhaps he may have seen us drive away. Anyhow, he accused me outright of having been unfaithful to him; and I denied it, but I could see he didn't believe me.' She sighed. 'If they meet, there'll be another murder, I'm afraid.'

But Mallett was no longer listening. 'One last question,' he said abruptly, 'before you go. You say you gathered what was the reason for Charleroy's depression, or whatever it was you noticed in his manner when first you met him.'

'Yes. Yes, I did. But, Superintendent, you can't hold that against him. He told me of his own accord.'

'Told you what?'

'Oh, just that he had had a few words with Giles before he left the Hall. He said that Giles had acted like a madman, ordering him out of the house.'

'And the quarrel had to do with Miss Laforte?'

Pauline's look was stony, as she said, 'I don't know. I didn't inquire.'

'All right,' said Mallett, 'you can go.'

17

On the day before the inquest on Giles Gabb, Mallett was shown through the French windows into Mrs Charleroy's garden. Mrs Charleroy was already out of doors, cutting long-stemmed roses. She drew off her leather gloves as Mallett appeared, and closed the secateurs.

'Good morning, ma'am,' said Mallett politely, with a forward movement of the head and shoulders which he imagined to be a bow. 'I hope you'll excuse this early call.'

'Oh, good morning, Superintendent!' Mrs Charleroy sounded as if he were the most welcome of visitors. 'Won't you come inside? Or would you rather sit out here and smoke your pipe?'

Mallett pulled out the pipe which, still smouldering, he had just pushed away into his coat pocket. Together they sat down on a rustic seat at the side of the path, and Mrs Charleroy placed the basket of roses on the flag-stones beside her. When he turned to look at her, she met his look unflinchingly; but he fancied that, a moment before, her eyes had been darting here and there, making sure that no one was visible.

'I was passing by,' said Mallett casually, 'and I thought I'd look in. As a matter of fact, I'm on my way to Morgan's cottage.'

'Oh, indeed?' said Mrs Charleroy carefully.

'Yes. Not that I expect to find him there. Funny how elusive that fellow is. I expect he's up at the Hall by now. Still, I can leave a message with his wife, I suppose.'

'Yes, I suppose so.' Mrs Charleroy sounded vague.

'Time's getting a bit short,' continued Mallett, as though he had all day to spare. 'I must get him up to the Station to-day, if I don't find him at home.' He turned to her confidentially. 'Between you and me, he seems to have been the last person to see Giles Gabb alive – except the murderer, of course.'

'Really?'

'Yes. If his statement is correct, he saw Giles Gabb on the lake at about six that morning. Not that he's told the police. Oh, no! People, I notice, prefer to talk to almost anyone else except the man who's trying to solve the problem. Have you noticed that, Mrs Charleroy?'

Mrs Charleroy laughed somewhat artificially. 'I'm afraid I haven't had much experience of murders, Superintendent.'

'No. No. You wouldn't have.' Mallett pressed fresh tobacco carefully into his pipe, tucked away the strands neatly, and lit it again. Mrs Charleroy watched him uneasily. When next he spoke, she started.

'Is your son about just now?'

'I don't know. He may be. Did you want to see him?' She half-rose, and her leather gauntlets fell to the ground. Mallett picked them up and gave them back to her.

'No. Don't trouble, Mrs Charleroy. It doesn't matter. Perhaps if you'll spare me the time, instead?'

She sat down again, reluctant yet alert. Mallett's manner became more serious.

'Have you had any talk with your son about the events of Saturday evening and Sunday morning, Mrs Charleroy?'

'No,' said Helen, running her mind hurriedly over the past. 'Not since the actual morning of the murder, that is, when we were all told the news. Royce was there then, and so were the others.'

'You know he didn't spend the night at the Hall? Do you happen to know what time he came in that morning?'

Helen's heart missed a beat, but she answered calmly: 'He says he came in some time in the small hours. I'm afraid I didn't hear him.'

'And no one saw him until he appeared at breakfast, is that so? What time would that be?'

'About half-past seven, I believe.'

'You know he left the Hall at about eleven the night before?'

'Yes. Yes, he told me that.'

'And you know why?'

'I gather,' admitted Helen reluctantly, 'there had been some slight difference of opinion between him and—' She hesitated.

'Giles Gabb,' inserted Mallett firmly.

'Yes – and Royce thought it better to leave.'

Mallett nodded grimly. 'And do you know where he went then?'

'No. I'm afraid I don't, except that he went for a walk, to recover his temper.'

'Is that what he told you?' said Mallett. 'Well, no, Mrs Charleroy, he didn't go for a walk. He went for a ride. He went for a ride in somebody else's car. And what's more, he took a lady with him.'

'A lady!' Mrs Charleroy's astonishment was clearly genuine. 'Do you mean my niece, Miss Laforte?'

'No, ma'am. I mean Mrs Basil Gabb. Their movements have been traced to the Swan Bridge Inn at Stickleback; the innkeeper has identified them. Now— He pointed the stem of his pipe at her, and curiously, as she recoiled a little, Mrs Charleroy noticed the blue smoke curling out from the stem. 'All that is neither here nor there, so far as we're concerned. But what *is* to the point is, your son left this lady at about five o'clock that morning – and between then and seven-thirty, no one seems to know where he was.'

'But, Superintendent,' protested Mrs Charleroy, 'does it matter? Why should he have to account for his movements? You're surely not suggesting that he had anything to do with this murder, just because of a stupid quarrel he had with Giles? I assure you, Royce is utterly incapable of that sort of violence. He'd walk out of the house – but he'd never lie in wait for anyone hours later and shoot him treacherously like that! I know him. For one thing, his anger – if he was angry – wouldn't hold out for so long.'

Mallett shrugged his shoulders. 'I daresay you're right, ma'am,' he said. 'But in that case, will you see if you can get him to talk? I tackled him on the day of the murder – and he would tell me nothing. I shouldn't know as much as I do if Mrs Basil Gabb hadn't very properly given me her version of the matter, as well as confirming our previous findings.' He got up. 'What I want to know is, what did your son do between five a.m. and, say, six-thirty? We think that Giles Gabb was shot between five and sometime between six and half-past. I'm convinced your son is keeping something back, besides his drive with Mrs Gabb. It's understandable he wouldn't want to give away a lady; but when I questioned him, he couldn't give me a straight answer as to when he got back home. He contradicted himself. First, he didn't know. Then he thought it was in the small hours, before daylight. Then he jumped to the other extreme and said it was sometime between six-thirty and seven. Finally he shut up altogether and wouldn't answer any questions at all.' Mallett shook his head and sighed. 'Young people are so foolish! By the way, have you noticed anything odd about him – his manner, I mean – since that day?'

Mrs Charleroy thought. Her mind was busy with the picture of Royce tearing away in a car with a strange young married woman beside him; and yet Mallett's questions demanded that she should keep her wits about her. 'He *has* been a little upset,' she said reluctantly. 'This business has naturally upset us all.'

'H'm,' said Mallett. 'Well, have a word with him, will you? The inquest is to-morrow – but the matter won't end there. I'm sorry to bother you; but I knew your brother the late Colonel, and I'd like to help you if I can. By the way, I've been re-reading your brother's memoirs. Interesting life he must have had. I gather you were out in the Sudan with him yourself at one time. I noticed one of your water-colours in the book. Very pretty, I'm sure.'

Mrs Charleroy inclined her head. She too was standing now, with her basket of roses in her hand. She was almost as tall as the Superintendent, and now she looked him full in the eyes.

'Your son was with you too, at one time, wasn't he?'

'Yes, Superintendent, he was.'

'How old would he be then? Sixteen or seventeen? I gather he could handle a rifle almost as well as his uncle – like the rest of you.'

Mrs Charleroy answered firmly. 'My son is an excellent shot. So are my brother's two children. And so am I. But all the same, Superintendent, none of us shot Giles Gabb: neither my son, nor I, nor my niece or nephew. It's not done in our family to shoot human beings in cold blood. I hope you'll accept that. I hope you'll give up the false trail you're following now, and find the real murderer.'

Mallett made his substitute for a bow once again. 'That's what I'm trying to do, ma'am, to the best of my ability. And that's why I ask you: have a word with your son, and get him to give a straightforward account of what he did after he left Mrs Basil Gabb that morning. If he's the sort of fellow you say, he won't be afraid for his own skin. And if he knows something, and won't say, let him remember he's hindering our investigations, perhaps enabling the murderer to get away. I leave it to you, ma'am. Good day.'

He turned abruptly and went away.

Helen Charleroy watched his broad back disappear through the French windows. Now that he was gone, she could hear her heart beating fast, high up in her throat; and her knees trembled. She put down the basket of roses again, and sat on the rustic seat, to regain her strength. She closed her eyes...

A voice beside her ear roused her. She opened her eyes, to find Winifred standing in front of her, holding out a letter on a tray.

'It's for Mr Royce, madam,' said Winifred. 'But I can't find him anywhere. The gardener brought it. He was told to wait for an answer.'

Mrs Charleroy looked at the thick white envelope and the bold hand-writing. Gingerly she stretched out a hand and took it off the tray.

'I'll give it to him,' she said. 'Who brought it? Morgan, did you say?'

'No, madam,' said Winifred with a toss of the head. 'It's the gardener who works for Mrs Basil Gabb, over at the North Lodge.'

Mrs Charleroy spoke with asperity. 'Tell him he needn't wait for an answer. Mr Royce is not here.'

18

Sunshine flooded through the French windows into Mrs Charleroy's morning-room. The faint scent of the bowl of Ophelia roses on her escritoire mingled with the perfume of pot-pourri and lavender from other years. Hubert Olivier, ushered in by the maid, sniffed the air and felt apprehensive. The personality of Helen Charleroy saturated the room, insinuating itself into the mind of the unwilling visitor. He sat down on one of the chintz-covered chairs, and stared without appreciation out at the pretty garden, that might have been a picture embroidered in silks, or painted on a calendar, so exactly did it fulfil the ideal of 'lovesome thing, God wot.' But to Hubert, at the present moment, it was not lovesome.

Mrs Charleroy entered. 'My dear Hubert! So kind of you to come!' She gave him her long thin hand. 'I know you must be terribly busy, but I thought perhaps you might be visiting the Hall, and so I ventured to ask you, for the sake of old times.'

'Old times'! Hubert groaned inwardly. He fancied, from Mrs Charleroy's smile, that she was aware of the acute embarrassment she was causing him, and that it gave her some enjoyment. 'Scheming women: how I hate them!' he thought, wishing that he could have made use of his own shrewd sharp young wife to protect him from this exasperating encounter. But Madeleine would soon have got to the bottom of the whole business, and everything would have been raked up again. In keeping Mrs Charleroy's note to himself and accepting her invitation, he had probably chosen the lesser of two discomforts.

'You know I'm always at your service,' he said, giving her hand a slight pressure in both his own.

They sat down.

'Well now, first of all,' she said, 'tell me about the inquest. You know, Hubert, this dreadful business has upset me terribly, because of the children. Poor Arden! She thought at first it was suicide, you know. Now tell me: does this verdict mean that the police have some definite theory they want to follow up; or are they completely at a loss, and do they just want further time?'

'It wasn't a verdict,' explained Hubert patiently. 'The inquest was adjourned *sine die*. They could of course have returned a verdict of "Murder by some person or persons unknown," but apparently it was thought better to adjourn. It probably means that the police have neither the time nor the inclination to set out whatever facts they now possess; and that again probably means that they are pursuing some line which they hope will soon give them a much more definite case to put forward.'

'In short, they have a definite suspicion against someone?'

'I wouldn't go so far as to say that. Let us say they are exploring the possibilities – which may be several – and leave it at that. Mallett is in charge of the case, you know. He's a good man – a dangerous customer, because he's unorthodox in his approach; and yet he looks so much like a policeman that people are apt to underrate him.'

'Yes,' said Mrs Charleroy, 'I agree with you – about his ability, I mean.'

'You know him, then?' said Hubert.

'I didn't until yesterday. That's one of the reasons why I asked you to come and see me.'

Hubert looked up, surprised. There was a harsh, even anxious note in her voice that he never remembered hearing before, even when she was most intent on her purposes. 'Good God! You don't mean to say he's been here?'

'I certainly do.'

'Just investigating? Or did he give you any reason to imagine——?'

Mrs Charleroy folded her hands in her lap, and gazed out into the garden.

'I suppose, Hubert,' she said, 'you'd call me a scheming woman.'

The words so exactly corresponded with his thought that he was unable to think of an answer. He could only smile deprecatingly. But she was not interested in his reaction; she was pursuing her own train of thought.

'One gets that name,' she continued, 'when one has an object in life, and is willing to do a good many things to achieve it. Of course, very few people have the right to say that of me, because very few people know anything about me.' She smiled. 'But you at least have had some material to go upon. What would you say?'

He laughed, embarrassed. 'Well, really, Helen——'

'Well, really, Hubert!' she mimicked him. 'Why should you be so scrupulous – in your choice of words, I mean? I'm not scrupulous, either in word or deed; and as you see, I'm rather proud of it. That's what's so shocking, isn't it? If only I had the grace to be a little ashamed!'

Hubert brushed aside her tiresome badinage. 'If you'll tell me what's the matter –' he began a little irritably.

'Oh, but there's no hurry, is there?' she said. 'I did hope you'd stay and have lunch with me. The children may be here, or I may be quite alone. I never know what to expect, just now. But it would give us plenty of time to talk. And I like to talk sometimes: I like to remember old times.'

Again the words jangled in Hubert's ears. He wanted to jump up, to shout at her, 'I understand what you're getting at, you old harridan: you're trying to blackmail, in your own tortuous way. Well, you can't. Your hold over me is broken. You can't do anything, now.' Instead, he sat there smiling back at her, even nodding as if at pleasant recollections of by-gone days...

Four years ago, Hubert Olivier had been a guest at Herons' Hall. He had been brought along by somebody else, to take the place of a defaulter; and he had done his best to make the most of the occasion. The Colonel was, as usual, away on one of his hunting expeditions; and Mrs Charleroy was installed as regent. He could see her still, queening it at the head of the dinner-table, with her ropes of pearls, her long flashing ear-rings, and her diamond rings on almost every finger. He had made himself very pleasant. He had been asked again...

Her voice broke in on his recollection. 'You saw Arden the other evening, I suppose,' she was saying. 'Did you think she had changed?'

Ah, now she was coming to it! And yet, it had all happened so naturally! It was natural for a man like him to pay court to ladies, to make them happy and therefore at their best, by an air of deference, a way of leaning over the backs of their chairs, a well-phrased piece of flattery in season. Yet as a rule he watched himself pretty closely: he kept the courtship on the distant, romantic plane. True, he had actually set before himself the advantages of marrying Mrs Charleroy. There she was, a widow, good-looking, rich, the sister of one of the best-known and most influential men in the country. How old would she be? Getting on for fifty; and he was thirty-seven; a barrister, but too poor to leave his home town; glad to pick up the trivial bits of work passed on to him by his much more prosperous brother the solicitor. A marriage with Mrs Charleroy would help him; and he did not think he would be refused. She had a son at Oxford; but what of that? Royce would soon be off on his own devices. So Hubert had leaned over her chair-back and amused her with his jokes, that set her long ear-rings dancing, and flattered her with his tender yet non-committal attentions. For he never had committed himself: oh, no! Something had always held him back, kept him from saying those last few words for which she was obviously waiting – something other than the existence of Madeleine Parkes, which in the flush of this new acquaintanceship he had almost forgotten. And then, just when his resolution was on the point of crystallizing, Arden appeared...

'Arden?' he said, raising his brows. 'Well, really, I wasn't given much chance to form an opinion. But so far as I could see, yes, she had changed, a good deal.' He gave a hurt laugh. 'And evidently she thought the same about me, for she didn't seem to recognize me.'

Mrs Charleroy almost purred: 'Oh; you mustn't be hard on the poor child. She always was shy among strangers; and she was rather upset at the time. Giles had proposed to her, you know, that very afternoon.'

'How extraordinary!' said Hubert. 'I didn't know.'

It was extraordinary indeed, when one considered that if Giles had lived, she would be returning to the house that had always been her home. He remembered Arden at seventeen, tall and fair and with the indescribable bloom of youth which to him had seemed a kind of shimmering aura, a golden haze through which the real young woman, or girl, was only dimly discernible. He had not thought that he at his age was any longer capable of that kind of love, at once humbling and uplifting, ridiculous and completely grave. It did not fit in at all with his life, or his idea of himself. He felt like a man who has been suddenly snatched off the ground by a captive balloon broken loose from its moorings: he knew he would come to earth again, but when, and whether with limbs fractured or whole, he did not know. Meanwhile, the sensation of being carried off one's feet was delicious. He became a youth again. He played tennis, he rode, he fished and swam and walked and danced. He lost a stone in weight, and recovered the lines of his youthful figure. Arden, back from her school in Switzerland, took him for granted, as part of the new life at home. Mrs Charleroy – Aunt Helen now – watched sardonically, and waited for a chance to put him back in his place. But again, he did not commit himself: this time, not through reluctance but through diffidence and fear.

How far did Arden's glamour depend for him on the fact that she was an heiress, as he thought? He never stopped to ask himself the question; there was, for once, no clash between feelings and interest, so why stop to analyse? The real question was, would Arden consider him? At that time he had succeeded in banishing completely from his mind the uncomfortable problem of what was to be done about Madeleine Parkes…

'You must have been pleased,' he said to Mrs Charleroy, somewhat maliciously. 'Everything was turning out according to plan.'

Yes, of course, a marriage between Giles and Arden: that had been her idea! She was, as she had said, a woman of strong purposes. She had never been reconciled to the loss of her position, as virtual mistress of Herons' Hall. When her brother's death in the Sudan had been reported, and it became clear that he had left neither her nor his children any means of support, Hubert remembered her cold fury; she revealed it to him, as she calmly burdened him with one responsibility after another, with the whole straightening out of their affairs. She had, for instance, entrusted him – or his brother, she didn't care which, so long as she got good service at a low cost – with the sale of Herons' Hall. There was no money for its upkeep; and so it must be sold, if possible just as it stood, furniture and all. And there was one proviso: the new owner must be persuaded to allow her to live somewhere on the estate – to lease her a piece of ground for building, or to let to her one of the lodges. If Hubert did all this, she gave him to understand, she would further his cause with Arden. Nothing was said about anything so crude as a bargain; nevertheless, she made her meaning perfectly clear.

But then, a strange thing had happened to Hubert: his older, wiser self began to take control again; and the haze surrounding Arden began to lose something of its radiance, now that she was no longer the heiress of Herons' Hall. He still saw her as charming and interesting, very desirable, no doubt; but did he still want to marry her? He was not so sure. Wouldn't he find himself, now, working like a slave to keep her, and possibly her aunt, her brother and her cousin as well, in the position to which they were accustomed? And if he couldn't do this – and he certainly couldn't, unless he were heavily backed by capital and influence – wouldn't he sink into the position of the scape-goat, the despised husband who has married above his station and is associated with the decline in the family fortunes? More and more, as Mrs Charleroy pressed her upon him, Arden began to seem to Hubert a luxury he couldn't afford. Arden herself, of course, had not yet been consulted. At least, some time before her father's death, he had written her a letter which in a court of law would count as a proposal of marriage: a letter the remembrance of which troubled him sometimes. But as Arden had never answered it, or shown any sign, when next they met, of having received it, he assumed that she hadn't taken it seriously, or hadn't realized what it meant. Then, one day, the storm broke.

It was after that week-end holiday of his on the moors, at Pauline's father's place. Basil Gabb was there, not yet engaged to Pauline, and Madeleine Parkes, her friend, old Dr Parkes' daughter. Hubert was glad to see Madeleine again. He had been a bit worried about her in the past, for he wasn't quite sure how far she considered the understanding between them as binding, and how much she could prove if she did. He had flirted and danced with her all the winter through before he got to know the family at Herons' Hall; and though during the first days of his passion for Arden, he had dismissed Madeleine from his mind, yet she was there, waiting to re-enter, the moment she was allowed. Now that Herons' Hall was on the wane, he was glad to see Madeleine, fresh, bright, smart, and the daughter of a man whose money, house and position would not vanish overnight. On that week-end, as they walked across the moors, he proposed to Madeleine and was accepted.

It was therefore a considerable jar when Mrs Charleroy opened the conversation with: 'Well, Hubert, when are you going to ask Arden to name the day?' He stared at her open-mouthed. He said, 'But, Helen, I've never thought of the matter seriously. Arden is a very charming girl, but –' Mrs Charleroy did not spare him. She cut through his lame excuses; she found out the dilemma in which he had placed himself. She informed him coldly that he was dropping Arden because of the change in her position, and that he was a complete cad.

When he asked her what made her think he was breaking any promise to her niece, she told him bluntly that a proposal had been made in writing: she had seen the letter lying about in Arden's room, and had decided that it had better be preserved – by herself. 'But Arden never answered it!' he had protested. 'Her ignoring it was tantamount to a refusal.' 'Not at all,' said Mrs Charleroy. 'She had no time to consider it before the news of her father's death arrived. Of course she would be far too scrupulous to accept you then, and far too proud to do so now. You've counted on that, and rightly. But I shall keep the letter. It might interest your new fiancée to know that you are not really free to marry her.'

Of course she would do nothing. Hubert knew that. And if she showed the letter to Madeleine, what would she gain? Madeleine wouldn't give way; and as for a breach of promise suit, they would never bring it. The publicity would be as bad for them as for him; and his defence, that his proposal had never been accepted, might come off. So they had parted, on very bad terms: Mrs Charleroy to the south of France, where she proposed to live with the children until the Hall should be sold: and Hubert back to the old life of a small-town lawyer, popular, quite well off, well received everywhere, but just a little discontented. His engagement to Madeleine was fulfilled in due course. His friendship with the Gabbs had flourished. Finally, he sold Herons' Hall to Simon Gabb; and some acid letters passed between himself, his brother's firm, and Mrs Charleroy, over the price, which was Simon's, not hers... Hubert forgot, incidentally, to press Mrs Charleroy's point about a piece of land on the estate; but she had counted on this, and forestalled him. She wrote to Simon Gabb herself, and obtained her request without any difficulty, to Hubert's chagrin.

No, there had been nothing she could do to harm him. There was nothing now, except the damage that a skilled and malicious tongue could inflict, by comments dropped here and there in the right place. And Madeleine, too, though she would never let him down in public, had a sharp tongue and a great gift for making home life uncomfortable, if she were annoyed…

So here was Helen Charleroy again, with one foot in the doorway that led straight back to Heron's Hall; still using Arden as a kind of bargaining-counter; but this time thwarted by the hand that had murdered Giles. What did she want of Hubert now?

'Everything was turning out according to plan.' She did not trouble to deny it. 'Tell me,' she said, 'have you had any conversation with the police over this affair?'

'A little,' said Hubert, wondering, 'but not since the morning they discovered the body. I was with one of the doctors when he examined it and decided that Giles had been murdered. He asked a few questions about you, by the way; and I answered them: nothing very particular, just general questions about the previous owner of Herons' Hall; and that led on to the rest of you.'

'Did they say anything about Royce?'

'Royce? I don't remember. No, I don't think so. Why?'

'Because they suspect Royce of this murder.'

'Royce?' repeated Hubert, and laughed. 'Oh, but that's absurd! Why should Royce shoot Giles? Especially just when Arden was about to bring Herons' Hall back into the family!' The laugh died as he saw that Mrs Charleroy was in deadly earnest.

'Listen, Hubert,' she said. 'That big red-haired Superintendent came here to know if I could provide Royce with an alibi; just that. And I couldn't.'

'You couldn't? But there was no need, was there? Let me see: Royce stayed at the Hall, didn't he, like the rest of us, because of the storm? Well, he must have been about the next morning, at breakfast and so on. Or do they suggest that he followed Giles to the lake and shot him? And if so, what for?'

'Royce stayed at the Hall,' said Helen, 'but only until Giles turned him out. There was a quarrel – over Arden, it appears – and Royce left, at about eleven. He didn't get back here until early morning; when exactly I don't know and he won't say. He won't tell the police, either; he won't say anything about his movements, either on that night or the next morning. But the police have found out where he went after he left Herons' Hall. He went for a wild drive, in somebody else's car, with Basil Gabb's wife; and he left her at about five next morning. Nobody saw him again until Winifred, my maid, came downstairs that morning, and Royce appeared, as if from his room, and asked for his breakfast. That was at about half-past seven. So you see there are two and a half hours unaccounted for; and the police believe that Giles Gabb was shot at some time between five and six that morning! The Superintendent broke all this to me very gently; but he did say that he knew, from my brother Charles's book, that Royce was a good shot; and he did point out that Royce not only had an excellent motive, but was certainly in the neighbourhood at the material time. He suggested that it would be a very good thing if I could get Royce to speak: they had tried, and failed.'

'And have you tried?'

'I have. However, I know my limitations. I knew I should fail, and I did. Royce will say nothing about what he did on *any* part of that night and morning. Of course, he's under the impression that nobody knows of his escapade with Mrs Basil Gabb; and I can understand why he won't talk about that. Poor boy, he is all chivalry! At least, I suppose it must be chivalry, though his manner is merely sullen and rather rude. But what I can't understand is why he won't say what he did between the time he left her and the time he got home. You see, he doesn't attempt to maintain that he came straight home, even then. He says he thinks it was about half-past six; I managed to get that out of him, now I come to think of it. But where was he between five o'clock and then?'

'He doesn't know you know about his adventure with Pauline?'

'No, not yet.'

'So you didn't tell him you knew he left her at five?'

'I couldn't, without letting him know I knew all about his other movements. And I couldn't do that without making him feel that he had been watched and spied on, which would have been quite fatal in his present mood. But *you* could tell him, Hubert.'

She leaned forward and laid a hand on his knee. She was thinking of nothing, now, except her son and his safety; and Hubert found himself being drawn by the irresistible pull of her need and her sincerity, into the orbit of her schemes again.

'I?' he said feebly. 'What could I do? He wouldn't listen to *me*.'

'Yes, Hubert, he would – if he felt you were his legal adviser. He is in danger – in great danger. He must be made to see it. You must make him tell the truth, if only to you. Will you look after him, for my sake – for all our sakes? After all, we are old friends, and I have no one else I can trust.'

Hubert melted. The old quarrel, the old humiliation and grievance, melted away beneath the flattery of her appeal. 'I'll do what I can,' he said, patting her hand, and wondering if Madeleine would make difficulties. 'When can I see him? Is he anywhere about now?'

'You'll probably find him in the garden somewhere,' said Helen briskly, her point gained. 'He spends most of his time furiously sawing wood, and keeping out of our way.'

Hubert stepped out through the French window. As he passed the summer-house, he heard voices and laughter, and caught a glimpse of Billy and Jessica, their heads close together over a box of trout-flies.

'Ah,' thought Hubert. 'Helen again! What a woman!' In his mellowed mood towards her, he saluted her with admiration for the resourcefulness of her schemes. But this time he was wrong: for this was something with which Mrs Charleroy had had nothing to do, and could neither help nor hinder.

19

Mallett sat in the swivel-chair at his desk in the police-station at Chode, with Dr Jones facing him. He laid a large red hand on the pile of typescript before him.

'Well, there you are,' he said. 'Here are all the reports. Go through them if you like. Everything fits together very sweetly until you get to the centre of the puzzle, as it were, and then there's a blank.' He filled his pipe. Jones reached over and took the pile of rustling papers.

Over by the window, Dr Fitzbrown was walking round the long table on which the exhibits were arranged. There was the heel of Pauline's evening slipper, stained with the mud of the drive; there were the discoveries made on the island: the deed-box, the small black note-book, the rifle-case; there was the shot-gun on which Giles's body had been propped. In the centre was the copy of Sir Charles Laforte's memoirs, open at the title-page; under the title was a verse by Adam Lindsay Gordon, so heavily underlined in thick pencil that the paper had been furrowed up here and there:

> 'Yet if once we efface the joys of the chase
> From the land, and outroot the stud,
> Good-bye to the Anglo-Saxon race,
> Farewell to the Norman blood!'

'Suppose you tell us what's new,' said Fitzbrown. 'I don't see anything very new here.'

'Nothing new to look at,' agreed Mallett. 'But plenty of new information, all the same. The rifle, for instance—'

Jones looked up. 'You saw old Gabb? What did he say?'

'Yes,' said Mallett. 'I saw him yesterday morning. He was inclined to be crusty. He wanted to know what we were doing, and why, if we couldn't find his son's murderer, we didn't call in expert help. I asked him if he had done his part, namely, gone through the papers found in Giles's desk. He said he had, and that they contained nothing of importance…'

'Nothing of importance, Mallett,' said Simon, taking the sheaf of papers from the drawer of his desk. 'I was surprised. I thought the boy was busy with some new design which would astonish us all and make our name as famous as Mannlicher or Snider. But these are just jottings about other types, rough notes from books, and so on. There's nothing here.'

'Just as I thought,' said Mallett calmly. 'That's why his desk wasn't locked, and not because he had nothing of any value to conceal.' He told Simon of the discovery on the island. 'I kept this out of the inquest,' he said, 'along with every other bit of evidence that mattered. But you see the point, Mr Gabb: your son believed that somebody was tampering with his desk. He believed that his work wasn't safe in this house, and he removed everything he considered of any importance to the island. Now one might have thought that that was a delusion: the result of overwork and so on, preying on a rather overwrought mind. I might have thought so, from what you told me about him. I don't know about you?'

Simon Gabb, all attention, was gazing at Mallett with a new wariness. He did not answer the question. Mallett continued:

'Yet if we had thought that, we should have been wrong; because in spite of the carefully-hidden *cache*, the difficulty of getting to the place without being seen, and so on, Giles's deed-box was found and ransacked. Nothing was left of any importance in the *cache*, either. The only thing overlooked was a diary tucked away in a secret compartment of the deed-box. Whether he himself removed the other papers, or whether they were taken by the thief, one can't be sure; but—'

'But if you can't be sure, how can you be sure there was anything to steal?' said Simon sharply. 'What makes you think that this *cache*, as you call it, wasn't a further stage in the boy's obsession about his work?'

'I'll show you,' said Mallett. He went to the door and beckoned. One of his men entered and placed before Simon's astonished eyes the rifle-case that Fitzbrown had discovered leaning against a tree.

'Now, sir,' said Mallett, opening the case and revealing the rifle, 'will you have a look at that?'

Simon Gabb picked up the rifle gingerly. 'Is this the gun that shot him?' he said grimly.

'We think so,' said Mallett. 'Though, mind you, we can't prove it. This gun was unloaded when we found it. It had recently been fired, but there were no cartridges left in it. We can't say when exactly it had last been fired. Then again, we have never found the bullet, so that we've had no chance of making the usual examination. But your son was shot with a rifle – and here on the island we find this rifle of the expected type. How it got there is another matter.'

'Couldn't the shot have been fired from the island?' said Simon.

'I don't think so. Consider the distance between the island and the boat-house where the body was found. It must be about half a mile. Assuming that visibility was good, the man who wanted to kill another man without fail would hardly risk a range of more than three hundred yards, would he? But visibility was not good that morning. Yet if your son was shot near the island, how was it that he was found in the boat-house? It would mean that the killer took the risk of towing the boat containing his victim back into the boat-house; and whereas he might risk the trip himself on a misty morning and hope not to be recognized, he would be a very conspicuous object if he were seen towing another rowing-boat. No, I think we can still assume that Giles was shot as his boat was coming into the channel by the boat-house; which means we still have to ask how this gun got there. Well, let's leave that for the moment. Will you have a look at it, Mr Gabb, and tell me what you make of it?'

Simon began his examination of the rifle. He no longer handled it as if it were red-hot; he inspected it minutely, every inch, at some points using a pocket magnifying-glass as well as his spectacles. At last he looked up:

'Well, Mallett, you've certainly got something here. You say it was hidden?'

'Yes. It was extremely well hidden. It was in its case, propped up against a tree on the side away from the path, and festooned round with trails of ivy. We shouldn't have discovered it then if Fitzbrown hadn't happened to stumble on his way back down the path.'

Simon laid the rifle down reverently. 'This,' he said, 'is the result of Giles's work. This is the new type, or something approaching it, for which we were all working.' He broke the breech again, and looked down the barrel; then he measured the diameter again with a gauge. 'This isn't quite my line, you know,' he said. 'Giles was the firm's expert in small arms. But if you'll let me have it for twenty-four hours, I'll get a report on it from the works. I'll do more: I'll try to find out who made it There are no identification-marks on it: it's an experimental weapon, and therefore no doubt the only one of its kind. But it's most likely that it was made to Giles's specification in our own workshops. He had a free hand in this business, and he didn't tell his plans, even to me. But the works foreman would know. Giles had complete confidence in him.'

'Then you think it's the actual result of his experiments?'

'I do. It's a .256 of the Mannlicher type, with refinements. I don't know what these are; they can't be seen by a mere inspection like this. But what I do know is that it has been specially made. It's not a Mannlicher, nor any of the known deviations, not even any of our own projected patterns of this type. And if it was specially made to Giles's own design, you can be sure it embodies something new: a trifle perhaps, but something that will give that extra range, or higher muzzle velocity, or flatter trajectory, with, say, a heavier more blunt-nosed bullet, that every armaments firm is working for.'

'Then the design would be well worth stealing?'

'It would indeed.' Simon hesitated for a moment. Then he said, 'Look here, Mallett, I've got something to tell you that I ought to have mentioned before. But it involved a question of honour – my son's honour – and I couldn't bring myself to do it. What you've just told me clears him entirely.'

Mallett shook his head sadly. 'Why will you people always imagine you're the best judges of what to tell the police and what not? And then you get impatient because we don't lay our hands on the criminal within twenty-four hours. Well, go ahead, Mr Gabb: what is it now?'

Simon had the grace to look ashamed. 'It's just this, Mallett: there *has* been a leakage of information. We were informed of it a while ago, and warned to be careful. A man was arrested at Le Havre – a man wanted for other reasons by the C.I.D. – and he was found to be carrying various secret documents containing military information. Among these was the specification – luckily not complete – of a new small-bore rifle of military pattern. The firms who were making this class of stuff on Government contracts were circularized from New Scotland Yard—asked to investigate. The letter, being highly confidential, came straight to me. I didn't take much notice, the first time. I knew I could trust Giles, and he was the only one whose work counted from that point of view; and I thought I could trust him to handle his own business and not confide anything of that nature to any but trustworthy men. So I ignored it. Then a couple of months later another letter came. This time I happened to be in Scotland having a little holiday; and the letter was opened by Basil, and sent on to me there. He didn't attach much importance to it; but I began to worry. I don't know why – one has intuitions about such things – but at the back of my mind I had a persistent feeling that it was ourselves who were involved: that there was trouble brewing for us, big trouble, if the leakage were traced to ourselves; and endless worry and annoyance meanwhile. However, I still hoped I was imagining things.'

'Did you mention the matter to anybody else? Giles, for instance?'

'No, I didn't.' Simon looked down. 'I was afraid of the effect on him if I did. I knew his nature. He was suspicious and morose enough already. I thought it might upset his work.'

'You mean,' said Mallett, 'you weren't quite sure he wasn't in some way responsible.'

Simon gave a sigh. 'Well, it was possible, wasn't it? I didn't pretend to understand Giles. I knew he had a queer streak in him, amounting to mental aberration sometimes. I knew he had this genius for the mechanical side of our business, and together with it an absolute loathing of bloodshed. I knew he had a dislike of blood sports, and that though he was a first-rate shot and used to shoot and fish himself, I've often heard him ranting on the subject. And latterly I've heard him talk of killing men as the greatest of all blood sports – ever since there's been this possibility of war talked of again. I thought he might, by some perverse sort of reasoning, think it right to let his secret go as soon a he found it – not to let one country monopolize it. You see what I mean?'

Mallett nodded. 'But it seems to me, in that case he'd have thrown his new rifle into the lake, not arranged to have it multiplied all over the world, unless of course he wanted his fellow-mortals to exterminate one another as quickly as possible. – But go on. I gather the matter didn't end there?'

'No. A week before Giles was killed, I received a visit from a detective-inspector of the local C.I.D. at Broxeter. He told me in strictest confidence that definite information had come to hand regarding a further leakage, and that there was reason to suppose that it could be traced to our firm. It was proposed to send a special detective down, to take up his stand in the works in some capacity and watch developments. I mentioned this visit, first to Basil, then, after a good deal of hesitation, to Giles.'

'And what did he say?'

'Nothing. His reaction was exactly what I had expected. He turned very red and walked out of the office. After that, he didn't go near the works. He spent all his time on the lake with his new friends – except that he seemed to be busy late at night in his study. His mother was afraid he'd overwork again and have another breakdown. But I told her to leave him alone.'

'Did they send the man down from the Yard?'

'No. Frankly, Mallett, I didn't like the look of things; so I got into touch with them at once, and led them to believe we were on the track of the trouble, and if they left us to deal with it, it would be far better than arousing suspicion and alarming whoever was guilty by introducing a stranger into the works. They didn't agree; but it caused delay. Meanwhile, I was going to look into the matter myself. I had faced the fact that even if my son were involved, I had to trace this leakage.'

'Did you mention it to anyone else at all?'

'No. That is, not until the evening before Giles was shot. Then I told my brother James about it. I rely a good deal on his practical sense; and I wanted to keep the matter in the family. We didn't go so far as to concoct plans; but we were going to do so next day. Of course this other business put a stop to all that, temporarily, though James is still with me.'

'Perhaps it will have put a stop to the leakage as well,' said Mallett thoughtfully.

Simon looked up sharply. 'Then you think——'

'No, I don't. No, Mr Gabb, it wasn't your son who was giving away his own secret. He took very great pains to hide it, there's no doubt of that. But he was aware, before you told him, that someone was tampering with his papers; and what you said merely confirmed his suspicions. He moved all his important papers from his desk to the island after you told him of the receipt of the third letter, which, you must remember, was the first he'd heard of any official proof of these leakages; and if he spent his time fishing and shooting with his friends, he used them to cover up daily visits to the island. Otherwise his suddenly going there every day would have been most conspicuous... I imagine he had to have his notes and calculations within easy reach. He worked here in the evenings, and went back to his *cache* during the day, either to hide fresh papers there, or to consult his own notes. And he kept the model rifle on the island, too – the one he had had made for experimental purposes. It's ten to one it was made for him in your factory, isn't it? Will you confirm that for me? I shall want to see the foreman, or whoever was in his confidence, if that's so.'

'I'll do that. Leave it to me,' said Simon.

'And lock it up carefully. It's probably the only one of its kind in existence.'

'I will. By the way, you said there was a diary, I believe.'

'Yes: written in some special system of shorthand. I'm having it transcribed. There were some diagrams and figures in it, which are being studied. You shall have the note-book back when the examination is completed.'

'Is there anything that throws light on the business?' Simon spoke nervously.

'I'm not prepared to say yet,' said Mallett.

'Well, that's the rifle practically settled,' concluded Mallett, rubbing his hands together, 'though the confirmation hasn't come back from Gabb yet. Now if I'm right in supposing that the shot was fired from the boat-house, the murderer for some reason yet to be explained decided to conceal the rifle on the island.'

Dr Jones looked up from his study of the typescript. 'Takes a bit of explaining, doesn't it?'

'You mean because of the risk he ran of being seen, rowing across there after the shooting? It was a misty morning, remember.'

'Yes, but not too misty for a man to be seen rowing on the lake. Remember, the gardener saw Giles himself, from his bedroom window, so he says.'

'I remember,' said Mallett. 'I'll come back to that presently. Let's take your point first. After all, he had to get rid of the rifle somehow, hadn't he? He couldn't let himself be seen carrying it about the garden afterwards!'

'Quite so,' said Jones patiently. 'But why take it to the island? Why not, for instance, drop it into the lake?'

'It would be found.'

'Of course it would. But that wouldn't matter so long as the person who fired the shot wasn't anywhere around. There'd be no finger-prints left, once it had lain in the lake mud for a couple of hours. By the way, did you find any finger-prints on this gun?'

'None except Giles Gabb's.'

'Your murderer wore gloves, no doubt.'

'Why not?' Mallett was getting a little annoyed.

'Oh, nothing, nothing. But if this was the gun that shot Giles, can you tell me just why the murderer didn't get rid of it in the obvious way? Can you say why he went to the trouble of pulling Giles's body out of the rowing-boat into the motor-boat, rowing across to the island, planting the gun there in its rifle-case – unless of course you think he was carrying the rifle-case too—'

Mallett made a sound like 'Pah!', but Jones continued unperturbed:

'– and rowing back again, all at imminent risk of being seen, when by so doing he robbed himself of the one chance he had of getting away with the murder? Fitzbrown! You knew at a glance this was no suicide. Why?'

'Because he had been shot with a rifle, whereas he was leaning on a shot-gun.'

'Exactly. Then why the devil did the murderer get rid of the rifle – which would have made the thing look like suicide – and prop Giles up on a shot-gun, which the merest tyro could see had not been the weapon that killed him? Was he trying to make a suicide look like a murder? Or was it a murder, and did something go wrong?'

He turned back to his study of the typescript. Mallett pulled at his red moustache.

'Then you want us to suppose,' he said, 'for the sake of argument, that this special rifle was not the one that killed Giles? If so, where is the one that did?' He got up, and paced up and down, his hands behind his back. 'It seems fantastic: here is the perfect weapon, as every sportsman, not to mention soldier, would agree: the perfect weapon for an "anatomically deadly shot," as old Sir Charles would call it. And yet we have to ignore it and postulate the existence of another rifle, and begin searching all over again! No, no, I can't do it.'

'Then you stick to the island theory?' said Jones without looking up.

'And what about the other boat?' persisted Fitzbrown. 'What about your theory that there was someone else out on the lake that morning besides Giles?'

'Yes,' said Mallett. 'But I don't think there was one. I think there were two.'

'Two others besides Giles?' said Fitzbrown incredulously.

'Yes: two others. And one of them, I have reason to believe, was – but I'd better give you the evidence of Morgan the gardener. Here it is.'

He took, from the remaining pile of typescript, two sheets fastened together, and passed them to Fitzbrown.

Morgan, gnarled and surly, shuffled into Mallett's room at the Police Station, and glanced to right and left. He was annoyed and resentful at being taken from his really important work in the chrysanthemum-house and, as he saw it, almost haled off to jail by an uppish young police-constable whom he had known since the latter was a youngster to be chased out of Sir Charles's orchards. In front of him was this red-faced Superintendent full of self-importance; and at one side, another young officer busy sharpening a pencil, ready to take down all he said 'to be used in evidence against him,' Morgan did not doubt.

'Sit down, Morgan,' said Mallett kindly, pointing to a chair. 'We shan't keep you long. Just one or two things to clear up, you know.'

Morgan sat down, but he did not relax. He met Mallett's look with an uncompromisingly hostile glare. He gave his full name and address, and his occupation, grudgingly. He would have refused even that information if he could.

'Now, Morgan,' said Mallett, 'what time do you usually get up in the morning, eh?'

'About half-past five.'

'That's rather early, isn't it?'

'Not for *us*,' said Morgan, in a tone which implied a profound contempt for lazy men like the police, who don't get up till seven or eight o'clock, may be, according to their rank. 'I have to be on the garden by six-thirty.'

'"Plough deep while sluggards sleep,"' quoted Mallett. Morgan sniffed.

'On Sundays too, do you get up at half-past five?'

'Certainly, if I've got work to do. There's always work in a garden.'

'Doesn't Mr Gabb dislike seeing you working in the grounds on Sundays?'

'Him!' Morgan almost choked. 'He'd have us working all night too, if he could. However, it's not for him I work on Sundays. I just go along to see to the hot-houses and so on, and get the vegetables sent up to the house. On Sundays – mornings, that is – I work in Mrs Charleroy's garden.' His tone softened at the mention of the rightful owners, as he still considered the Colonel's family. 'Not that she wants me to; but it's the only time I get.'

'I see. Well, Morgan, on the morning when Mr Giles Gabb was murdered – which was a Sunday, you remember – you got up at five-thirty as usual. Is that right?'

'Well, I may have been a bit later,' conceded Morgan reluctantly; 'may be twenty minutes or so, that morning. My wife didn't call me, because of the mist.'

'Ah yes, the mist. Tell me now, what sort of a morning was it when you looked out of your window? Your bedroom window overlooks the lake, doesn't it?'

'Yes, it does,' Even this admission seemed to be dragged out of Morgan.

'And what do you see? Here –' Mallett pushed a large plan of Herons' Mere across to the gardener. 'This is your cottage, on the south bank of the lake, nearer the east, that is, the boat-house end, but not on the same side as the boat-house. I take it you couldn't see the boat-house because of the mist?'

'No, I couldn't,' said Morgan glumly.

'No. The lake is about a quarter of a mile wide there. Could you see the island?'

'Off and on, when the mist cleared a bit, I could just see it.'

'But it's farther away from you than the boat-house.'

'Yes, but it's bigger, and covered with trees. I could just see where it was.'

'But you didn't have a clear view? You couldn't have seen anyone landing on the island, even from your side?'

'No, I don't think so.'

'Could you have seen anybody rowing from the boat-house to the island?'

'No, I couldn't, not if they kept to their own side of the lake, that is.'

'As they'd have to do if they rowed in a straight line from the boat-house to the farther, that is, the north side of the island?'

'Yes.'

'Right. Now to come to the next point. You did actually see some-body rowing on the lake that morning?'

'Yes, I did.'

'So that this person must have been rowing along on your side of the lake. How far from the shore would you say?'

Morgan rubbed his grey short-clipped hair with a horny hand. 'About thirty yards or so, maybe.'

'And this person was rowing from the boat-house end to the island end of the lake? That is, from east to west?'

'Yes.'

'Rowing towards the island?'

'I don't know. I couldn't see where they were going.'

'Rowing quickly or slowly?'

'Oh, in an ordinary sort of way – neither fast nor slow, if you follow me.'

'Not in any hurry at all?'

'Oh no. Just at the rate they usually row when they're making for the fishing-ground.'

'What do you mean by the fishing-ground?'

'That's what they call this bit of lake here,' said Morgan, pointing to the west end of the lake, beyond the island. 'There's a deep pool there, and the bank overhangs part of it, and that's where they usually go when they fish for pike. There's always a pike or two hanging about there under the ledges.'

'Then you think that whoever was in the boat was making for the fishing-ground. What makes you think so?'

'Well, she – I mean they – had a rod in the boat.'

Mallett looked up sharply. 'You could see that?' he said. 'Then you recognized the person in the boat. Why didn't you say so to begin with? You should have come to us at once and told us that, as soon as you heard of the murder.' He bent an even more searching look on Morgan, and Morgan shrank away, avoiding his gaze. 'I thought,'

Mallett went on, 'you told the chauffeur and others, immediately after the discovery of the body, that you had seen *Mr Giles* rowing on the lake, at about six o'clock that morning. Then why did you say "she" just now? Come on, Morgan: you can do no one any good by concealing what you know, much less by lying. Who was it you saw on the lake that morning?'

Morgan was silent.

'You said "she",' persisted Mallett. 'There's only one lady who goes pike-fishing on Herons' Mere, and that's Miss Laforte. Was it Miss Laforte you saw?'

Morgan still said nothing.

'You don't deny it,' said Mallett. 'You were with the Laforte family for many years before you took on the same work under Mr Gabb, weren't you?'

Morgan nodded. 'Twenty years,' he muttered. 'Just after Miss Arden was born.'

'And naturally you still feel a loyalty towards them. I quite understand that. I respect you for it. But you must understand, Morgan, this is murder. We must find out the truth, whatever it may be; and that means, when the criminal is discovered, innocent people are freed from any suspicion. It doesn't follow that because Miss Laforte was on the lake that morning, she shot Mr Giles. But if you don't tell me what you saw, I can't prove that she didn't. And if it comes out later that she was there and both you and she concealed this fact from the police, isn't that the best way to make the police think she's guilty? Do *you* think she's guilty, perhaps?'

Morgan looked up, stung at last into replying with fervour. 'Oh no, sir – no!'

'Then don't behave as if you did,' reprimanded Mallett, though he was interested to see the tears that had sprung into Morgan's eyes, and the change in his manner from surliness to appeal. Morgan's glance wavered, and fell again; it was clear that the charge of having suspected

Miss Arden of anything so unthinkable as murder had first shocked him, then filled him with shame.

'Come on now,' said Mallett. 'Tell me what you saw. You looked out of your bedroom window: what time would that be exactly?'

'About ten to six, I think,' said Morgan in a low subdued tone.

'And you saw Miss Laforte rowing past in a leisurely fashion, fairly close to your side of the lake: close enough for you to see the pike-rod in the boat; and you therefore judged that she was making for the fishing-ground.'

'That's right.'

'You saw no one going there before her?'

'No – but –' Morgan's agitation suddenly rose again to the pitch of distress, as he fought with his inner knowledge and his reluctance to speak.

'But what?'

'I saw someone coming after.'

'Someone coming after? Rowing along on the same side of the lake, following Miss Laforte, you mean?'

'Not rowing, sir. Paddling – paddling the canoe. There's a canoe in the boat-house as well as the motor-boat and the two rowing-boats. It was him I meant when I said I saw Mr Giles on the lake that morning. I mentioned it without thinking, as soon as they told me he was shot. I thought when I spoke it must have been him, but afterwards when I heard what really happened, I didn't think it could have been.'

'Why not? Didn't you recognize him?'

'Well, no, not exactly. It was just a guess, as you might say.'

'But you recognized Miss Laforte.'

'Yes, but the canoe was farther away from the shore, and the mist seemed to be thicker just then. I didn't take much notice. I was just going to go downstairs, and get my breakfast when I saw the canoe, and I thought, " That's Mr Giles, going along to the fishing-ground after Miss Arden." He was wearing an oilskin and a sou'wester, and that's all I was able to see.'

'What time was this?'

'Quite soon after Miss Arden went by: five minutes or so, I should say.'

'And what made you change your mind later and think it wasn't Mr Giles?'

Morgan shifted uneasily. 'Well, for one thing Mr Giles never used the canoe.'

'That's not enough,' said Mallett. 'He might take the canoe if both the other boats were out.'

'The canoe's no good if you're going pike-fishing,' said Morgan stubbornly. 'It'd overbalance. You'd overturn as soon as you cast your spinner – and if a pike took your bait, he'd pull you overboard in a jiffy.'

'Yes, but suppose he weren't going pike-fishing. Suppose he merely wanted to follow Miss Arden.'

Morgan shook his head. 'It wasn't Mr Giles,' he said.

'You're sure?'

Morgan nodded.

'Then you must have a reason.'

Morgan nodded again, slowly. 'I didn't understand it at the time,' he said. 'And I've often thought about it since. You see, after I'd had breakfast, I came out of the house and down to the garden gate, not hurrying, as it was Sunday. It was about half-past six then, I suppose, and the mist was getting thinner as the sun came up. It was fairly thick still in the middle of the lake; it often lies there after it's left the sides. You couldn't see across to the other side. I walked down to the gate lighting my pipe, and when I looked up, I saw Miss Arden rowing by. She was farther away than when I'd seen her before, because she was making more or less in a straight line for the boat-house; and after a minute or two she pulled right away into the bank of mist in the centre. I don't think she saw me. But the funny thing was, she was towing the canoe!'

'Towing the canoe?'

'That's right. The canoe was empty, you understand, and she had it tied up to her boat, and she was towing it back to the boat-house.'

'And the man in the canoe?'

'I don't know. I never saw him again. He must have got out somewhere along the banks, I suppose, or on the island.'

Mallett tugged at his moustache. 'And you say this was about six-thirty?'

'Yes, or maybe a little before.'

'You didn't see what Miss Laforte did when she reached the boat-house?'

'No. I still couldn't see the boat-house from where I was. There was still a scarf of mist in between.'

'What did you do then?'

'I walked round by the path as usual, but I didn't see anybody. Of course, Miss Arden would have had time to put the boat and canoe away and get pretty well back to the Hall before I got round.'

'You passed the boat-house without looking in?'

'Yes. I never thought any more about it.'

'You realize that probably Mr Giles's body was there then?'

'I do now, of course.'

'You saw nobody at all between the boat-house and the Hall on your way up?'

'Nobody at all. There was no one about that morning except me, until Mr Gabb came out for his usual morning walk before breakfast.'

'What time was that?'

'About eight o'clock, I think, as it was Sunday. Other mornings he was about an hour earlier, that is except when the dark mornings and the bad weather stopped him from taking any walk.'

'One last point: did you hear any shots at all?'

'Well, sir –' Morgan rubbed his head. 'To tell you the truth, I can't be sure. Looking back, I think I did. And yet, it was such an ordinary thing to hear shots round the lake, what with them shooting at the ducks with a shot-gun, and aiming at the target with their rifles, that I never paid much heed to them. And now, I can't be certain if I really did hear a shot or two that morning, or whether it was some other day.'

'Well, never mind, Morgan. Now don't mention any of this either to Miss Arden or to her aunt. You'll only worry them for nothing. Leave it all to me. It'll all come right, you'll see.'

Morgan shuffled away, somewhat comforted and entirely mollified. But if he had turned and seen the look Mallett sent after him, he might not have been so completely reassured.

'Well, now,' said Mallett, as Jones in his turn, having received the sheets from Fitzbrown, laid them down. 'That was Morgan's unexpected contribution. What does it mean? Who was the man in the canoe? Has Morgan invented him, in an effort to shield Miss Laforte? If not, was it Giles or was it, as he says, some other man?'

'It can hardly have been Giles,' said Dr Jones. 'He would hardly have had time to disembark at the far end of the lake, run round the path, and get himself shot in that boat-house, before Miss Laforte's return.'

'Why do you assume he was shot *before* Miss Laforte's return?' said Fitzbrown. 'Why couldn't he have been shot after? Oh, I know you gave it as your opinion that he was shot between five and six probably; but you wouldn't claim to be able to place the time of death to within half an hour?'

'No,' said Jones with acid politeness. 'I would not. But you will notice that if Miss Laforte arrived first, with her rowing-boat and her canoe, and moored these in the boat-house, the murderer would then have had a choice of craft, and would not have had to lug Giles's body out of *his* rowing-boat into the motor-boat. We have already agreed that there could be no possible reason for such a feat unless the murderer urgently wanted to use a rowing-boat, and the one containing Giles happened to be the only one available.'

'But,' said Fitzbrown, thumping the table in great excitement, 'it follows then that Giles was murdered during the period between Miss Laforte's leaving the boat-house and her return. Morgan saw her passing his cottage at about five-fifty. So we can say she left the boat-house between five and ten minutes before. He says he saw her returning, towing the empty canoe, at about six-thirty. Give her another five or ten minutes to get back, and you have the two *termini post* and *ante quem*: that is to say, Giles was shot between five-forty and six-forty!'

'Why couldn't he have been shot before she took her boat out?' Mallet interposed.

'Oh, I say, Mallett!' remonstrated Fitzbrown, protecting his theory. 'Give the poor girl credit for some heart! We know she wasn't deeply enamoured of Giles; but she'd have to have had a heart of flint and nerves of steel to have set out pike-fishing from the very boat-house in which she had just discovered Giles's corpse!'

'Unless,' said Mallett, 'she did find the body, and set out in the other boat to look for the criminal – though I did get the impression from Morgan that she wasn't hurrying, that's true.'

Dr Jones snorted. 'Or unless,' he said, 'she shot him herself. Or do you think she's too much of a lady? She was a pretty good shot herself, apparently.'

'In that case,' remarked Fitzbrown, 'no doubt the gentleman in the canoe was pursuing *her*. It wasn't one of your men in disguise, was it, Mallett? Now that would be what I'd call smart service!'

Mallett looked at his watch. 'Well, you know pretty much how things stand.' He took his hat. 'I'll leave you here to browse over the rest of the material. I am now going to see Miss Laforte and ask her for myself.'

20

A rden sauntered down the flagged path to the tool-house. Royce did not look up as she appeared, but she could tell by the increased vigour of his sawing that he was aware of her presence.

'What on earth are you doing that for?' she said at last, not being able to think of anything else to say, and irritated by the spectacle of someone uselessly expending energy.

Royce did not answer. He went on sawing so violently that suddenly the long saw twisted in his hand, sprang out of its groove, and fell with a clatter on to the flagged floor.

'I wish you'd leave me alone,' he said, pushing back his fair hair from his scarlet forehead. 'Why are you all snooping round watching me? You never used to. I'm not used to so much attention. It gets on my nerves.'

Arden leaned against the door-post, and watched him with a queer look, half-maternal and pitying, half-curious and even searching. But she spoke rather scornfully.

'Why the woodland pose?' she said. '"And Father wore a Walden look, And plied a hatchet near a brook."'

Royce pushed the log off the trestle, sat down, and mopped his forehead. 'Oh, what a bore all this business is!' he said irritably. 'How I hate things that go on and on and you can't get away from them!' He turned to her roughly. 'I suppose you think I'm terribly callous? I ought to be thinking of you, and Mother, and even poor Giles.'

'Well,' said Arden, still watching him closely, but keeping the note of provocation in her voice, 'I don't see why we should all have to think of *your* sensitive soul, or nerves, or whatever's the matter with you, to the exclusion of our own—'

He turned round, stung, and would have interrupted her, but she waved his protest aside.

'—which is what you achieve by going off by yourself all the time and not coming in to meals and refusing to speak to anybody. I don't see what *you* have to be so upset about.'

'Don't you?' he said in a low voice, looking down at his hands, which were blistered with sawing and powdered with fine wood dust.

'No, I don't,' said Arden bravely, though a fine ear, listening carefully, might have detected the note of anxiety in her voice.

Royce gave a little laugh. 'My dear girl! Where is your intelligence? Didn't you see Hubert leaving here?'

'Well, yes, I did,' admitted Arden.

'And he had been closeted with Mother for a long time, hadn't he?'

'I think so.'

'And you mean to say you don't know what it's all about? Come, come, you're not trying.' He got up and confronted her. 'Don't you know they think *I* shot Giles?'

'You?' said Arden weakly. She shrank from meeting his eyes. 'Why on earth should they think it was you?'

He stared at her for a moment, incredulous. Then he threw back his head and laughed. 'Ah, I see! So *they* sent you, did they? Hubert failed, so Mother thought she'd try *you*. Well, don't worry, I shan't tell them anything. Let the police find out. It's their job.'

Arden brooded for a minute. Then she looked up. 'Look here, Royce,' she said with new decision, 'don't you think you and I are playing the fool in this business? Sooner or later we shall have to come clean, you know. I don't think we can go on hoping to fend the police off indefinitely.'

Royce's expression changed. As she watched him, she saw the lines of anxiety form round his mouth, making his face look thinner and older. 'What do you mean?' he said. '*You* aren't mixed up in this at all, Arden, are you? I know you think *I* am, and I can guess why. But you didn't really have anything to do with it?'

Arden slipped past him and sat down on the trestle. 'Hubert's staying to lunch,' she said. 'Do you know why? Because that man Mallett has rung up to say he's coming here again this afternoon.'

'Again?'

'Aunt Helen was rather mysterious about it,' pursued Arden. 'She asked me if I'd be here. So I can only think he wants to see *me*.'

Royce came and stood in front of her. 'You're not bound to see him,' he said vehemently. 'You're not bound to tell him anything. Hubert knows that. Let Hubert see him instead.'

'Hubert would love to,' said Arden. 'But really, there isn't much he can do about it if we don't tell him anything, is there?'

Royce sat down beside Arden on the trestle. 'Listen, Arden,' he said. 'I swear to you I didn't shoot Giles. I swear to you I never even saw him that morning. But I know it looks as if I did, because I had the chance. I was around. I can't explain how that came about, because it involves – somebody else. But I didn't kill him, either purposely or by accident.' He paused. 'I know you didn't, either.'

Arden glanced at him sideways. 'Although I was "around" too, as you put it?'

'You don't need to admit it,' urged Royce strenuously. 'They'll never get anything out of me.'

'So you did see me on the lake that morning?' said Arden.

'Yes, yes, of course I did. I was – following you. What else would I be doing? But that's nothing. It's irrelevant.' He looked down. 'I thought perhaps, at first, you hadn't seen me. Then I saw from your manner, you must have… I think they'll arrest me quite soon now. I suppose they've been leaving me alone in the hope I'd give something away… Of course, if you think it better to say you saw me, I don't mind. But I really don't see why you should come into it at all.'

Arden gave a low laugh. 'Can it be you really think I did shoot him?' she said. She caught him by his shoulders and turned him towards her. 'Why, yes, I believe you do! This is wonderful! Each of us protecting the other! How very touching! Only it seems we shall succeed in landing each other in the dock, if we don't stop being chivalrous and show some common sense instead. – Why on earth should I of all people want to kill poor Giles? Wasn't he supposed to be going to give me back my lost rights in Herons' Hall?'

'It might have been an accident,' muttered Royce, 'or in self-defence or something. Giles was a violent sort of fellow at bottom, I always thought. And anyway,' he burst out vehemently again, 'I know *I* didn't shoot him. I never even saw him, I tell you! I know he said he was going down there early, and he told you not to bother to come; but I saw no one but you, and that was a pure fluke. Naturally, after what had happened the evening before, if I'd seen Giles, I wouldn't have gone anywhere near the lake. I happened to see you, and I followed you, I don't even know why.'

'I never saw Giles either,' said Arden.

'You didn't? Why did you go down to the lake, then?'

'Oh, I don't know. I didn't sleep very well. It was so strange being back there again; and I was rather worried about what had happened the evening before. I knew he wanted me to come fishing early, and it was only when he saw you there that he changed his mind and told me not to bother. At least, so I thought. And as I couldn't sleep, I thought the best plan would be to go down and keep the original arrangement, and then perhaps go straight home. I didn't want to face all those people at breakfast again, and yet I couldn't very well leave without seeing Giles at all…'

Royce interrupted her.

'Look here: if I tell you what my movements were exactly,' he said excitedly, 'will you tell me yours? Then we can decide what to tell this Superintendent fellow, whichever of us it is he wants to see.'

'I think,' said Arden, 'we shall have to tell him the truth, you know.'

'Oh, I don't care what *you* tell him,' said Royce cheerfully, 'so long as I know you're clear of it all. As for myself: I shall know how to look after myself all right.'

'More chivalry?' murmured Arden. 'If I were you, I'd let *her* look after *her*self. She looks to me quite capable... Well, go ahead. Or shall I begin, as I arrived first?'

Half an hour later, Royce and Arden were still sitting on the trestle in earnest conversation. On the floor, a map of the lake had been drawn in the sawdust, with cubes of wood representing the boat-house, the island, Morgan's cottage, and Herons' Hall with its two lodges.

Royce gave a groan. 'And the awful thing is, she thinks she's in love with me!' he said. 'I get notes from her every day. She sends them by the chauffeur or one of the gardeners – not Morgan, I'm thankful to say. I never know when they're going to arrive. That's one of the reasons I stick down here. I dread to see them approaching. But they find me out – and I'm sure they all know. Even Winifred does: I can see by the way she tosses her head when she sees me. And as for Billy and that wretched Gabb girl he's going around with, they giggle together for hours in the summer-house, and I'm convinced it's over me.' He turned to Arden anxiously. 'Does Mother know? I simply daren't go near her in case she starts in on me. She's had one or two shots already...'

'I don't know,' said Arden. 'She hasn't said anything to me. She's worried about you, but I don't think it has anything to do with Mrs Gabb.' Arden gave the name a slightly malicious emphasis. 'I think she's chiefly worried by your queer behaviour and the attitude of the police.'

'Oh yes, I see.' said Royce. 'Well, honestly, Arden, I'm less worried by the police than by – *her*. I'm afraid she wants to get a divorce out of Basil – she as good as says so – and she's going to play up her affair with me for all she's worth. Not that he has any real grounds, you know. I didn't follow her that night. I rushed out of the house partly because of you, partly because of Giles – and the rest just came about.'

'Where exactly *did* you go?' said Arden inquisitively.

'You swear you won't tell?'

'Oh, don't be so silly! It's bound to come out. You might as well tell me, then I shan't look conspiratorial if I'm asked. I always like my lies to have a solid basis of truth, as I told you once before.'

Royce described his midnight excursion with Pauline. 'I was a fool,' he said. 'Not that anything really happened; but if she says it did, just to get a divorce out of Basil, where am I then?'

'Then you're not in love with her?'

'In love with her! I loathe her!' shouted Royce. 'That is, I'll regard her as a dear, dear friend if only she'll let me off and stop pestering me. But if she goes on as she is doing, there'll be another murder.'

'Shut up!' said Arden. 'There's someone coming. – Look here, I think I can get you out of this without bloodshed if you'll do as I say. Or rather, leave it to me. But if you hear I've announced our engagement, you must back me up. Don't worry: I'll stage a quarrel later and let you off; you don't even need to buy a ring. It'll all be very secret – but I'll see it reaches the ears of the fair Pauline.'

Royce turned a bright crimson. He opened his mouth to speak, but before he could collect his thoughts sufficiently, Billy appeared grinning in the doorway.

'Come on, break it up!' he said. 'That policeman's here again.'

Royce got up slowly. 'For me?'

'No, not for you – for Arden. Come along, sister.'

Arden got up and went away. Royce sat down on the trestle again and held his head in his hands. Billy approached him, concerned.

'I say!' he said awkwardly. 'Aren't you letting this business get on your nerves? Hadn't you better snap out of it? Why not come down with us to the lake? We aren't allowed to take the boats out, but we're going to try a bit of spinning from the bank, or perhaps in the home pool. Come along! It'll do you a world of good.'

Royce shook his head.

Billy lingered for a while, but getting no further response, went away.

21

Hubert stood waiting in the pathway as Arden came along. Arden was sauntering, and humming to herself, and once she paused to pinch some green-fly off one of the roses. When she came up to him, she greeted him with her sweetest smile.

'Oh, hullo, Hubert! How nice of you! I suppose you've come to protect us all?'

Hubert, taken aback by her unexpected friendliness, answered with less than his usual aplomb. 'Your mother wants William and myself to watch your interests. I hope you'll allow me to, Arden.'

'Why, of course, Hubert, if you think it's necessary. As a matter of fact, I was hoping to see you before you went. I wanted you to do something for *me*. Can you spare me a minute? Let's sit down here.' She moved to a rustic seat under a rose arbour, and invited him to join her.

Hubert followed rather dubiously. He was a little afraid of Arden, because of her old appeal for him, which was not quite dead. He was very much afraid of Madeleine, who could and would make his life extremely uncomfortable if she thought that there was any recrudescence of this love affair. Already he envisaged great difficulty in making her believe that his interest in the problems of this family was purely professional. He would have to send his brother William next time.

'It's only a small thing,' she was saying, 'and yet it's something none of us can do. *You* would be the ideal person.'

'Anything I can do,' said Hubert without conviction. 'But do you think you ought to keep the Superintendent waiting?'

Arden took no notice. 'It's about Royce,' she said. 'If you're looking after his interests, I think there's one thing you ought to know.'

Hubert raised his eyebrows. Arden seemed full of mystery, yet there was no trace of anxiety in her manner. 'My dear Arden! Do be careful what you say to the police, won't you? In fact, I don't think, if you have any new information about Royce's movements, you ought to see the Superintendent now at all. I think you ought to consult William first.'

'Oh, don't worry about the Superintendent,' said Arden. 'I can manage him all right. What I want *you* to do is to go and see Mrs Basil Gabb, and warn her off.'

'Warn her off, Pauline? What on earth has *she* got to do with it?'

'A good deal. Don't you know that on the night before Giles was shot, Royce and she went for a drive together in Harry Gabb's car, and didn't get back till five next morning?'

'Well, yes, your aunt has just been telling me something about that. But I don't see—'

'And don't you know that while Royce has been doing everything he can, including arousing everybody's suspicions, by trying to protect *her* good name, she is doing everything she can to drag him into a divorce suit?'

Hubert said incredulously, 'But why should she want to do that? She's comfortable enough with Basil. And now that Giles is dead—'

'It appears,' said Arden, 'that she thinks herself violently in love with Royce. I gathered from all Royce told me that she will go to any lengths to get rid of Basil: she's sick to death of him, and if he won't give her a divorce, she'll drag Royce into it and make Basil divorce her.'

'And Royce?' said Hubert.

'Royce doesn't want to marry her. He wants to marry me. He only went off with Mrs Gabb that night because he had had a quarrel with me and thought I was going to marry Giles. – Now you see how it is. I want you to go and see Pauline and put it to her – tactfully, of course – that there's nothing doing. Make her see that if she gets rid of Basil now, she'll be left high and dry, because Royce can't marry her. Tell her he's engaged to be married to me, and make out that I'm the kind of female who won't let a man go, once she's got her talons into him. You can embroider the story with your own narrow escape, Hubert dear. *I* don't mind.' She laughed sweetly, and laid a hand on his arm.

Hubert answered constrainedly: 'I'm glad, Arden – glad about you and Royce, I mean… I suppose you won't announce the engagement yet awhile, until this business is cleared up?'

'There isn't any engagement,' said Arden, getting up. 'It's just the quickest way of getting rid of Pauline. Make it a secret marriage if you think it would be better. I've told Royce not to deny any of it. – Well, good-bye for the present. Good luck!'

She sauntered away, leaving Hubert sitting in the rose-arbour, staring after her in dismay.

Mallett eyed Arden keenly as she came into the room. He wondered if she would prove to be truthful or a liar, accommodating or hostile. It was his habit, when beginning an interview, to try to make a lightning guess at the character of the person before him, and later to compare his guess with the results. His lightning judgment on Miss Laforte was that she was by nature truthful, but that she would prove an equally dauntless liar if she believed it to be necessary. It remained for him, therefore, to convince her that it was not necessary. She must, however, be a cool hand, since if Morgan's evidence meant what it seemed to mean, she must have been the first to find Giles's body in the boat-house; and she had said nothing. She had not even run away home, but had coolly moored her boat beside the others, and gone back to Herons' Hall, to create the appearance of having never left her room.

Mallett held out his hand. 'I knew your father slightly,' he said, 'though he wasn't much at the Hall. And quite recently I've been re-reading his book.'

'Have you?' said Arden. 'He wasn't as bad as he sounded, you know. Actually, he was the soul of kindness, and I don't believe he ever hurt a living thing, except according to the laws of sport. It was just that he had a blind spot. We have it too: his children, I mean.'

'Really?' said Mallett, surprised.

'Oh yes. When you're blooded as young as we were, and taught the technique of hunting, you can't *feel* sensitive about killing things, however much you may decide to *think* it's wrong. That was at the bottom of the quarrel between me and Giles, you know.'

'I gather he had moments when he reacted violently against blood-sports,' said Mallett. He drew up a chair opposite hers, in front of the French window. 'The copy of your father's book I read was one which I found in Giles's study – and it was heavily annotated.'

Arden nodded. 'You see, he couldn't cure himself of feeling violently on the subject, though he thought his feelings were sentimental, or even hypocritical, and tried to get over them. To him, we and everything about us stood for something he hated – and envied. He vented his rage on my father's book, I suppose, as he sometimes vented it on me.'

Mallett nodded sympathetically.

'I was terribly sorry for him,' she said. 'I sympathized with him, though I couldn't *feel* the same. And then, he was cursed with this inventive genius – and with being the son of a man who made guns. Sometimes I thought the conflict in his mind would really drive him mad. I thought he'd commit suicide. Superintendent, are you quite sure he didn't?'

Mallett nodded again. 'Yes, quite sure. Mind you, Miss Laforte, you're right in thinking he might have done so. Did he ever threaten suicide to you?'

'Only in a general way, when I wouldn't agree to marry him. I didn't really flatter myself I would be the cause, though. What makes *you* think he might have done so?'

'I'll tell you,' said Mallett, 'in confidence, for the moment: he left a diary. It was written in a very minute shorthand, and carefully hidden. It supports what you say of the mental torment he was going through.'

Arden drew in her breath sharply. 'Where is the diary now?'

'Still in the hands of the police.'

'Will anyone else be allowed to see it?'

'It will be returned eventually to his father.'

'And yet you say you're sure he didn't commit suicide, Super-intendent?'

Mallett paused, and decided that the moment had come to overthrow Arden's defences. 'Yes, quite sure,' he repeated, 'and so are you, Miss Laforte. And we both have the same reason.'

He paused, but no question came. Arden was staring out into the garden, her chin resting on her clasped hands. She did not alter her position, but he saw her knuckles whiten suddenly. He leaned forward:

'What made *you* decide, when you found Giles's body in the boat-house that morning, that he had been murdered?'

Again he paused, but still she did not answer.

'You did so decide, didn't you?' he went on. 'If you'd thought it was suicide, you would have given the alarm at once. But you knew it was murder, didn't you, when you saw the body there propped up with a shot-gun, the body of a man who had been killed with a rifle? So you went back to Herons' Hall and said nothing.' Mallett shifted in his seat. 'You're a brave girl, Miss Laforte. But it's always a mistake to try to shield people. In nine cases out of ten, you merely succeed in drawing down suspicion on to the head of the very person you're trying to protect.'

There was another pause. 'Why don't you think *I* shot him, then?' said Arden at last. 'Or do you, perhaps?'

Mallett shook his head. 'For two reasons: first, you had a boat: you were out on the lake in one of the two rowing-boats. But the murderer had none, and needed one. Second, you probably wouldn't have been strong enough to lift Giles's body from the rowing-boat into the motor-boat, even if you'd wanted to.'

'So if one was on the lake in a boat, that seems to you a proof of innocence?'

'So far as I can see at present, yes.'

'Then if the canoe was out on the lake at the same time, you'd say whoever was in it was cleared of suspicion too?'

'Yes, I think so. It was the fact that the other two craft were not there that caused the murderer to go to the trouble of lifting the body from one boat to the other. You were in the other rowing-boat; your cousin Royce Charleroy was in the canoe, wasn't he? Now will you please describe to me without wasting any more of our good time – yours or mine – exactly what your movements were between, say, five and seven that morning, and as much of your cousin's as you observed?'

It was five o'clock in the morning. Arden lay in bed and wondered why she had been such a fool as to come back into this house, now that it belonged to strangers. All along, she had been against returning, even to live in the South Lodge, pleasant though that was, and suited to their means. But she could not think of a powerful enough reason for refusing; and since Aunt Helen seemed so keen on it, why should she oppose her, when all she felt was a disinclination, at the back of which was the slightest trace of fear? Yes, she admitted, when the boys pressed her, that it would be good not to live in a suburb, a modern villa with a patch of lawn ruled round with flower-beds; good to have Herons' Mere to fish in, if the new owner proved accommodating; good to be surrounded by trees and fields, and perhaps to have the run of their own gardens again. So Arden gave way, with scarcely a protest. She was by nature rather lazy, unless deeply concerned; she would not use all her considerable force of character unless she was convinced of what she wanted. And the trouble was, she was not quite sure.

So they had come; and the inevitable had happened: they had met the new people. It seemed to Arden that she had foreseen it all: that there would be curiosity, chance meetings in the woods and on the lake path, conversations, then visits to the house by Giles. There would be a Giles, and he would fall in love with her. It was all so neat, such a fitting way to end the story of their exile, that she should retrieve the family seat by marrying the new son and heir. It might all have been arranged by Aunt Helen herself. But unfortunately, Arden did not and never could love Giles. She understood his strange and difficult character; she appreciated his genius, and saw all too clearly that it was 'to madness near allied'; but she would have married old Morgan the gardener sooner than Giles. And as his passion for her increased like a raging fire, so she shrank away – not visibly, but in her mind. At first she had thought that his curious hatred of her father and all his kind would be transferred to her; but she soon saw that his gusts of fury against her and the nature she was born with merely served to fan the flames. *Odi el amo*: never was there a man to whom that applied more truly.

And now she had to face the situation and end it. What a task! But last night had been too much altogether. First there had been Royce's stupid behaviour with Mrs Basil Gabb, then his still more stupid outburst in Arden's room; then her own idiotic impulse to annoy Royce still further, to pay him out by a night's misapprehension for having annoyed her during the evening. And then there was the utter bad luck of Giles's interruption. What a ridiculous situation! There she and Royce had been seen standing like a pair of fools, hand in hand. She could never say to Giles, 'We are cousins, almost brother and sister. He's always in and out of my room, just like Billy.' And anyhow, as she had never given Giles any right to control her behaviour, no explanation was called for. Yet the tableau rankled in her memory. She had wanted to tell Giles calmly and kindly that she couldn't marry him, that she could only be his friend: all difficult enough to say in any circumstances. But now, Giles would merely think that she had been flirting with him. He had behaved with considerable dignity. He had kept his temper in front of her, and his cool improvised excuse for coming to her door had been conveyed with perfect calm.

What happened afterwards had not been so good, though. She had heard their voices raised, his and Royce's, on the stairs. She had heard him order Royce out of the house, and her blood had boiled with indignation. He, one of the intruders, ordering Royce out of what had been his own home! The impudence of it took her breath away – until she remembered that it was perfectly legitimate, that it was they who were now the intruders. An easy way lay open, by which she could get back the right of admission for them all to Herons' Hall, and even avenge herself on Giles some day, maybe... But she could not take that way. No. To-morrow morning she would leave this house and never set foot in it again. They would all go away, abroad, to Italy, somewhere where one could live cheaply in lovely surroundings. Aunt Helen must be persuaded. But first of all, she would keep her appointment with Giles.

The sound of Royce's footsteps running down the stairs had scarcely died away when she heard voices again: Giles's, and this time a girl's. It did not take Arden long to realize that this was Giles's cousin Lucy, and that she was reproaching him for treating her badly, for going off with 'that Laforte girl.' She could hear Giles answering occasionally in low monosyllables, trying first to quieten her, then angrily repulsing her. She heard the final declaration... The encounter had lasted a few minutes only. Silence reigned in the corridor. A door closed. Outside, raindrops pattered from the leaves of the trees. There was the sound of a car being started, some distance away. The sound receded...

'So,' continued Arden, 'after what had happened the evening before, I decided I would meet Giles down by the lake, as we had arranged in the first place. And there and then I would explain to him that the best plan would be to marry his cousin and keep Herons' Hall in the family: that I was quite sure he and I would never know a moment's happiness if we lived together. I thought it would be easy to say all this in the cold light of morning; and then I would go straight home and never go near Herons' Hall again.

'So I got up and dressed. I crept down quietly in my stockinged feet, because I had left my Wellingtons downstairs the evening before. I wondered if I would find them still there, and what I would do if I didn't, or if I couldn't find the boys' boots either. In our day, all the boots were collected from the cloak-room and taken down to the kitchen to be cleaned, and then put in the bedrooms; but this wasn't a sporting household luckily, and I found the boots all there, just as we had left them. All, that is, except Giles's pair. I thought it likely that he had taken them and gone down to the lake already. I felt rather mean creeping about the house before anyone else was about, and yet there was a queer feeling of familiarity about it all: I had done it so often before, when we were at home.

'Well, I opened the front door and set out. The morning was as you'd expect after a heavy thunderstorm. It was quite still, there was water everywhere, and branches and twigs from the trees. The mist was thick on the park, and I couldn't see the boat-house until I was about twenty or thirty yards away. When I arrived, I found the door open, and one of the rowing-boats gone; so I knew Giles had arrived. I wondered if perhaps I had better wait for him there at the boat-house. But I began to feel damp and cold; so I decided I'd take the second boat and row after him. It was getting light, but visibility was much too bad for shooting, so I assumed he would have gone to the fishing-ground: that's what we call the deep part at the end of the lake, where the biggest pike are.'

'You didn't think he might have gone to the island?' said Mallett.

'It did cross my mind; but I didn't see why he should want to. He only went across to the island to readjust the target or reckon up his score after practising from the bank; and he had been there the day before. Anyhow, I thought he'd be sure to come on to the fishing-ground, and that would be the best place to find him. So I rowed round the lake on the south side, keeping fairly close to the bank because I didn't want to be enveloped in the mist, which was quite thick in the middle of the lake, but was clearing up on the edges.'

'What time did you reach the boat-house, do you think?' said Mallett.

'Oh, about twenty to six, I should say.'

'And you rowed round to the west end of the lake, and did not find Giles. What then?'

'Well, then, after waiting a few minutes, I began to feel cold again. I decided perhaps he had gone round on the other side, or even perhaps on to the island after all. So I struck across the lake in the direction of the island. As I was cutting across, I heard what sounded like a rifle-shot—'

'Only one?'

'Only one, yes. So I thought Giles must be on the other bank aiming at the target, though I couldn't imagine how he could see even that far in the mist.'

'What time would that be?'

'Let me see: I should say about fifteen to twenty minutes after I left the boat-house. It must have been nearly six by then. The mist was thinning considerably now that the sun had risen. I was just thinking of changing my direction and rowing round the island to the other side of the lake when I was surprised to see my cousin Royce going by, paddling the canoe. He didn't see me. He too was making for the fishing ground. I slipped in under one of the alders on the island, and watched him disappear. Then, as he didn't come back again, I pushed out, rowed back a little way – and to my surprise I saw he had tied up the canoe to a branch and gone away. I realized then that he had taken the canoe to save himself the trouble of walking all the way round the lake; and I thought it was rather cool, to borrow what was now the Gabbs' canoe, not ours, and leave it there to be found by one of them to put away, just so that he could get home a quarter of an hour sooner and have breakfast. I wondered where he had spent the night. I knew Giles had turned him out of the house, and I had thought he would go straight home; but obviously he wouldn't have been about at that time in the morning unless something odd had happened.

'I decided that I would make good the liberty he had taken with the canoe. I rowed across, untied it, took it in tow, and made for the boat-house. By now I was thoroughly cold, depressed and hungry. I didn't care whether I met Giles or not, and I decided I wouldn't wait for him if I didn't see him on my way back, but would go straight home to breakfast…'

She paused. 'I think you know what I found in the boat-house, Superintendent. It was a terrible shock to me. You see, as I was rowing in, as soon as I got into the channel, just before you reach the boat-house doors, I just shipped my oars and drifted. I didn't look behind me. It wasn't until I had tied my own boat to the ring and stood up, that there in the motor-launch, leaning forward, I saw him propped up by the gun.'

'The first rowing-boat was back in its place, of course?'

'Yes. I had to step into it to get across.'

'What time was it by now?'

'Well, I had hung about a good bit, watching Royce, then waiting to see if he would come back, then rowing over to the fishing-ground, then taking the canoe in tow. It must have been not far short of half-past six by now. The sun was up, and the mist was clearing fairly quickly. I could just see the island from where I stood.'

'So at least half an hour had passed between your hearing the rifle-shot and finding Giles?'

'Yes, I should think so.'

'What did you do then?'

'I ran to see if I could do anything for him. I saw at once he was dead. My first thought was suicide – and it fitted so well with all I knew of Giles that for a minute I didn't use my eyes. Then I looked again at the wound in his temple, and I saw that he was leaning on a double-barrelled shot-gun, an ordinary 12-bore.'

'And then you realized it was murder.'

'Yes.'

'And you also realized that the man who had passed you on the lake was your cousin Royce Charleroy, and that he had, the night before, had a violent quarrel with the deceased?'

'Yes.'

'It didn't strike you as odd that he should have taken the canoe after shooting Giles, and left it at the other end of the lake to provoke inquiries? Surely that was a stupid thing to do, for a man wanting to avoid attention?'

'I didn't think very hard at the time. I was merely terrified. The only thing I could think of doing was to avoid being asked questions myself, if possible, and leave everything as it had been before. I unmoored the rowing-boat I had been using, and pulled the canoe in behind it. Then I tied my boat up again and closed the doors over the lake. My one object was to get back into the house without being seen. I hated the thought of going back to the Hall, more than I can ever say; but I felt it was the only way to avoid getting implicated, and having to admit what I'd seen. Luckily it was Sunday morning, otherwise I might have met old Mr Gabb setting out on his morning walk. As it was, I was in the house and back in my room by seven, and no one saw me. I waited there until the hue and cry began. Then I fetched my brother, and told him we'd better clear out. He would insist on going to Royce's room, and of course he was astonished to find that Royce hadn't slept there, unless he'd made his own bed, which wasn't likely. However, I told him some cock-and-bull story about the maid having been in there already, and I got him away before he could find anyone and begin asking questions... Since then, I've been acting ignorance, concealing information from the police, and telling various lies.'

Mallett knocked out his pipe on the step. 'A waste of talent,' he said. 'From what you say, I should judge your cousin must have been half-way across the lake when the shot was fired. And luckily, your evidence is corroborated by Morgan, a somewhat less partial witness.'

He was about to heave himself up out of his chair when there was a sound of excited voices outside; and in a moment Billy Laforte and Jessica Gabb appeared in the doorway.

'I say, Superintendent, look here!' Billy held out under Mallett's astonished eyes a rifle, thick with lake mud and hung with green lake weeds.

Mallett pushed back his chair. 'Where did you get this?'

'Just outside the channel, down by the boat-house.' The two told their tale conjointly, interrupting one another and turning from Mallett to Arden and back again. 'We went down there hoping to get a boat out. There seems no special reason why we shouldn't now, does there? After all, I mean, it can't do poor Giles any good, our all making ourselves miserable indefinitely, can it?' Billy turned piously to Jessica for assent.

'The boat-house was locked,' continued Jessica, 'and there was no one about, not even a policeman, and it was too much trouble to go back to the house and ask. So we thought we'd try from the bank near by.'

'I am teaching her to spin,' said Billy proudly. 'She's quite good at it already. She used to have views, you know, and all that, but when I explained that the pike eat the trout and—'

'Oh, never mind that!' cut in Jessica impatiently. 'Anyway, he was teaching me to spin, and I was getting on all right, except when I didn't reel in quickly enough and the spinner sank and got caught in the weeds. However, we managed to get it clear each time...'

'And then,' interrupted Billy, 'I was getting her to make longer and longer casts, across from one bank to the other: you know the place, Arden, just where the channel begins to broaden out. You stand on the concrete ledge on one side and cast right out under the opposite bank. I knew there was a pike lying up under the edge, but it was a bit weedy and she wasn't always fast enough; so at last I took the rod from her just to show her again—'

'And he cast,' said Jessica, 'beautifully, right under the bank. I felt I could do it all right myself then, so I tried, and I cast, and it went just where his had. But when I came to reel in, the beastly spinner had gone down to the bottom and stuck fast. And I couldn't move it at all—'

'So I shouted to her to leave it alone,' said Billy, 'and I ran round the boat-house to the other side, while she kept the line taut. I stuck my arm down into the water and into the mud; and I felt something hard...'

Mallett had been listening with only half an ear as he examined the result of their fishing. 'And my men are supposed to have dredged this channel,' he said disgustedly.

'Oh, but you'd never have found it if it hadn't been for us,' Billy assured him. 'It was right close to the bank, just where the old pike lies, and smothered in mud and weeds.'

Mallett looked up. 'Well, keep this find to yourself,' he said. 'Miss Gabb, do you know if your father is at the house or at the works?'

'I'm sorry,' said Jessica, 'I haven't been near the house since breakfast.'

Mallett called for brown paper and string, and tied up the rifle in a nondescript-looking-parcel. A car was waiting for him outside. He was driven quickly to Herons' Hall; but Simon Gabb was not there. A telephone call confirmed that he was still at the works. And Mr Basil? Yes, Mr Basil was there too.

'Back to the Station, Robins,' said Mallett, 'as quick as you can. We're picking up some exhibits and going on to Broxeter.'

As the car swung out of the drive gates, Mallett, glancing round, saw Hubert Olivier coming towards the North Lodge. He told Robins to stop, and called out:

'Want a lift back to Broxeter, Olivier?'

Hubert shook his head. 'No, thanks. I'm going in here.' He indicated the small coupé standing outside. 'My wife's car; and my own's further back. *Embarras de richesse!*' He laughed.

'Right.' Mallett waved the police car on. He wondered on what mission Olivier was going to the North Lodge while Basil was away. The fellow seemed to be everywhere, these days.

22

'You are absolutely sure of that?'

Three men – Mallett, Simon Gabb, and Basil – confronted Challoner, the foreman of the small arms factory; but under their concentrated gaze he did not waver. He was a short stocky man with stubby black hair, and black eyes with an intensely serious expression; it was easy to see why Simon Gabb had said that he was completely to be trusted. They were interviewing him in Simon Gabb's untidy office, filled with the documents of many years: yellowing papers, blue prints, odd pieces of metal pushed on to shelves and forgotten.

'Absolutely, sir,' said Challoner. Before him on Simon's desk lay the two rifles, one from the lake and one from the island.

'You are prepared to swear that they are identical?'

'In design, sir, yes.'

'And that this one' – he pointed to the second rifle which was still dim with lake mud – 'has been copied from this?'

'Yes in so far as they could. It's copied in all essentials. In fact, it's copied in every detail, but the material and the workmanship are inferior. I should guess that it had been carried out by some small firm that didn't have the best tools. Still, it's a very serviceable weapon.' He picked it up and took imaginary aim.

'And the original is definitely the one you made for Giles Gabb, to his specification and design.'

'Yes.'

'You say it was unique? The fact that this second rifle resembles it is no coincidence?'

'That's impossible, sir.' Challoner fixed his solemn black eyes on Mallett. 'You see, Mr Giles was constantly experimenting, the last couple of years, with new ideas for rifles and cartridges. Like everyone else, he wanted a longer range and a flatter trajectory – therefore an increased muzzle velocity. He was trying to work up a muzzle velocity of three thousand five hundred feet per second, or more. He used a standard calibre barrel of small bore, for the sake of economy; but he was experimenting with all the other parts: the breech-bolt, the rifling, the shape of the bullet, the composition of the charge. This one, for instance' – he broke the breech and looked down the barrel with screwed-up eye – 'this one has a shallow rifling, six grooves of two to one section, twisting once per spiral of twelve inches. The cartridge—'

'Can you show us one of the cartridges?' interrupted Mallett.

'I'm sorry, sir, I can't. We only made a couple of gross specially for Mr Giles, and he took them away with him. I haven't even got the specification. But I can tell you they were of the stream-line or boat-tail pattern, developed to an even greater degree than the current types. Personally I didn't agree. I said to Mr Giles, "With a small-bore rifle like that, and your bullet sharpened at both ends like a shuttle, what's going to happen? Your bullet'll have such penetrating force, it'll go right through your man and out the other side; and unless you get him through the head or the heart, you'll be no better off. You'll be letting the light through him, that's all.'

Challoner gazed round at them as if expecting all sensible men to concur. His solemn face expressed no shadow of realization of the meaning behind his words. To him, as a gunsmith, men were simply the target for the rifle.

'But Mr Giles wouldn't listen,' he went on. 'He was all for distance and speed. He said, 'We must eliminate head-resistance: therefore we must have a fine point. We must eliminate tail-drag: therefore we must have a cut-away tail. I'm trying for long-distance accuracy, Challoner. I'm trying to make a rifle such that no allowance for distance will have to be made up to half a mile. Therefore at short distance it'll be foolproof. What does it matter if your bullet sometimes goes through a man, provided you can get him on the exact spot you want to up to two hundred yards, and hit him at any distance you can see over? A man isn't like an elephant: there are very few places where you can plug a hole in a man and not do vital damage.' Well, I saw his reasoning, of course, and I made the cartridges as he said. How he came off with them, I don't know. But one thing's certain: Mr Giles would never have been satisfied. Sooner or later he'd have been back here with some new idea, and the old one would have been scrapped again.'

'So you made this to Mr Giles's design. Now tell me: did the design or specification ever leave your possession while you were working on it?'

'No, sir, never once. Mr Giles was most particular about that.'

'What happened to it at night?'

'Mr Giles took it away with him. He wouldn't even trust it in the safe. He was coming every day to the works at that time; and he took the plans away at night and brought them back in the morning.'

'But someone else must have worked on it beside you?'

'Oh yes, several men, naturally. But none of them knew what he was doing, if you understand me. Nobody except myself knew the whole design. They were just told, " Get out a bullet-casing of this pattern," and given the material. Another fellow made me a small quantity of nickel alloy. Another man did the rifling of the barrel as specified. This required special machine tools, which were separately made. So they none of them knew what each part was for, and couldn't have made use of it.'

'Then whoever copied this rifle must have had the whole design and specification before him? He couldn't have pieced it together from information got from separate workmen?'

An expression that might have been Challoner's substitute for a smile crossed over his face. 'I reckon I would have seen a fellow going round asking all those questions,' he said. 'No, sir, it just couldn't be done. Whoever made this copy must have got the design from Mr Giles.'

'You don't think Mr Giles got some other firm to make it, by way of experiment?'

'Why should he?' said Challoner. 'Why should he go out of his way to let another firm into his secret, and pay money besides, just to get an inferior job of work done, when all he had to do was to give his orders here?'

'You're right,' said Mallett. 'Well, Mr Gabb,' he said to Simon, rising, 'this confirms my original impression, that the theft of the design was an inside job – inside your own household, that is. It must have been done by someone who had access to your son's study – who "borrowed" the design and then returned it, after having taken a copy; and who then employed some man working in a small way, say the owner of a repairs garage or something of the kind, which would give cover to any other illegal business. We shall have to comb the neighbourhood, and farther afield. – Now there's one thing, Mr Gabb—'

There was a tap on the door, and James Gabb entered.

'Excuse me,' he said, crossing the room to speak to Basil. He showed Basil a grimy-looking card. 'There's a man in your office who says he has an appointment with you.'

Basil took the card and went out.

Simon said to Mallett:

'You remember my brother, Superintendent. He's been here since the day after Giles was shot. He's kept his eyes and ears open, and he says there's absolutely no reason to suspect any leakage from the works, so far as the men or Challoner are concerned. He has checked over the references *et cetera* of every man employed in the small arms factory, and his opinion confirms my own.'

'That's so,' said James. 'In all cases where there could possibly be access to any confidential data, they've been here for years, and we know all of them personally. And wherever there could be any doubt, any man recently taken on, in fact any man of less than five years' standing, I've gone into his record, and satisfied myself in every way. – What's this?' he said, catching sight of the deed-box, which together with the two rifles stood on Simon's desk. 'Isn't that Father's old deed-box? I haven't seen that for many years.'

He went up to it and ran his hands lovingly over the highly-polished walnut surface and the inlaid brass fittings. 'This brings back some old memories, doesn't it?' he said to Simon. 'You know,' he went on, turning to Mallett, 'our father used to keep all the certificates in here – birth, marriage and death – and the grave receipts and even his IOU's.' He laughed. 'I remember how I used to wish I could have it for myself one day. But of course my brother here got it, being the eldest.'

'Ah yes,' said Simon. 'Well, you could have had it if I'd known. It wasn't much use to me. It was pushed away on one of the shelves here for many years; then it got moved into Basil's office, to make more room. Then finally I think Giles took it away, to keep his papers in at home. He'd have done better to get a good safe put in. They're not much use, those old things.'

'The outer lock isn't much good,' interposed Mallett. 'But there's a secret compartment. Did you know?'

Simon and James both looked surprised. 'Now you mention it,' said James, 'I do seem to have heard Father say something about it.'

Mallett inserted a key in the elaborate-looking lock. 'This part is easy,' he said, opening the box. 'I was able to open it, when I found it on the island, with one of my bunch of keys. But unless you knew about the secret compartment, I don't suppose you'd find it. That is, I suppose you wouldn't try.'

He inserted his pen-knife in the groove round the pen-tray, found the catch, and lifted up the tray, revealing the hidden space. 'I brought this along here,' he said, 'because I wanted to find out who owned it originally. I found it on the island, and at first I decided to leave it there, in case whoever was after Giles's secret went back; but he didn't. Presumably he either had all he wanted, or thought it would be too dangerous. So I sent a man over to collect the box, and here it is. The people at the South Lodge assured me it was not the property of the late Colonel, so I reckoned it must be yours. You say it belonged to your father, Mr Gabb, and then to you? It was left here and moved to your son's office, and later taken away by Giles?'

He was noting these facts down in his note-book when the door opened and Basil re-entered. 'It was nothing,' he said irritably to his uncle. 'Some fellow wanting work.'

'I'm sorry,' said James. 'I thought his card said—'

'Just a trick to get an interview,' said Basil. 'Hullo, what's this?' He glanced at Mallett. 'You got it open?' He bent curiously over the deed-box and studied the mechanism of the, hidden spring-clip.

'Did *you* know about it?' said Mallett quickly.

'Oh yes,' said Basil. 'Giles discovered it one day.' He turned to his father. 'You remember, it used to be in here, then you moved it to my office. Giles found it there one day when he was prowling round; and you know his passion for taking things to pieces. He said he'd heard Grandfather say there was a secret compartment. He tapped it and tried the various joins, and after a bit he found the clip. Then he said he'd like to have it in his study at home. So I said "all right," and he took it away.'

'When was this?' said Mallett.

'I don't remember exactly. About six months ago, I suppose.'

'I see. Well, gentlemen, thank you for all your help. I don't think there's anything more I can ask you at the moment. The next thing is to find the man who made that second rifle – and the man he made it for. I'll send an officer to collect these. Good day.'

23

Hubert, when he reached the North Lodge on the mission entrusted to him by Arden, was surprised and a little dismayed to see his wife's coupé standing before the gates. Ordinarily he would have thought nothing of it. Madeleine and Pauline were old friends; they had been at school together, and now that marriage had brought both of them to this district, they saw a great deal of each other. Madeleine was apt to be jealous of Pauline. She considered herself much cleverer, if not more attractive, for she was pretty, *petite* and shrewd, whereas Pauline was large, handsome and somewhat slow; therefore Madeleine could not help feeling that there was some unfairness in the fate that had allotted to Pauline a young if difficult husband, the son – the second son, it was true, but still, Basil's position was assured – of a man whose industry made millionaires; and to herself nobody better than Hubert, a professional man whose income, even if he were successful, could never amount to as many hundreds as the Gabbs made thousands.

Hubert knew all this, and knew that Madeleine thought she had done him a favour in marrying him; but he remembered the anxiety with which she had pursued him, her fear lest he should feel the pull of the old love irresistible; and he was content. He now had a piece of knowledge about Basil's wife that made him feel superior to Basil; but he did not intend to share his knowledge with Madeleine.

It was odd that she should contrive to be here at just this moment: she had an uncanny flair for news. Hubert wondered if his own visit to the Charleroys, of which he had not told her, had anything to do with it; and how he could contrive to get rid of her.

The maid who opened the door looked at him doubtfully; but when he gave his name, she seemed reassured.

'Mrs Gabb is not at home to anybody to-day,' she said. But Hubert brushed aside her hesitations:

'That's all right. My wife is with Mrs Gabb now.' He followed the girl to the drawing-room.

She tapped on the door and leaned her ear towards the panel as if knocking at a sick-room. Hubert hovered just behind her in the shadows. The maid tip-toed in and gave his name, in a whisper, apparently, for Hubert heard nothing from within until Pauline's voice said wearily:

'Oh yes, all right, show him in. And bring tea.'

Hubert entered, by now hypnotized into tip-toeing likewise. The curtains were partly drawn: the sick-room atmosphere grew more oppressive at every step. In the dim light he saw Pauline stretched out on a settee at the side of the fire, and Madeleine perched on a *pouf* beside her. Pauline had obviously been crying; her eyes were red, and she had to remove a damp lace handkerchief from one hand to the other in order to greet him. His wife did not seem surprised to see him.

'I rang up William,' she said, 'and he told me you were coming over to see Mrs Charleroy.' She turned to Pauline. 'Isn't it awful, my dear? He and William are going to have to spend all their spare time over this business, protecting these people's interests; and you know, they won't get a penny for it. Mrs Charleroy hasn't a bean, and if she had, she'd still expect Hubert to do it for love – wouldn't she, darling?'

She smiled up at Hubert with the touch of malice he expected whenever the family at the South Lodge was mentioned.

'Still,' she went on, 'I'm glad you came. I've been having a heart-to-heart talk with Pauline, and I want you to back me up. – You don't mind Hubert's knowing, do you?'

Pauline's shake of the head expressed resignation rather than consent. She knew that she could not prevent Madeleine from telling her husband. She hoped that if she conceded this, Madeleine would perhaps be satisfied, and refrain from telling the whole of Broxeter besides.

'You see, darling,' Madeleine continued in a voice rich with its load of scandal, 'Pauline has been behaving rather foolishly – in a way,' she added hastily, to forestall any rebellion on Pauline's part. 'On the night Giles was murdered, she went for a ride with Royce Charleroy. They didn't get back till five. And although nothing much *happened*, so she says—'

'It didn't,' interposed Pauline sulkily.

'Nevertheless, she felt she had fallen in love with him. And as she had to all intents and purposes spent the night with him, she thought she'd get Basil to give her a divorce.'

Hubert had been listening with only half an ear to the familiar story. Meanwhile, he had been watching Pauline, and it seemed to him that her whole attitude, her listless look, expressed a very genuine misery.

'Just a minute,' he interrupted. Madeleine's voice jarred on him, and he wanted to give Pauline as well as himself a moment's respite. 'If I might ask, Pauline,' he said in his gentlest tones, 'what was wrong between you and Basil? Was it recent, or—'

Pauline dabbed her nose with her small handkerchief. 'Oh, I don't know,' she said, 'I suppose I oughtn't to have married him, really. I realize now I wasn't in love with him at all.' Tears filled her fine grey eyes. 'I didn't know, then, what love was.' She turned away.

Hubert gave her a moment to recover. Her clumsiness, due to sincerity, gave his own heart a twist. 'Poor girl!' he thought; and then: 'How she will improve, after this!'

'But you haven't any specific complaint against him?' he persisted gently.

Pauline waved the sodden handkerchief. 'Oh, he has been very difficult lately! For one thing, he has been out such a lot, working at the office till all hours, and worried to death over these new contracts. Still, I blame myself mostly, if he has been queer. I suppose it was my fault, for egging him on – for complaining that he had no real position in the firm, unlike Giles, who was treated like a god, deferred to, able to come and go as he pleased, just because everyone thought he was a genius; whereas Basil, who was steady and dependable, couldn't take a half-day off without leave. I did sometimes rub that in, I'm afraid. As if it mattered!'

Hubert was silent. He understood her feelings very well. He knew that to her, who had fallen in love, ambition seemed now a petty unwanted ridiculous thing. No doubt, as the months went by, she would change her mind again, as he had done, and be the poorer for it... Madeleine's sharp voice broke in:

'But Pauline dear, you must remember, things are different now. After all, now that poor Giles has gone, Basil is the eldest son – the only son – and it's your duty to take up your position as the future mistress of Herons' Hall, if only for your child's sake. If you don't, somebody else will.'

Her voice was charged with significance. Hubert turned to look at her. 'Who?' he said sharply.

Madeleine bridled. 'Isn't it perfectly true,' she said, 'that Billy Laforte is running round all over the estate with the Gabb girl? Well, we know what that means, my dear!' She turned back to Pauline. 'That woman, his aunt, has her plans well laid. And now that Arden has lost her chance, she'll see to it that she plays her second string for all she's worth." She laughed.

Hubert grimaced at her insensitiveness; but he dared not protest when Arden's name was involved. Madeleine continued:

'You can't imagine the cleverness of that woman. Oh, I know! I've got good reason to. First she tried to get Hubert for herself, then for Arden.' She laid a hand on Hubert's arm. 'You were quite good enough for them then, my dear, when they still lived at the Hall. All she wanted then was a husband – for herself, or failing that, for Arden. But now she's out of the Hall, she'll never rest until she's got herself back again. She'll do it if she has to kill off poor old Polly Gabb and marry Simon herself. But meanwhile, she's been granted a marvellous windfall in the shape of Jessica.'

'I don't think *she* planned it,' deprecated Hubert.

'Maybe not,' snapped Madeleine, 'but there it is: a piece of luck, just as her only chance seemed gone. And what I say is, Pauline's a fool if she leaves Basil now. For one thing, Royce is only a boy, and quite unstable. You're several years older than he is, a married woman with a baby. Even if Basil did give you a divorce, I don't suppose Royce would marry you. And if he did, what future would there be for you? You couldn't live here.'

'There *are* other places,' muttered Pauline with unexpected insubordination.

'I know. But you need money – and where's it coming from? Your father would cut you off, you know he would. And Royce Charleroy couldn't keep you, not in the way *you're* used to. He couldn't keep you in silk stockings for a year. Do you know what I'd do if I were you? I'd go straight to Mr Gabb and insist on his turning them out of the South Lodge. Say you want it yourself. Say there are too many trees round this Lodge and it doesn't suit the baby. Anyway, get rid of them. You'll never be happy till you put all this foolishness on one side and become your old self again.'

Pauline bounced uneasily on the settee. 'I know you're right, Madeleine,' she said in a strained voice. 'I know it's all no good. It's just as well Basil wouldn't give me a divorce. And I do realize that the state of affairs between us is mostly my fault. If he's possessive and jealous, it's because he loves me. One does these awful things to other people when one loves them; and if they don't love one back, they feel – as I felt about Basil. I understand that now. And I'm going to do as you say. For one thing,' – she smiled wanly – 'I know just

one fact you don't know. I know why I couldn't have Royce, even if
I were free.'

Madeleine leaned forward in greedy anticipation. Hubert watched
Pauline and admired her.

'You see,' went on Pauline, 'actually he's madly in love with Arden
himself. He told me so – or rather I got it out of him, that famous night.
He was terribly upset: he had just heard that she was engaged to Giles.
Also he had had a row with Giles. Whether it was about her or not, he
didn't want to say; but Basil overheard it and he says it was. Anyway,
Royce told me enough to make it all quite clear. And since then—'

'Have you seen him since?' said Madeleine.

'Yes, just for a moment. He tried to avoid me, but I made him stop.
He was walking in the woods. He made me feel he absolutely hated me.'

'Why, whatever for?'

Pauline turned to look at her, as if seeing her for the first time. 'Don't
you understand? For making him go out with *me* and kiss *me*, when
actually he needn't have bothered – for he knew by now that Arden had
never been engaged to Giles at all. She lied to him that evening; and
when I met him, he was hating both of us: me for having caught him
in a weak moment, her for having made him entangle himself with me.
I've sent him several notes since then, asking him to forgive me, but I've
had no reply. Probably he tears them up and throws them away unread.'

'Maybe he does,' murmured Hubert.

'In my last one I told him not to worry: I'd given him up.' Her lips
trembled.

'Perhaps he didn't get it,' said Hubert. 'Write another one, and I'll
give it to him myself. By the way, did you tell the police any of this?'

'Yes,' said Pauline, 'most of it. I had to. Why?'

'Because I think Royce has been doing one thing for you, Pauline.
He may not be in love with you, but he's been trying to protect you.
He refused to tell the police anything about his movements that night;
and you see, his escapade with you didn't give him an alibi, if he left

you at five. But he didn't know you'd told them the story, and he's been behaving in a most suspicious manner, therefore, ever since.'

'I don't see that,' said Madeleine. 'I mean, I don't see he's so very noble in keeping it back, if it doesn't give him an alibi. If it did, now – but then he'd probably have told.'

'I don't think he would,' said Hubert. 'But the point is, if he accounted for his movements at all, he'd have had to have mentioned you. And he didn't. So the police sent for you.'

'I remember,' said Pauline, thinking of Royce rushing out of Giles's study, as red-eyed then as she was now. 'They don't suspect him, do they?'

'Nobody knows,' said Hubert. 'Somehow I don't think they do. You can see, though, can't you, that his quarrel with Giles, no doubt over Arden, and his leaving you at five, definitely brought him into the running. Therefore to behave suspiciously by refusing information for your sake was no small thing to do.'

Madeleine broke in impatiently. 'Oh, don't encourage her, Hubert!' she said, 'just when she's beginning to get over it! It's only an infatuation, anyway. I want her to make it up with Basil and forget about it as soon as ever she can.' She turned to Pauline. 'You say yourself everything Basil did was due to his love for you.'

Pauline went on quietly, speaking rather to Hubert than to Madeleine. 'There's one reason why I want to end this business, that I haven't told you.'

'Yes?' said Hubert. He recognized in her voice a new note of determination.

'Yes. The truth is, Hubert, I don't think it fair to Royce – or Basil – that it should go on any longer. In fact, if I could, I *would* get the Charleroys out of the South Lodge, just as Madeleine suggests – but not for the same reason.'

'Why then?' interposed Madeleine. 'What better reason could there be?'

'Because,' said Pauline slowly, 'if Basil meets Royce, there'll be trouble. I don't think Basil would seek him out; and as for Royce, he's hardly aware of Basil's existence. But suppose they meet—'

'But why?' persisted Madeleine. 'I thought you said you told Basil everything that happened.'

'I did. And it was a good thing I did, because I think he knew all along. I think he did follow me that night, and saw me get into the car with Royce, and saw us get out at the Lodge and go in together, and then come out again and go off in the car. He may even have been somewhere about when we came back next morning.'

'What makes you think so?' said Hubert.

'Well, partly the way he behaved when I saw him. He pretended to have come straight from the Hall; but his manner to me was quite savage, before he had heard a word of what I had to say. He questioned me – he almost attacked me – as if he knew the answers. Do you know what I mean? And if you knew Basil as well as I do, you'd know that that was most unlike him.'

'But you had been quarrelling the evening before,' objected Madeleine.

'Yes,' said Pauline, 'but usually, after one of those quarrels, he would have gone to the opposite extreme next day. He'd have been almost absurdly contrite, and afraid lest I'd taken what he'd said seriously, and anxious to make it up. I've never known him anything but over-repentant next morning. This time he was even more violent than the time before. And since then, from one or two remarks he let fall, I've come to the conclusion that he knew all about Royce and me and believed the worst. He certainly didn't believe me when I said Royce was not my lover; he merely said he wouldn't divorce me, and so I should be spared the humiliation of being turned down by a murderer. That was when he broke the news to me that Giles had been murdered. And to-day I made a discovery which bore out what I thought.'

She sat upright on the settee, for the first time abandoning her languid attitude, and put her feet on the ground.

'Yes,' she said, 'there can't be any other explanation. I went into his dressing-room to look for something; and in a corner of the wardrobe I found a blue suit of his, an old one rolled up into a bundle and pushed away. It was still damp smelling, absolutely musty, and beginning to grow mould inside. Now why should he hide it like that, if he hadn't been afraid I should see it and realize he'd been out in the rain that night, instead of over at the Hall, as he said?'

'How funny!' said Madeleine. 'What did you do with the suit?'

'I sent it to the cleaners – the Smart Service, in Broxeter, where I always go.'

'But wait a minute!' said Hubert. 'Wasn't he wearing a dinner-jacket that night?'

'Yes, of course,' said Pauline.

'And a coat too, surely,' said Madeleine.

'Yes,' said Pauline. 'He was wearing his light grey coat, I remember. He's had both of them cleaned since then. He told me he had taken them – at least, I asked him what had become of them and he said he had taken them himself.'

'Funny he didn't take the blue suit too,' said Madeleine. 'He must have forgotten.'

'Yes, but wait a minute,' persisted Hubert. 'What I want to know is, how did he get the blue suit soaked, if he was wearing a dinner-jacket at Herons' Hall?'

'Well, what I think is this,' said Pauline. She had forgotten her troubles, and her energy had returned. 'I think he followed me after the quarrel, and saw me meet Royce and take him into the Lodge. He waited outside, not wanting to break in on us, or perhaps wanting to see exactly how long Royce would stay. That's when he got the grey coat and the dinner-suit splashed with mud. Then when we left together, Basil must have gone in – the maid wouldn't hear him, she didn't hear us, she sleeps like a pig – and changed his wet clothes, just as I did. It was then he put on the old blue suit. Then he went out again – and again got wet, getting back to Herons' Hall.'

'But why should he go back to Herons' Hall?' objected Madeleine. 'Wasn't the natural thing for him to do to wait for you at home? Why should he turn out of his own house again, on an awful night like that?'

'Oh, just to catch me out in a series of lies, I suppose,' said Pauline. 'Basil is like that. All jealous people are. They'll put themselves to endless inconvenience to find out what will torment them to know; and even then they're not satisfied unless they can prove they've been deceived as well. Anyhow, it wasn't raining later: the rain had stopped before Royce and I left, I remember.'

'In that case,' said Hubert, 'how did he get wet at all, the second time?'

There was the sound of a car drawing up outside and turning into the garage. The three, whose heads had been conspiratorially close together, withdrew guiltily to their earlier positions. Pauline rang for more tea. Basil entered.

24

W hen Mallett got back to the police station, he found Fitzbrown still in his room, engrossed in the typed transcript of Giles's diary.

'You still poring over that?' said Mallett, as he directed the attendant constable to put the two rifles and the deed-box back on to the table.

'Yes,' answered Fitzbrown absently. 'Jones handed it over to me. He said it was interesting, but beyond him: borderline cases aren't his forte.'

Mallett sat down heavily and took out his pipe. 'Interesting, yes,' he said, 'as revealing the man's state of mind. If he had committed suicide, it would have given the reporters a wonderful opportunity for quotation. But he didn't commit suicide. He was shot. And I can see nothing in this journal that gives any clue as to any person he was afraid of.'

Fitzbrown looked up. 'I don't know about that,' he demurred. 'He was aware that somebody was after his secret. Unfortunately the notes only go back to the middle of April, but he seems to have been uneasy even then. Listen to this:

'*Apr. 18th*. Just as I thought: somebody has been at my desk again. Luckily all plans and diagrams on me, except the ones already destroyed. Must try something else.'

'That's rational enough, anyway,' said Mallett.

'Yes,' said Fitzbrown. 'That's why it's so startling to come across sudden lapses – land-slides as it were, or what's that term they use in geology when horizontal strata show a vertical break, so that the lines of deposit, instead of running continuously and sweetly in their parallels, suddenly are all out of alignment?'

'A fault, isn't it?' said Mallett.

'That's it – a fault. Well, Giles's mind shows faults: sudden breaks interrupting the sequence, which nevertheless continues at a lower level. It's most odd. To give you an example.' He flicked over the pages of typescript. 'After having satisfied himself that his desk really was being tampered with – I take it the comment "broken thread" refers to an actual thread of cotton or something which he had tied across the lid of the desk as a trap—'

'That's it,' said Mallett. 'I found a bit of black thread hanging from one of the knobs of the inner drawers, before I'd read that diary; and I guessed what it was. It's a common trick.'

'But of course the expression "broken thread" is symbolic too,' went on Fitzbrown, captivated by his own argument, and hardly hearing Mallett. 'He comes back to it later on, that is, to the associations it awakens in his mind. However, that wasn't the example I was thinking of. The passage I meant was where he starts by saying that he is being watched and spied upon. By now he has brought the deed-box from the office, and for a while this seems all right. Then he begins to suspect tampering again. He begins by talking about prying eyes, and then suddenly he goes on to say that eyes are of two kinds, glass and jelly, and he thinks the former are the worse, when it comes to prying out the secrets of a man's mind, which, he adds, is not made of jelly but of small cells which are extremely active, and if one could stop them from acting, it would be an excellent thing.' Fitzbrown glanced up at Mallett, who was studying the second rifle. 'Of course that clearly refers to the circle of glass eyes in the animals' heads in the study, and the effect they had on him. So too, I think, does this bit about "a ring of fire – a rabbit in a cornfield."'

He turned over more pages. 'Then you have completely matter-of-fact statements, such as that he used the new rifle with the new "shuttle" cartridge and scored a series of bull's-eyes at two hundred yards; that he tried it again at service range of six hundred yards and was astonished at its accuracy. Then here are his results at long range of twelve hundred. But he thinks that certain improvements could still be made. Here's a rough sketch of a cartridge...

'He doesn't actually mention his first encounter with Arden Laforte; but we get a few references to "A. D." and "Took them all trout-fishing to Swan Bridge Inn." He has one entry headed "Heredity," which says:

"The same man begot the book and the daughter. Must they be the same inside? I am cruel; I am sensitive. The pike I caught to-day groaned when I hit him with my hammer (so much for the silent tribe of prolific fish). I am sorry for him, but I hit him again, to kill him and stop his groaning. The more sensitive I am, the crueller I become. I want to kill men, more and more men, but best of all myself. The male spider is not faced with any decision.'

And so on, lots more of it. Very queer stuff, don't you think?'

'Very queer,' said Mallett, abstractedly.

'You know,' said Fitzbrown, 'really this fellow should have been a poet. He would have gone far. Arrange that stuff above in separate lines and you get modern poetry:

"I am cruel,
I am sensitive...
I want to kill men,
More and more men,
Best of all, myself.
The male spider is not faced with any decision."

The delightful inconsequence of the last line... Oh, hullo, Bob, you're just in time to take part in a discussion on poetry.'

Dr Jones entered. He glanced sharply at the rifle Mallett was holding. 'What, another? Where did you get that? Out of the lake, apparently.' He took it from Mallett and examined it, while Mallett explained where it had been found, and what they thought about it at Gabb's.

'A replica,' said Jones thoughtfully. 'And you found it in the lake, near the boat-house. Still no sign of any bullet or cartridge?'

'Not yet.'

'They hadn't missed any at Gabb's – any of the special type made for Giles Gabb, I mean?'

'Apparently not. Giles took them all himself. Why?'

'Because the man who copied the gun probably wouldn't copy the cartridge too. He'd use some standard kind of the same calibre, or try to steal a few of the new type. Even if he had the facilities, he'd find it hardly worth while to go to the trouble of making cartridges, especially for a small-bore rifle, where you have to have such a high degree of accuracy. Well? Have you decided which rifle shot Giles—this one or the one on the island?'

'This one, obviously,' said Mallett. 'Else why should he have thrown it away?'

'Quite so,' said Jones. 'But what you want to ask is, why having thrown it away, did he then row over to the island? Why, having shot his man, did he want another gun?'

'I see you think you know the answer,' said Mallett.

'Yes,' said Jones with decision. 'I think I do. Having shot his man with *this* rifle, he threw it away, into the lake, probably in a funk, and because he couldn't be seen walking away from the place carrying a rifle. Then he realized that his best plan would have been to stage a suicide; and he had thrown away the rifle that was supposed to have done the job. The shot-gun which Giles was carrying was no use; but he – the murderer, that is – knew for certain that there was another rifle, exactly similar to the one he had thrown away, somewhere on the island.'

'Why should he know that?' said Mallett.

'Because,' said Jones, 'he was the man who had been tampering first with Giles's desk, then with his deed-box. You'll find a reference to that in the diary, Fitzbrown, near the end, where he decides that the deed-box too has been opened, and he will henceforth keep all his goods on the island.' Jones perched himself on the table and wagged a stout forefinger towards them both. 'What I see happening is this: Giles, having discovered that the deed-box was being tampered with, removed it to the island, where he devised the hiding-place. But he still kept the diary in his desk for a day or two, being confident, perhaps, that the shorthand would baffle any intruder – not because it isn't perfectly good shorthand, but because it's one of the lesser-known systems, and is written very minutely.'

'Yes, that's so,' said Mallett. 'We had difficulty in getting it transcribed ourselves. We had to send it up to town. There was no one in Broxeter who knew the system, hence the delay in deciphering it.'

'The intruder, however,' went on Jones, 'could and did read it, and therefore learnt about the *cache* on the island, and the rifle which had been taken there. Whether Giles discovered that the diary itself had been read, one can't say; but probably he didn't know. If he had, he wouldn't have left his stuff on the island, much less put the diary as well into the deed-box. He evidently thought that his things were safe there: the rifle hidden, the diary in the secret compartment, the deed-box in its *cache*.'

'Funny he didn't keep the diary in his pocket,' said Mallett.

'Fishermen don't keep anything in their pockets except their *impedimenta*,' retorted Jones. 'They don't carry round anything they don't want to lose, or get soaked or smelling of fish.'

'When do you suppose he took the deed-box and rifle to the island?' interposed Fitzbrown.

'I don't know,' said Jones. 'But all things considered, I should say it was about a week before he was shot. That's when the entries in the diary cease; that's when he began spending all his time on the lake with his friends.'

'And also,' said Mallett, 'that fits with something the old man told us. He said that the first time he mentioned the matter of the leakages of information to Giles was about a week before he was killed, when he – Simon Gabb, that is – got the third message from the C.I.D. saying they proposed to put a detective into the works. He told me that Giles said nothing in reply, but turned very red and walked out of the office: and *since* then he had spent all his time on the lake with his friends.'

'Exactly,' said Jones. 'Giles knew that it was true: that there had been tampering, and that as it was his invention and he was in charge of the papers, he was in a way responsible. It was a great shock to him to hear that there was an actual leakage—'

'Especially as they had kept it from him before,' said Mallett. 'Simon Gabb told me he had said nothing to Giles about the two previous communications he had received. He tried to maintain that this was out of consideration for Giles's queer mentality, but actually he admitted that it was because of his fear lest Giles himself were involved.'

'I wonder,' said Fitzbrown over his shoulder, 'if Giles himself suspected anybody. There's no hint of it in the diary, if he did; but he would be bound to think it might have something to do with his new friends, wouldn't he? I wonder if that was why he kept them out on the lake every day that week: to observe them, to see if any of them attempted to get to the island or betrayed any suspicious knowledge…'

The telephone bell rang. Mallett went to the desk to answer.

'Yes?' He craned his neck forward to answer, and his second 'yes' was spoken in a sharper tone. Mallett's side of the conversation consisted almost entirely of 'yes,' but he managed to convey by the recurring monosyllable a steeply-rising crescendo of interest. He put down the receiver with a word of thanks, and picked it up again immediately in order to call the Chief Constable's office at Broxeter.

'Hullo. This is Superintendent Mallett. Is the Chief in? All right, put me through to the Deputy Chief. Hullo, Simpson. This is Mallett. About the Gabb murder: I want you to do something for me immediately. Will you send a man to the Smart Service Dyers and Cleaners, Commerce Street branch? Yes, at once. He is to ask for a navy-blue suit of clothes left there about noon to-day for Mrs Basil Gabb. And let's hope to the Lord they aren't as smart as they claim to be, because I want that suit in the same state as it was when delivered. What? Oh well, if they've started to clean it, I'll have it all the same, though it won't be much use. In that case, I shall want a report as to what was wrong with it. No, not bloodstains this time: mud-stains. Eh? No, not the same thing at all: mud – M-U-D. Yes. That's right. Hurry, will you? And let me have it back here as soon as you can. Thanks very much.'

He put down the receiver, and looked at his watch. 'A quarter-past five. There's just a chance, though rather a remote one. I believe these cleaners have a van that goes round to their various branches and collects the goods, which are then taken to the works to be cleaned. If she missed the morning van, and the evening one hasn't yet called, it may be—'

'What *is* this?' said Jones, coming forward. 'Have you heard the View Halloo or something?'

'That was Olivier,' said Mallett. 'You know, the lawyer-fellow who spent the night at Herons' Hall, and went down with you, Dudley, when you first saw the body. He thinks he's got hold of something.'

'And has he?'

'I don't know. But I'm bound to investigate.' Mallett endeavoured to sound nonchalant, but his green eyes were alert, and he pulled at his red moustache impatiently. 'Olivier was speaking from Mrs Charleroy's telephone, so he couldn't say much: but what he did say was, he and his wife had been having tea with Mrs Basil Gabb, and she had mentioned a suit of her husband's which she had found rolled up in a cupboard; it was very damp and she had sent it to the cleaners' in Broxeter. Olivier suggested that this might interest us…'

'Well, I'll be off,' said Dr Jones. 'I've got my surgery. Coming, Fitzbrown?'

Dr Fitzbrown laid the typescript down reluctantly, and rose. 'You know, Mallett,' he said, 'that diary has one significance for this investigation that you've overlooked. You think it's merely an interesting psychological document, which might have been relevant if the man had really committed suicide. I think the man who murdered Giles Gabb read, among other things, Giles's diary, and that it was Giles's diary which made him think what a good idea it would be to fake Giles's suicide. The diary, if discovered, would confirm the view that Giles had shot himself. So if you can find a man in Giles's entourage who can read Baxter's Basic Shorthand—'

25

Pauline still lay on the settee and dabbed her nose with her handkerchief.

'I do think,' she said complainingly, 'you need not be quite so rude to my friends. You practically drove them out of the house.'

Basil paced up and down the hearth-rug a couple of times. He was scowling and preoccupied. 'Oh, shut up,' he said, 'and give me a cup of tea – that is, if you're quite sure it's not too much trouble.'

His tone was so unlike that to which she was accustomed that she stared back at him in alarm. If she had cared at all what happened to him, she would have ordered him to bed and taken his temperature; for though they often quarrelled and Basil often reproached her, she had always hitherto had the comfortable feeling that his ravings arose out of his devotion to her. Now his tone was sneering, and she could read nothing into either his voice or his look but dislike, if not hatred. What had come over him?

'Well, hurry up,' he snapped, seeing that she did not move. 'You weren't too indisposed to pour out tea for those two. What were they doing here, by the way?'

'Good gracious, Basil,' said Pauline, trying to assert her old influence, 'you're surely not going to object to my seeing Madeleine now! We were at school together. I knew her long before I saw you.'

Basil made an impatient gesture. 'Not her. Her husband. What was that fellow doing here? He's a lawyer, isn't he? He and his brother are acting for your friends at the South Lodge, did you know that?' He gave an unpleasant laugh. 'Olivier hopes to get up some sort of defence for Charleroy, so I hear.'

'What!' said Pauline, unable to prevent the sudden leap of her heart. 'Is he arrested? Have they accused him?'

'Not yet,' said Basil. 'But I'm told the Superintendent was there again to-day.' He came over to Pauline and stood by the settee, looking down at her in a way she did not like. 'It can only be a question of time. And you – you'll have to give evidence. You'll drag my name in the dust. You'll brand me as the man whose wife had a liaison with a murderer.'

With each phrase his face seemed to come a little closer. She pressed farther back among the cushions, and her limbs grew rigid. She had never before noticed the deep lines at the corners of his nose and mouth, the brooding, boding look in his eyes. It was the mask of tragedy that was looking down at her; and she had never before seen in it anything but the face of the man who was so much in love with her, whom she rather despised.

'You know what Olivier came here for,' Basil was continuing. 'He came to get all the information he could get out of *you*. That's what they were here for, both of them. But you're too big a fool to see it.'

He had been kneeling with one knee on the settee beside her, as he leaned over her with this new menace in his voice and eyes. But at the last words, he relaxed and turned away contemptuously.

'Of course,' he said, 'if all this comes out, don't expect *me* to help you. I'm through with you. In fact, I'm through with you in any case. And don't expect me to put myself in any false position for you. I shall divorce you, and keep the child.'

'But Basil,' Pauline faltered, 'what has come over you all of a sudden? The other morning, when I asked you to release me, you refused. And anyway, there really is nothing between me and Royce Charleroy.'

'You expect me or anyone else to believe that?'

'I know you can't prove it,' retorted Pauline. 'For one thing, Royce Charleroy is in love with his cousin, Miss Laforte. You said so yourself, and it's true. And you're wrong about Hubert and Madeleine. As a matter of fact, they were trying to persuade me to make it up with you, and let everything be as it was before.'

Basil threw back his head and laughed. 'So I was to be allowed to have my wife back at their hands, was I, now you'd all found out that Charleroy wouldn't be available? Thanks very much! But in future I've decided to carry on alone. Maybe I'll get on better that way. Now that I'm the head of the family – or will be when Father goes – I don't want you getting in my way with your extravagance and your stupid notions of your own superiority. *I'm* going to be master henceforth.'

Pauline said nothing. She did not know on what lines to tackle him. Was he mad, or drunk? Would it all pass like his previous gusts of passion, and leave him even more weary and subservient than before? Even now, he was showing signs of collapse. He passed his hand over his forehead.

'Well,' he said in a strained voice, 'give me some tea, a strong cup, please. I have to go out again this evening.'

She poured out the tea, and handed it to him. Her languid pose was ended. She seethed with indignation, in proportion as he weakened; and through her mind there raced projects for revenge. But she kept her temper and said mildly:

'What, again? Must you? This is the first time you've come home early for a month at least.'

He drank the tea greedily and held out the cup to be refilled.

'I must. The works are very busy. Everything falls on me.' He coughed, somewhat awkwardly. 'If I'm not back, don't wait up for me. I may not be back to-night.'

Pauline raised her eyebrows. So that was it! Well, she'd see about that. If there was anything of that sort going on, she would have him watched. Hubert's brother would arrange something… She rose in renewed dignity. 'If you *do* spend the night in Broxeter,' she said, 'you might call at the Smart Service for me before you come home to-morrow. I sent a few things there this morning, and they're supposed to be ready in twenty-four hours.'

Basil looked recalcitrant. These daily commissions of hers: how gladly he had undertaken them when they were first married, and how his initial pride had been gradually worn down to boredom and exasperation! 'Can't you get them sent out?' he said irritably. 'I haven't time for that sort of thing these day's.'

'No,' said Pauline. 'They don't deliver beyond the seven miles' radius. Anyhow, there's no need to make such a fuss. You took your own dinner-suit there the other day and called for it again; and if you think that's different from fetching something to oblige *me*, let me tell you that the principal item was your blue suit, which I found rolled up in a bundle in your dressing-room, all damp and mouldy. Why you didn't take it in with the other things, or give it to me, I can't imagine.'

She stopped. Basil was staring at her, and his face had gone a ghastly white. 'You?' he said. 'You sent it? When?'

'This morning. Why? What's the matter?'

Basil laid his cup down, and came towards her, pacing slowly, like a feline about to spring. She recoiled towards the door.

'Did you tell Olivier – or his wife? Was that what they came to find out?' His hands were crisped in front of him, and he seemed about to seize her by the throat.

'No, no,' she stammered, confused. 'At least, they never asked me, I'm sure. If I told them, it was just in conversation—'

'Oh, get out of my way!' shouted Basil. He pushed her aside with a violent thrust of his forearm which sent her staggering back against the wall.

A few minutes later, she heard the engine of his car being started up in the garage. She ran upstairs and to the window that looked out on to the main road. She was in time to see Basil's car swing out of the drive gates and turn in the direction of Broxeter.

As she was about to leave the window, her eyes caught sight of another car moving slowly along the other side of the road. The second car drew out and took on speed. She saw the faces of its occupants, the driver and a companion; and she had no doubts as to their profession. Basil was being followed by two police-officers in plain clothes.

26

'I had a bit of a job to pick it up, sir,' said the police-constable, laying a brown paper parcel on to Mallett's desk. 'It had actually left the shop when we called there, and was on its way to the works, but we phoned up and got them to send it back to us. Sorry I'm so late.'

Mallett undid the parcel and took out the three pieces of Basil's blue suit. The waistcoat he threw on to the floor without looking at it. He examined the trousers more carefully, especially the knees, which were stained: but his real interest was obviously centred in the coat. Like the other garments, it was crumpled, damp and growing mould in places. Mallett held it up and turned it round and round, while Fitzbrown and Jones stood one on each side, looking like two critical tailors about to take the measurements necessary for an alteration.

'You think this proves he was out in the rain that night?' said Jones.

'No,' said Mallett. 'He had the dinner-suit on when he was watching Charleroy and his wife. Then he changed into this suit. But the rain had stopped by then.'

'Then how does the suit help you? And how did it get wet, anyway?'

Mallett, holding the coat by the loop, twirled it slowly round. 'You know what a housewife does when she's ironing?' he said with a twinkle. 'No? Perhaps you don't, not being a married man like ourselves. Well, she sprinkles the clothes with water and rolls them tightly together, and in that way she gets the moisture all through them. Now these clothes were rolled up in a tight bundle. The reason why they're wet is because *one* part of them was soaked, and the moisture penetrated throughout.'

'Do you mean he fell in the lake?' said Jones.

'Not exactly. But he took a dip. Look here.' He picked up the right sleeve and held up the cuff. On the rim of the cuff, in the otiose buttons, and for four or five inches upwards, there was a green stain. 'He made the mistake of trying to brush off the mud while it was still wet,' said Mallett. 'Then when he couldn't do it, he rolled the whole thing up into a bundle and hid it until he could find some means of disposing of it. He laid the coat down, and picked with a pin into the holes of the buttons. 'We shall find that this came from the bottom of the lake, I think,' he said, 'and that it's the same as we have here on our second rifle.'

'Then that's why he wanted the boat,' said Jones, 'to get to the place where he'd dropped the rifle, and not to get to the island.'

'Why not both?' said Fitzbrown. 'I wonder why he dropped the rifle to begin with.'

The telephone bell on Mallett's desk rang insistently. The young police-constable answered.

'Yes. Yes. All right, keep cool,' they heard him say. 'Where is it?' He reached out for a pencil. 'North Lodge, Herons' Hall—'

'Give me that,' said Mallett, snatching the receiver. 'Yes, Mrs Gabb. Mallett speaking. Yes, all right. I'll be along. Yes, the doctor's here. I'll bring him.' He dropped the receiver. 'Got your car?' he said to the policeman. 'You can drive us there. Hurry! Jones – Fitzbrown – you'd better both come. There's one man murdered and another fighting mad – two men holding him down already. Coleman!' The sergeant appeared. Mallett gave orders for a second car to follow. He was about to hurry off when the young police-constable from Broxeter stopped him.

'Excuse me, sir,' he said.

Mallett, checked in full cry, rounded on him ferociously. But the policeman held his ground.

'I *must* give you this, sir,' he protested, appealing for reason even in a crisis. He held out an envelope. 'The girl in the shop gave it to me. She said she found it in the coat. Not in a pocket: they always go through the pockets, and these were all empty. But it seems there was a hole in the lining of the right-hand pocket, and as it was a pointed object, sir, it worked through to the bottom of the lining. She felt it there, and thought it was a lead weight; but owing to the shape, sir – the pointed end—'

Mallett tore open the envelope and shook out the object on to his palm. It was a slender cartridge, about two inches long. The projecting end of the bullet was finely pointed and tipped with aluminium; and on the case was rubber-stamped: 'G.G.3.'

27

For Pauline, the evening dragged along.

She watched, rather listlessly, the bathing of the baby, and saw him put into his cot for the night. She wondered how much longer she would be allowed to have any part in him. She had very little now, so efficiently was everything arranged – by herself, of course, but sometimes she wished that the rules laid down for her own convenience could occasionally be broken for the same reason. She spent an hour in her room, dressing for dinner, though she knew she must dine alone.

When it was time to go downstairs, she took a book; but she had not the habit of reading, or the ability to pick out the right book from the shelf; and so she found herself sitting idly once again in the drawing-room, gazing into the leaping flames of the fire, and wondering why she, who had been so popular at school, such a leader, should now in the prime of her youth find herself so completely alone.

She no longer thought of Royce, even with regret. It was not her nature to repine over anything hopeless. She hardly gave a thought to Basil either. If she had lost him, she no longer cared. If she had not lost him, she would be tempted to be sorry; for now was her chance. Now or never, she would break free from this encirclement, of marriage, money, comfort, convention, and find herself, find some outlet for this new energy; or she would be for ever baffled, and would settle down to a steady progress – no, not progress, process rather – through the remainder of her youth, through middle age, through old age, growing ever a little stouter, a little more sedentary, a little less capable of any feelings except pride and prejudice...

For a brief moment, the recollection of her feelings that evening, when Royce had sat beside her in Simon Gabb's drawing-room and looked at her with laughter in his eyes: the surge of feeling, unknown before, the weakness that had swept over her, recurred, and made her bite her lips with pain. But she mastered it, because it was hopeless. It was not of Royce she thought now, but of herself only. Where should she go? What should she do?

Dinner was over. It was dark now, and the heavy curtains were drawn. A wind had risen, and was lashing the tall pine-trees that flanked the Lodge on the north side. Then there was a sharp pattering of rain on the window, and the sound of the cars passing by on the main road changed to a swishing of tyres on the wet surface. Nine o'clock came, then ten. Perhaps Basil was not coming in. He had hinted as much. She wondered why he had been so annoyed about the suit... If he didn't come in very soon, she would ring the bell and tell the maid to bolt the doors.

Then she heard his car turn in at the gates. She knew all the sounds, the change of gear at the entrance, the bottom-gear crawl round the Lodge to the garage, the rolling back of the garage doors, the car being driven in, the closing of the doors, Basil's step in the hall. She knew to a second how long these separate processes took, how long, in normal times, it would be before the drawing-room door opened and she felt Basil's lips on her cheek, Basil's hand on her shoulder. Everything he did was so methodical, so exactly timed, that one shrank from it beforehand. To-night, perhaps, would be different. He had been so queer when he left. Her heart beat a little faster. She almost wished she had gone upstairs to bed. Suddenly she dreaded seeing him...

Surely he was being a very long time now. She had heard the garage doors roll back on their iron rail as usual; but she had not heard them close. Perhaps even now she would have time to get upstairs, shut herself in and pretend to be asleep. She left the drawing-room quickly. But once in her room, and, as she felt, safe, she was assailed again by curiosity. What was going on out there? She walked along to the end room, from which one could see the main road; and she was not altogether surprised to see, halted some little way along on the other side of the road, the side-lights of another car...

From her own room she could see neither the road nor the garage. Her room faced south and west, on to the trees that came almost up to the Lodge on this side. Raindrops ran down the panes. The night was inky black, and she could see only her own reflection. She put out the light, and looked out again, pressing close to the glass and trying to penetrate the darkness.

Then suddenly it happened: a sharp cry, a groan, men shouting, running, struggling, torches flashing...

Ten minutes later, Pauline was speaking to Superintendent Mallett on the telephone.

28

B asil drove the car up to the garage doors; and stepped out of the driving-seat. The wind caught him, the rain beat violently against him, the trees swayed and creaked above his head, as he splashed through puddles and laid his gloved hands on the heavy door. It ran back easily. As he returned to his car, someone stepped towards him out of the darkness: a short thick-set man wearing a trilby hat with oily brim pulled well down over the eyes.

'Good evening, Mr Gabb,' he said.

Basil swung round. 'How did you get here?'

The man gave a chuckle. 'Sorry to startle you. I came on a bus. I've had rather a long wait in the rain.'

'You fool, why did you come here? If you'd waited, I'd have come to you. As a matter of fact, I went out to your place after I'd been to – seen to other business; and it was all shut up. Why didn't you stay there, as I told you to?'

'Well, Mr Gabb, to tell you the truth—'

Basil silenced him hastily. 'We can't stand here. Anyone can see us from the road. Go into the woods there, behind the house. You'll find a tool-shed I'll join you in a minute, when I've put the car in.'

'All right, Mr Gabb,' said the man. 'But if you don't come back, I'll have to come and knock at the front door.'

Basil said nothing. He went back to his car, drove it into the garage, turned out the head-lights, and went to close the doors. Then, on second thoughts, he went back again, picked up something heavy from a work-bench at the side, returned again to the doors, and pushed them to. Then he followed the man who had waylaid him.

Ten minutes later, the argument was still going on.

'I'm sorry, Mr Gabb. I'm afraid I don't see it that way. After all, I'm not to know what you wanted the rifle for, or why you wanted Maxton's to make it. I did all you asked me. I took the plans there, and I pretended they, were mine. I paid them just like you said. Nobody can pick on me, as I see it.'

'Yes. But you took them elsewhere too, didn't you? You made a nice little bit out of the German consulate, for selling what didn't belong to you. But that time you didn't pose as the inventor: they wouldn't have given you a penny for that! Oh no, you told them the truth – that these designs were the latest ideas being tested by Gabbs' for their new small-bore military rifle. And now you dare to come here asking for more!'

'I'm sorry, Mr Gabb,' came the monotonous answer. 'But you see, I don't think you can prove it. I mean, how could you? Even if any leakage came out – if an agent gets caught – he doesn't give the names of those he's working for; and those he's working for don't give the names of any others who've helped him, if you see what I mean. Of course, I don't admit at all what you've been saying. All I'm saying is, in cases like that, you'd be surprised how hard it is to trace anything back. More likely it would be traced back to *you* than anybody, because after all the plans couldn't have got into their hands if you hadn't pinched them first, could they?'

Basil's teeth were chattering. 'I asked you to get the thing copied,' he said weakly. 'I trusted you. I paid you. You had no right—'

'I'm sorry, Mr Gabb.'

'Well, look here, what are you here for now? What did you come to the office for this afternoon? Don't you know the place is watched? Everybody is suspect. And you come here and give them the clue! How do you know you weren't followed?'

'Why should anybody follow me, Mr Gabb? *I* haven't done any harm.'

'If you're identified as the man who took those plans to Maxton's—'

'I don't think I shall be, Mr Gabb. I didn't take them there myself, you see. I got somebody else – and he's a long way off by now. I've got lots of friends. You make lots of friends in the motor trade, you know.'

'Well, anyway—' Basil raised his voice in exasperation, and dropped it as suddenly. 'Well, anyhow, what do you want now?'

'Well, Mr Gabb, if you won't give me a job at the works – and perhaps you're right there: perhaps it mightn't be very wise – I think you ought to give me a bit of help, to set up somewhere else. After all, it's owing to my helping you that I've got to leave Broxeter and start up elsewhere. Starting afresh in a strange place takes capital. And look at the good-will I'm sacrificing—'

'Good-will? You?' Basil gave a harsh laugh, and checked himself. 'What do you want? How much? Only mind you, you've got to leave this country. I won't help you otherwise.'

'Oh, I don't know about that, Mr Gabb.' The flat, monotonous voice went on, dripping on to Basil's brain like the raindrops falling on to the roof above him. 'I really couldn't promise to do that, with all my connections in this country. Still, I'll consider it if you'll make it worth my while.'

'How much?'

'Well, I couldn't do it on less than five thousand, Mr Gabb, if I stay here. And it'll have to be double that if I'm to go abroad. Everything's so dear overseas, they say.'

'Ten thousand pounds?' said Basil. 'You're crazy! I'm talking about a hundred or two – and you'll be lucky to get that. Come on, now, two hundred: take it or leave it. If I don't hear you've left Broxeter within seven days, I shall denounce you to the police as a spy.'

'I don't think you will, Mr Gabb. After all, it's much more serious for you than for me, isn't it?'

Suddenly a window in the Lodge above them showed brilliantly lit. The light shone down through the tiny window in the tool-shed, and cast a beam across to the opposite wall. Both men shrank back into the darkness behind. Basil was the first to recover.

'It's all right. It's my wife,' he said shortly, speaking rather to reassure himself than his companion. The light was extinguished. Basil rounded on him. 'What do you mean?'

'Well, Mr Gabb, after all, if the police get me, they're going to find out who wanted the rifle, aren't they? And then they're going to ask, what did you want it for?'

'Well, all you have to say is, I wanted it for experimental purposes. My brother and I were experimenting.'

'Yes, but they'll say, Mr Gabb, funny you didn't have it made by your own firm. And after all, it's bound to come out, isn't it, you used that gun to shoot your brother with?'

There was an intense silence. The raindrops pattered heavily on the trees on to the tar-mac roof. On the main road, on the other side of the high wall, not twenty yards away, the traffic streamed past. The wind soughed through the tops of the pines. Yet to Basil Gabb the whole world, like the inside of the tool-shed, was silent, waiting for him to move, to take action...

The man spoke again. 'I'm sorry, Mr Gabb...'

Basil laughed, but not aloud. He heard the words repeated, repeated *ad infinitum*: 'I'm sorry, Mr Gabb – sorry, Mr Gabb – sorry, sorry, sorry...'

Basil lifted the hammer.

The man turned. He saw his doom hanging over him, saw it descending. He cried out, a sharp inarticulate cry. The blow fell, with sickening thud. Basil felt his enemy fall across his feet, and heard his head strike the thin wooden side of the shed. Something fell with a clatter from a shelf above. Basil threw the hammer out, out into the wood, leapt across the body, and began to run towards the house.

Torches flashed in his face. He felt his arms pinioned. He struggled violently, shouting, cursing, kicking the shins of the two burly men who held him. His two captors growled, breathed hard, muttered 'Now then!' and 'You would, would you?' Little by little, in spite of his maniacal efforts, they began to master him. Another man came running. 'There's a fellow hurt in there!' gasped one of his captors, nodding to the shed. They got Basil to the Lodge door.

The front door opened. He saw the familiar hall, the stairway, the shaded pink light; he smelt the familiar smells of food and heat, polish and all the indefinable aroma that is one's home. Again a spasm of energy seized him; for a moment he shook his captors off and stood alone. But then he stopped, puzzled. He did not know where to go. This was his home, but it was not friendly. It was hostile, a trap. He saw Pauline coming down the stairs...

In a moment, the two men had hurled themselves upon him again and grasped his wrists in a grip that hurt. This time there was no escape. Yet he struggled on. After every fresh rest, when he had got back his breath, new strength seemed given to him. He wanted to make an end of it, to finish the job, to kill Pauline...

The door behind him opened again. The third man entered. 'There's a fellow in the tool-shed with his head bashed in.'

Basil laughed. '"Sorry, Mr Gabb." By jove, I bet he's sorry!' he said to himself.

'Get the handcuffs, Bill, out of the car. Mrs Gabb, will you call the police-station? Just call "Police." They'll give you Chode.'

Basil heard the familiar tinkle under the stairs as the receiver was lifted. He heard Pauline's agitated voice: 'Operator! Operator! The police! Hurry, please!' He ground his teeth, and like Samson, once again he put forth all his strength. It seemed to him that he lifted both his foes bodily off their feet and flung them against the walls. Purposefully, not hurrying this time, he began to stalk forward, seeking that voice, that voice of all others that he hated, the voice of folly, temptation, ruin... But he forgot to look behind.

'Hurry, hurry!' he heard Pauline saying into the telephone. 'There's been murder. He's mad. It's taking two men all their strength to hold him down.'

There she was, robust, handsome, stupid, unfeeling, his undoing… There she stood, arranging his final undoing now… Basil paused in the doorway, waiting to spring. The man with the handcuffs in one hand, and the wooden truncheon in the other, likewise paused, to make sure of his blow.

Basil felt a sharp pain shooting through his head. The picture of Pauline broke up into a thousand pieces. Each piece whirled round and round in a circle of white light, and shot away upward out of his vision. He fell to the ground with a crash, as Pauline replaced the receiver.

29

Hubert sat in Mrs Charleroy's drawing-room, surrounded by an attentive audience. Mrs Charleroy, Royce and Arden hung on his words; and if he mistook their interest for admiration, that lent vigour to his narrative.

'Of course,' he said, 'it was the merest fluke that I discovered it myself. But the police admit that if it hadn't been for that piece of evidence, they would have been a long time tracing this thing to its source, if they had succeeded at all.'

'You must feel very gratified,' said Mrs Charleroy.

'Well, I am, Helen, naturally: partly because it's a good thing to get to the bottom of it and prevent further crimes, but above all, for the sake of Royce and the rest of you. You would never have felt quite easy in your minds, would you, if the real murderer had not been found?'

Arden broke in sharply: 'Superintendent Mallett said Royce was cleared long before. He told me so that afternoon, when I talked to him. He said the times didn't agree. I dare say he suspected Basil all along.'

'Ah, but,' said Hubert sagely, 'it's not a bit of good, in a criminal case, suspecting or even knowing something you can't prove. It was the blue suit, and the cartridge they found in it, that pinned the crime on to Basil, even if it hadn't been for his second crime, which was undertaken because of the first. As it was, with that piece of evidence, all the rest fitted together beautifully, like a jig-saw puzzle. I was there when Mallett reconstructed it. This is how it all worked out:

*

'Royce returned with Pauline in Harry Gabb's car at about five o'clock. She wanted to slip in before daylight, and he dropped her at the gate and drove on, in order to leave the car in front of the fallen elm-tree, where he had found it the night before. We now know that their movements had been followed by Basil. He saw them go off for their joy-ride. He didn't follow in his own car because they would have been out of sight before he could have got his car out of the garage; and the car Royce was driving was much faster than his. He went into the Lodge as soon as they left, changed his clothes, and waited.

'He sat up until the small hours, and when they didn't return, his thoughts got gloomier and gloomier, until in the end he went back to his room and took out of the inner cupboard in his dressing-room the rifle which the police call Number Two – the one copied from Giles's invention. I'll return to that in a minute. When he heard the car returning, he slipped out of the house by the back way, carrying his rifle, doubtless under a mackintosh or overcoat. He saw Pauline go in, while Royce drove the car on to the elm-tree. Basil then followed Royce, possibly with no very clear idea of what he meant to do, except that he wanted to kill Royce. He did not of course know where his pursuit of Royce would lead him. It led him to the boat-house.

'Meanwhile, two other people had been there before them. First, Giles. Giles was well aware that his plans were being spied upon. He had suspected this previously; but a week before, he had learnt that the leakage was not only going on, but was known to the police. He transferred the plans, and the model rifle which had been specially made for him by Gabb's – the police call it Number One – to the island. The daily fishing on the lake with the two of you and Billy provided him with an excellent opportunity for watching his hiding-place. I don't think he suspected any of you. He must have known that the person tampering with his desk was someone with access to the Hall; and you had never visited the Hall until the night of the thunderstorm.

'That night, he had arranged to go fishing with you, Arden, early the next morning. But his discovery of you and Royce together in your room upset him, and – morose and suspicious as he was – he decided that you were fooling him and were all against him. He cancelled his date with you, Arden, and then, meeting Royce on the stairs, ordered him out of the house.

'But he himself couldn't sleep. He felt he had to go down to the lake and row over to the island, to make sure his precious secret was still safe. I imagine that the unexpected presence of all these people in the house upset him and made him doubly restless. He got up, then, and arrived at the lake while it was still dark, in order to avoid being seen. He took his shot-gun, being the kind of man who likes to carry a gun. He got into the first and nearest rowing-boat, rowed over to the island, inspected the *cache* and the rifle, and found, I think, that all was well. I – that is, Mallett thinks that the deed-box was not ransacked till later. He conjectures that it was about five-thirty when Giles arrived at the boat-house. It may have been earlier; but at any rate, it was before Arden arrived, and long enough before to give him time to get out of sight and hearing. Arden saw and heard nothing when she arrived, though she noticed that rowing-boat number one had gone, and knew that Giles must have taken it.

'Arden arrived, so she says, at about twenty to six. We know why she decided to keep her appointment with Giles after all. When she saw that Giles had taken the first boat and gone, she naturally assumed that he had gone to the fishing ground. She therefore took rowing-boat number two and, as she thought, followed him. By now, in spite of the mist, it was getting light enough to see a little way. Morgan the gardener saw Arden rowing fairly close to the shore at about ten to six; and ten minutes later he was able to see Royce further out, paddling the canoe.

'Now to go back to Royce. He left Pauline at about five o'clock, and having re-parked the car, he strolled down the avenue, past Herons' Hall, intending to take the path to the Mere. For one thing, it was his shortest way home; it was much quicker than walking all the way round by the road to the South Lodge. As he passed the Hall, to his surprise he saw Arden come out alone. He waited a few minutes to see if Giles was about, then followed her to the boat-house. He saw her take the rowing-boat and row out on to the lake. Again he followed her; and also it struck him that it would be easier for him to cross the lake than to walk round by the path to the Lodge. – Am I right, Royce? Correct me if I guess wrongly. – Finding both rowing-boats gone, he took the canoe. He paddled round to the other side of the lake, towards the fishing-ground; but not finding Arden, and thinking he had lost her in the mist, or that she must have gone over to the island, he decided to give up the chase. He tied up the canoe, then, and went home. The distance from that point to the South Lodge was five minutes' walk across fields. He left the canoe to be fetched by someone else; and arriving at the South Lodge, let himself in, went up to his room, came down to an early breakfast, and went out again. Then he learnt that Giles had been shot. First he was told that it was suicide, then murder. His reason for holding his tongue was chivalry: he wanted to keep Mrs Gabb out of it if possible, and he wanted to protect Arden. He did not know that Pauline had very wisely told the police of her own movements – and therefore his – at the outset.

'Basil was following in your tracks, Royce; but not so close as to be seen by you or – even more important at that hour – heard. He had to be careful to keep some distance behind you, lest he should step on a twig or something and give himself away. When he got to the boat-house, you had already got into the canoe and set off. You were out of sight, perhaps in a lucky swirl of mist: anyway, you were out of his clutches, and if he had wanted to shoot you, he couldn't have seen you. Then, as he stood there at the back of the boat-house, he heard the sound of a boat being rowed towards it.

'At first, no doubt, he thought it was you, Royce, coming back again. He probably did not know you had taken the canoe. Then, as the boat came into view in the narrow channel, he saw it was not you, but Giles.

'This was, we conjecture, at about six o'clock, or a few minutes before, when you, Arden, were at the other end of the lake, watching Royce go by. We can't be sure to a minute: but we know that it can't have been much later than six, because of what followed between then and the time when you, Arden, returned.

'Basil shot Giles. Let us leave out for the moment his reasons, and return to what he did afterwards. Let us say just this much about the act itself: it was an impulse, for he had come there expecting to find Royce; but it was not a mistake. It was an impulse following naturally on a long history, as the medical profession would say.

'Impulses are usually succeeded by an equally violent reaction. When Basil saw the boat drifting in towards him, with Giles's body slumped forward, he probably lost his head. One can imagine him running along the ledge to get hold of the prow of the boat and pull her in, without losing the oars. To do this, to get both his hands free, he had to get rid of the rifle. There was also the desire to get rid of an incriminating weapon. Acting on impulse again, therefore, he threw the rifle into the lake; and for the next few minutes he was busy hauling the boat in, shipping the oars, and so on.

'Then he conceived the idea of staging a suicide.

'He knew that Giles was regarded by everybody as a genius and also a little mad. He had read Giles's diary, and knew that it was filled with accounts of Giles's mental torments, and threats to commit suicide. But then he realized that he could not make it seem like suicide without the rifle; and this he had thrown away. His first idea was to get back the rifle. It was quite near, in water only about three feet deep, and he thought he knew where it had fallen, though one could not see the bottom of the lake because of the weeds and mud. He therefore decided to get out the boat and try to retrieve his rifle. He pulled Giles's body out of the rowing-boat into the motor-boat, and propped it up temporarily on Giles's shot-gun. He knew, of course, that no one would mistake the rifle-bullet wound for the effect of a shot-gun. Then he got into the rowing-boat and pulled over to the spot where he thought the rifle had fallen.

'But the lake is deceptive. Apparently what he did was to take off his mackintosh or overcoat, and then plunge his arm into the lake above the spot. This isn't easy. Even if you lie flat in the bottom of the boat, you can't plunge your arm right down without the risk of overturning; and then the area to be covered is very deceptive. It looks small until you begin searching; and then there are the weeds and the mud. Anyhow, as we know, he failed to find his own rifle; and time was precious. He gave up the search, quite soon, I imagine. Maybe he realized that even if he did recover the rifle, it would be a most dangerous thing to do, to place it there in the boat with Giles. It might be traced back to him, and then everything would come out. So he decided to row across to the island, and get Giles's own rifle instead.

'This also was a daring thing to do. He might be seen – though he relied to some extent in getting into the mist and keeping there. He knew that Royce was somewhere on the lake; but if he had been seen by Royce, he probably thought it cut both ways: he could pretend that he was pursuing his brother's murderer. Several people knew that Giles has ordered Royce out of the house that previous night, and that there was bad feeling between them over Arden. Basil could pretend that Royce was also the person trying to ferret out Giles's secret, and that that was what Royce was doing on the lake that morning, whereas he, Basil, had merely followed him. For these and possibly other reasons, Basil decided to row across to the island. I think we can assume that he did not know Arden was on the lake as well.

'When he got there, he had to search. He had not, we think, yet found out Giles's new hiding-place. But Giles had been there half an hour before, and the path to the *cache* in the rock was visible enough. Basil followed it. He saw the signs of disturbance round the stone; and it didn't take him long to lay his hands on the familiar deed-box. He opened it – he had a duplicate key – and removed all the papers. He tried, we believe, to open the secret compartment, because it was really necessary to his plan that Giles's diary should be somewhere where it could be read. He ought to have been able to open it: he had seen Giles do so, and he himself had done so at least once since then. But whether he had no pen-knife handy, or anything thin enough to slip into the groove, or whether in his haste he fumbled or forgot, we don't know. We only know that he failed to do the trick on this occasion, and was forced to leave the diary where it was.

'Time pressed. There was the much more important quest for the rifle. He pushed the deed-box back, stuffed the papers into his pocket, and turned to look for the real object of his search.

'We know he did not succeed. He naturally looked for the rifle near the rock where he had found the deed-box; but it was not there. It was lower down, leaning on the other side of a tree beside the path, cunningly concealed with ivy. Dr Fitzbrown found it later, when he stumbled and threw his arm round the tree.

'It must have been now about a quarter past or twenty past six. It was getting light; the sun had risen, and the mist would soon clear. Then suddenly – we conjecture from your story, Arden – Basil was disturbed. He heard the sound of oars on the other side of the island. That was when Arden, having put her boat in at the island, left again to pick up Royce's canoe. Actually, Arden, you must have been there for at least part of the time that Basil was searching. Perhaps your arrivals coincided, and therefore you didn't hear each other. Anyway, it seems probable that he heard you leave; and it hastened his own departure. He left in a panic, without the rifle. He rowed back to the boat-house, moored his boat, and fled across the fields back to Herons' Hall. He got back to his room without being seen; and from then onward one can picture him trying to clean the mud off his boots and off the sleeve of his coat. He waited in his room until the hue and cry was raised. He showed himself – with his outer coat on, no doubt – to several people;

and then he left on the pretext that he wished to join his wife, or break the news to her.

'From that time onward, having failed to give the impression that Giles had committed suicide, he played on the other string, of throwing suspicion on to Royce. The first thing he did when he got home was to tax Pauline with her midnight escapade. He knew that this didn't give Royce an alibi – that in fact it released him at just the right time, and would create a prejudice against him in everybody's mind. It was also a neater revenge than shooting him...

'Why did Basil kill Giles?

'That, as I said, is the last episode in a long history. But the essential factor in it is that Basil is the second son. He has suffered all his life from having an elder brother who everybody agreed had genius; whereas he, Basil, was considered merely reliable, useful, mediocre. The brilliance of Giles has blasted Basil's life, one may say; and when you add to this that Giles allowed himself all the liberties of the temperamental person – the right to work when he pleased and play when he pleased, the right to be a little mad on occasion, and then to return to the fold and be more revered and cherished than ever: you can imagine Basil's feelings, which were those of the ninety-and-nine well-behaved sheep, and the son who had not been prodigal. He suffered acutely, and nobody knew. Nobody noticed that he in his way was just as sensitive, or highly-strung, or unbalanced, or whatever you choose to call it, as Giles; and Basil had no genius to compensate him for his sufferings, to win him the admiration of others and keep him on good terms with himself.

'Still, I suppose he would have gone on plodding and suffering all his life if it hadn't been for Pauline.

'Pauline is a fine healthy specimen of womanhood; handsome, uncomplicated, rather stupid, impulsive, full of so far undirected energy. She married Basil because he wanted her to, very badly; and the Gabb family are millionaires. But she never could get used to the position of second son's wife. She wanted to reign at Herons' Hall, to queen it over the neighbourhood; and she had calculated that one day this would come true, as Giles was not a marrying man. If he had been, perhaps she would have married him herself. Furthermore, she wanted Basil to be a great industrial leader, an iron and steel king, something bigger and greater than his father; but she hadn't been long married to him when she saw that he was a cypher in the firm. Simon Gabb was still the director-in-chief, so far as administration was concerned: Giles was the brains. Basil would never do anything more exciting than run along the lines they laid down for him.

'Pauline therefore despised Basil; and she did not fail to let him know, for she has no sympathy with sensitiveness, if she believes in its existence. She didn't even take a great amount of interest in their child. I suppose she wanted to wait and see how it was going to turn out, before she gave it her attention. Basil noticed all these things. Her boredom with him, and everything about him, rankled extremely. He made up his mind to show her and everybody else that they were wrong.

'It was about six months ago, soon after their child was born, that Basil began tampering with Giles's papers.

'It seems that he had always had an idea that if he were given a chance, he could evolve designs for the Gabb factory that were as good as, or better than, his brother's. As a boy, he had played with mechanical toys, as Giles did, taken them to pieces and so on; but he always had the mortification of seeing that whereas Giles's efforts were applauded and admired, his own were ignored and brushed aside. And so it has been since he has grown up: if ever he has proposed any improvements on the technical side, he has been more or less told to stick to what he knows, and not meddle with matters too deep for him. This has always irked him; but Pauline's contempt provided the final spur. He became obsessed with the idea of inventing something which would make Gabb's more prosperous and more famous than ever; and the credit and the gratitude would be for him only.

'So when there was talk of this Government small-arms contract, and Giles began his new experiments, Basil decided to forestall him. He persuaded himself, though, that he must first see Giles's own designs, so that his own should outstrip them; and he began gradually tampering with Giles's papers, in the office, and then in his study at home. Giles, apparently, never had the slightest suspicion that the culprit was Basil. Like all the rest, he had a mild contempt for his lamb-like brother; he thought of Basil as a manager, a superior sort of clerk, quite unmechanically-minded, probably unable to understand the designs even if they were put before him. The proofs that he never suspected Basil are, first, that he decided to use the deed-box, and even opened the secret compartment in Basil's presence; second, that in his diary he used Baxter's system of shorthand, which owing to some whimsy of their father's, they had both been taught by a private tutor instead of the usual method.

'Basil began by borrowing the plans, copying them and returning them. Whether he himself really evolved any new design, we do not know, because he destroyed all his private papers, both at his office and at home, probably on the night when he realized that he might be arrested, the night on which he went after the blue suit. Probably he never did. Probably he was incapable of invention, and merely deluded himself. But when Giles's own new design for a small-bore rifle was complete, Basil made arrangements to have one made for himself. He got hold of a shady little garage man – Marks was his name – who appeared to be on the downward grade; and he offered to help him if he would approach a certain rival firm of small-arms manufacturers and ask them to make a rifle to this design. Marks was to pose as the inventor, and if the firm demurred, he was to offer to pay all the expenses of the experiment himself, representing that his faith in his invention was such that he was willing to put all his savings into having one made. Marks approached several of the larger firms and was turned down; but finally he found a smaller firm willing to do it for the cash; and this was the origin of rifle number two, copied from Giles's, but in inferior material.

'As for the cartridges, this was even more difficult. The firm that made the rifle hadn't the delicate machine-tools necessary for the production of this very fine cartridge; so Basil from time to time stole a few of Giles's own special brand, from one of the boxes in the study. One of these was subsequently found in the lining of his coat. It was marked "G.G.3," that is, Giles Gabb's special brand, the third experiment. Basil told himself, no doubt, that an accurate cartridge was essential to his own experiments, but he was not really concerned with a new type of cartridge; so the G.G.3 was good enough for him.

'This fellow Marks, however, was even more shady than he seemed. He realized, when he saw these plans, that they were of no ordinary kind. He knew that Gabb's were taking on more men, rumour said with a view to increased manufacture of small arms; and he grasped that he could make money out of this opportunity in several ways. He showed the plans to a man he knew, and so by devious routes he reached the doors of the German Consulate in Broxeter. From that time onward, the leakage began. Luckily it was discovered fairly quickly; and you'll be interested to hear that the German Consul at Broxeter, and certain of his staff, have been recalled by their Government, as unacceptable to His Majesty's Government. They are doubtless packing now, and busy burning papers. It's interesting to think that all these movements were started, really, by Pauline Gabb's impatience with her husband. Most historical movements, you know, Helen, can be traced back to similar apparently trivial personal causes – or so I believe.

'So you see, when Basil saw Giles and not Royce drifting in towards him through the mist, there was all that guilty knowledge behind his impulse; and in his hands was the proof of his guilt, the rifle that was the replica of Giles's own. There was no means of escape. The concrete walls of the boat-house imprisoned him, and if he moved towards the door, he would be seen. He might have hoped to hide the gun from any unsuspecting person; but not from Giles's morose and suspicious eyes. And he knew Giles's nature; treachery, the theft of his idea, the betrayal of it to outsiders, would meet with no mercy from him… The boat drifted nearer; the gun Basil was holding could damn him, but it could also save. Giles turned his head; Basil took aim…

'To come to the last scene of all; by the time that the blue suit was discovered, Basil was already in a tight corner. Marks was pressing him for money, and though he didn't say so yet, it was clear that he realized that Basil's rifle had some connection with the shooting of Basil's brother. Marks turned up at the office on the day that Mallett took the rifle to Gabb's for them to examine. He saw Basil, ostensibly to ask for work, actually to threaten. Basil got rid of him. But the damage was done.

'James Gabb saw Marks first, and thought he looked a shady character. James was there solely to act as detective, to try to find out about the leakage; and he thought it worth while to get the man followed. It so happened that his son Harry was in the office and had his car outside. James told Harry to follow the man, and if he lost him, to go to his garage and wait there and see what he did. The address of the garage was on the card. This was just in Harry Gabb's line. He followed Marks – who went by bus and tram – back to his garage, and when Marks left again, Harry trailed him all the way out to Herons' Hall. But first he rang up the Broxeter police; and they sent a car out to watch North Lodge and Basil. James and Harry had had their eye on Basil for some little time, and they were taking no chances. The visit of Marks to Basil confirmed them in their opinion, and they took matters into their own hands. They acted correctly in ringing up Broxeter and not Chode, because it was Broxeter who were interested in the leakage of information, whereas Chode were solely – theoretically that is – concerned with the murder.

'This is where I come in. When Pauline mentioned the suit of clothes, I thought at once of the night of the murder, and after I left the North Lodge, I rang Mallett up from here. I would have rung him from Pauline's place, but Basil had come in, and he almost turned

Madeleine and me out of the house. I wondered then if he suspected us of suspecting him. Mallett got Broxeter on the job, and they retrieved the suit. It proved all and more than we had hoped, for there were not only the mud-stains, but the forgotten cartridge that had slipped through a hole in the lining.

'Meanwhile, Pauline had let out to Basil that she had sent the suit to the cleaners. Imagine his panic and dismay! He had hidden it, no doubt, because he was afraid to have it cleaned. He was afraid that its mud-stained condition would excite the notice of the cleaners, and it would be remembered against him if ever his movements on the morning of the crime came to be questioned. He had read, I suppose, how often in murder cases the very fact of having sent a suit to the cleaners is apt to bring suspicion on a man who has anything to conceal.

'When he heard that Pauline had sent the suit, he seemed for a moment, Pauline says, ready to murder her; but instead, he rushed out of the house, and away in his car to Broxeter. He got to the cleaners – followed all the time by the Broxeter police car – but found to his horror that the suit had been collected, or rather sent after, by some strangers who were obviously the police. I don't know how much or how little the girl in the cleaners told him – whether for instance she mentioned the cartridge which she had found in the lining and had handed over to the police – but I imagine not, as that would have driven him to despair. He went next to Marks' garage, and found the place closed. After waiting irresolutely for a bit, he then got into his car again and drove to Gabb's. He spent an hour or more there, destroying papers and getting rid of the ashes from the grate. The offices were empty; the office staff had gone home. He was quite undisturbed. The police officers, having no authority to force an entry, waited outside. At last, having done all he could, Basil returned to the North Lodge, arriving there shortly after ten o'clock.

'Marks was waiting for him. There was a conversation in the tool-shed, some of which the two policemen overheard. But they were on the other side of the high wall cutting off the grounds of Herons' Hall from the main road, as it seemed impossible to approach the shed and not be seen. When, however, they realized that things were getting dangerous for Marks, they ran round to the front – and were just in time to catch Basil as he made a dash for the garage. By now he was running amok, and they had a difficult job to hold him down until the Chode police arrived. Marks was dead, and Basil was raving. They found the hammer in the wood next day.

'Well, that's how we piece it together,' concluded Hubert. 'A very neat job, I think. The inquest on Marks will be held to-morrow, and William and I will be representing Basil's interests. I'm just on my way to see old Mr Gabb now. Of course they'll find Basil "Guilty but insane".'

'Was he insane, do you think?' said Arden.

'Who can say?' said Hubert cheerfully. 'If he was, then he concealed it pretty well up till now. Or you may say he didn't get the credit for it. Everybody was so busy watching Giles that they never thought of Basil – steady, dependable Basil – as being the real case for the psycho-therapist.'

'I don't think Giles was mad,' said Arden. 'He was merely two people in one, only the two people were irreconcilable. There was a third, though, that was Giles – and he was sane.'

Hubert rose. Mrs Charleroy accompanied him to the door.

'What will happen now to Herons' Hall?' she said.

Hubert turned and regarded her shrewdly. 'My dear Helen, exactly what you think. Old Mr and Mrs Gabb will leave. Pauline will leave. You and your brood will be left in possession. The only Gabb to remain will be Jessica. She will shortly become Mrs Laforte, and mistress of Herons' Hall. You, as her husband's aunt, will migrate over there to look after the two young people. Rooms will be found for Royce and Arden – very convenient, as they wish to get married, and he has no money and no job.' Hubert patted her arm. 'I'll see if I can hurry the process. I flatter myself that Simon Gabb will take my advice on most things from now onwards.'

'Yes,' said Helen thoughtfully. 'You've certainly brought that off, Hubert. Doesn't it seem hard, though, that he had to lose both his sons in order to get the benefit of your advice?'

Hubert looked hurt. 'Some people might say,' he replied tartly, 'that it was *your* return that brought the Gabbs bad luck. You didn't intend to – but you wanted above everything to get back there, didn't you? I remember old James Gabb saying to me on that very night how he wondered if Simon had done the right thing in buying that place just as it stood, furniture and all. He said it didn't belong to them, and never would: it was like living in a house of ghosts. Shortly after that, your family walked in – and trouble began.' He laughed.

'Oh, don't be offended, Hubert!' said Helen. 'I'm sure none of us meant any harm. Yet it happened, as you say. Life is strange… Well, let's bury the hatchet, shall we? I appreciate your offer of help; but there's something I want your advice about most urgently.'

'What is it?' said Hubert, groaning inwardly. He was getting less and less inclined to give his advice for nothing now that it was beginning to acquire a rising value in the market. 'Anything I can do, of course.'

'It's about Billy and Jessica,' said Helen. 'Naturally it suits me very well to see him happy and settling down with such a nice girl, in his father's house, that should have been his in any case. But – can I conscientiously see him marry the sister of Giles and Basil Gabb, both of whom may have been insane, and one of whom is a fratricide? Can I really, Hubert?'

She twisted her long fingers together, and her agony of mind was apparent; for there stood Herons' Hall, to return to which was the dream of her life; and there stood Billy and Jessica, waiting to take her back to it. But between them, was there an angel with a flaming sword?

Hubert gave a soft chuckle. 'My dear Helen,' he said, 'how stupid of me not to have relieved your anxiety. Certainly' – he kept her in suspense a moment longer – 'certainly I wouldn't advise such a marriage if there were any fear of the taint's being passed on. But – didn't you know? No, of course, how could you? I only heard myself the other day – Jessica is not the daughter of Simon and Polly Gabb. She is not related to them at all. She's their adopted daughter. It seems that after Basil was born, Mrs Gabb couldn't have any more children; and as she and Simon both longed for a daughter, they decided to adopt one. They told nobody, not even Basil and Giles until they were grown up; and Jessica was not told till quite recently, when she left school. It was a big shock to her, I believe, and had the effect of making her very hostile towards them all for a while. Then Billy came along and put everything right. So you see, Helen—'

'Oh!' gasped Mrs Charleroy, swept for once off her feet, 'oh, Hubert, what a load you've taken off my mind! Billy isn't my own boy, but I feel just as if he were. And now they can all be happy – dear, dear children!'

Her eyes filled with tears of relief and gratitude. Laying her hands on Hubert's black sleeve, she pressed a kiss on his cheek.

Hubert ran down the path, red in the face and muttering to himself in his embarrassment. He jumped into his car, swung it round violently, and set off at full speed for Herons' Hall. Arden and Royce, watching from a window, laughed and laughed.

30

'But we won't go and live at Herons' Hall, will we?' said Arden later. 'No matter how many others do – no matter what Aunt Helen schemes?'

'No, darling,' said Royce. They were walking along the lake-side in the moonlight, looking across to the dark island with its trees silhouetted against the luminous sky.

'You'll get a job – or I will – and we'll go abroad, somewhere where it's sunny and one can live cheaply, and wear what one likes and catch one's own food?'

'Yes, darling,' said Royce dreamily.

'Billy and Jessica can carry on the old family tradition. It will be amazing to see them settle down. They will, though, as soon as they get into Herons' Hall. But you and I never will.'

Royce did not answer. He had no great confidence in his power to cope with the future, no ambition, no desire to look ahead or to outstrip anybody or even to make money in order to buy things for Arden. He had only a vast, unbelievable happiness. He wanted to preserve that, somehow, for both of them. For that he was willing to work, even to live in a house and catch trains and sell things, though he hoped it would not be necessary. 'There must be some way of life left for people like me,' he thought, 'who only want to live their own lives, to "sit in the centre and enjoy bright day." Selfish? Well, at least, nothing we do or think or plan in secret could ever lead to madness or murder or war...'

'Good night, Miss Arden, good night, Mr Royce,' said Morgan, going home.

Superintendent Mallett, Dr Jones and Dr Fitzbrown left Simon Gabb's house together. Hubert, standing on the top of the flight of steps, was saying a last few words to Simon.

'Well, everything's fixed for to-morrow,' said Mallett. 'Have you two got your own cars here?' He paused with one foot on the step of the police car. 'Awful cad, that fellow Olivier.'

'Awful cad,' nodded Dr Jones.

'Awful cad,' repeated Dr Fitzbrown.

THE END